THE GHOST VILLAGE MURDERS

DORSET CRIME
BOOK 9

RACHEL MCLEAN

ACKROYD
PUBLISHING

Ackroyd Publishing

ackroyd-publishing.com

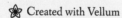 Created with Vellum

DORSET MURDER MAP

From the Dorset Crime series by Rachel McLean

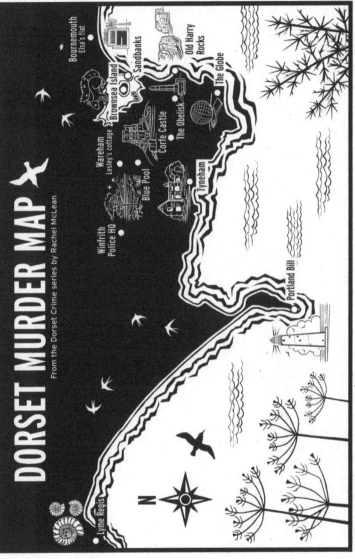

- Bournemouth
  - Elsa's flat
- Sandbanks
- Brownsea Island
- Old Harry Rocks
- The Globe
- Corfe Castle
- The Obelisk
- Wareham
  - Lesley's cottage
- Blue Pool
- Tyneham
- Winfrith Police HQ
- Portland Bill
- Lyme Regis

N

Illustration by Maria Burns

rachelmclean.com

THE GHOST VILLAGE MURDERS

CHAPTER ONE

"Where's she gone?"

Faye Reed tugged on her boyfriend's hand as she surveyed the abandoned village. He turned to her.

"Who, Daisy?" he asked.

She nodded.

Kyle looked at her. "She went to look at the schoolhouse, didn't she?"

Faye shook her head. "It's locked, this time of night."

"Huh?"

Faye gave him a look. "You heard me. She went to have a look, knocked on the door, then went off that way." She pointed past the church, the only fully intact building in the place.

Kyle shrugged. "She's probably scouting the place out, finding somewhere for a party."

Faye flashed her eyes. "Reckon we'll get some time to ourselves?" She leaned her head on his arm.

Kyle's gaze was over her shoulder. She turned to see his mate Didier's red Fiesta pass them, making for the car park.

The window opened and Sid, sitting in the back seat, leaned out. "Alright, you two? No snogging in the ghost village!"

Kyle winced. "Sorry," he muttered.

Faye pursed her lips. "I knew it was a bad idea."

"You're not the only girl. Daisy's here."

"Yeah, and I don't know where the bloody hell she is."

"Right."

"Yeah." She tapped her thigh with her fingertips. Daisy did this: she should be used to it by now.

"Why don't you go find her?" he suggested. "I'll follow on."

She sighed. "You'll just stay with your mates."

"I won't. Find Daisy. I'll be right there."

She looked into his eyes. "Only if you give me a kiss first."

She watched a smile break across Kyle's face. He had the cutest smile.

He leaned down and kissed her. "See ya in a minute, gorgeous."

"See ya."

She blew him a playful kiss as she walked away.

They were in Tyneham village in South Dorset. The place had been abandoned in the Second World War, but now it was open to the public, at the weekend and in the holidays, and at dusk it made the best place for a party.

No one within miles to hear them. No one to tell them what to do.

Except – she shuddered – she'd thought she was getting Kyle to herself, but his bloody mates had tagged along.

She strolled away from him, past the schoolhouse. The door was locked. She walked over to the church. Locked too.

"Daisy!" she called. "Where are you?"

She'd better not have gone off with one of Kyle's mates...

Faye rounded a bend to find two boys standing in front of a

ruined house, passing something between them. At the sight of her, their hands dropped.

"Lou Watson and Chris Daniels," she said. "What are you up to?"

"Nothing," said Chris. Lou was stuffing something in his pocket.

She shook her head. "Got any beer?"

The boys looked at each other. "Er... no," said Lou. "Too young."

She laughed, pointing at his pockets. "Not for that, though?" She shook her head. "You seen Daisy?"

"She went that way," Chris said. He pointed past them, towards the trees.

Faye frowned. *Daisy, what the hell?*

She was getting sick of losing her friend. Maybe next year, when they were in Year 13, she might stop doing this.

Maybe not.

"Daisy!" she called.

Nothing. She walked round the ruined house, passing into another clearing. "Daisy!"

"Over here!"

Faye stopped. "Where are you?"

"Over here!"

That doesn't help me. "Look, I'm by a ruined house. You must have passed it. You come back."

"I... I can't."

What?

"Just come back." Faye walked on, passing another house. She turned to look back where she'd come from. She couldn't see Kyle.

He'd be with Didier and Sid. *Bloody Didier.*

"Daisy, you're making me worried. Just come back."

"I told you, I can't." Daisy's voice was louder now.

Faye tramped on through the undergrowth, cursing her friend. She was missing valuable snogging time.

"Daisy!" she snapped. "Get back here right now or I'll—"

"Who are you, my mum?"

Daisy was right in front of her, standing on the other side of a fence.

On the fence was a sign: *Keep Out. Dangerous Building.*

"Can't you read?" Faye asked.

"Oh, don't be a wuss."

"Who says wuss?"

"I do."

"So why can't you come back?" Faye leaned on the fence.

Daisy was facing away from her, towards the house. Her legs seemed to have been planted in the grass.

"Daisy?" She was acting weird.

But then, for Daisy, that wasn't unusual.

"Daisy, what's going on?"

Daisy glanced back at Faye. Her face was pale.

"Daisy?" Faye felt her skin turn cold. "Why don't you get back over here?" She scanned the ground. There were mines around here. And the sign...

She backed away from the gate.

"Daisy, come back over the gate. It's not safe."

Daisy shook her head. "It's not me I'm worried about." She pointed towards the house. "It's her."

"Her?"

There were no other girls in their group. Once Faye had found out Didier was tagging along, she'd talked Daisy into it too.

So who was Daisy talking about?

She followed Daisy's outstretched arm. She was pointing

towards the abandoned rectory. Faye couldn't see any woman, or girl.

"Who? Daisy, come back. I want to find Kyle."

Daisy shook her head. She swallowed. "Her. The woman."

"There is no woman. Are you winding me up?"

Daisy took a step towards the building.

"Daisy," Faye said. "It's not safe. Please—"

Daisy looked at her. "For God's sake, Faye. Why aren't you listening? There's a woman in there, and I think she's dead."

CHAPTER TWO

DCI Lesley Clarke picked up her keys from the table and looked at her wife Elsa. "Where is she?"

Elsa shrugged. "She's eighteen, sweetie. You can't control her movements."

Lesley checked her watch. Eight thirty. She needed to be at work.

"I suppose you're right," she grunted. "Can you tell me when she gets in?"

Elsa put a hand on Lesley's shoulder. "I'll send you a message."

Lesley stroked her wife's face. "What would I do without you?"

"You'd have an eighteen-year-old daughter who's perfectly fine and can look after herself."

Lesley narrowed her eyes. "She's supposed to be at college this morning. Could she be on her way there already?" It was unlikely.

The front door opened. Sharon paused halfway through, looking between Lesley and Elsa. Her face fell.

"Shit," she muttered.

Lesley put her bag on the floor. "I'm not going to ask where you've been. But I would prefer it if you had the courtesy to let me know when you're going to be out all night."

Sharon's gaze was on the carpet. "Sorry, Mum. I lost track of the time."

"You've got your phone with you."

"Yeah."

"So you could've texted me."

Sharon looked up at Lesley. "Who texts?"

Lesley clenched her fist. "WhatsApped me, then. You know what I mean. I was worried."

Sharon was wearing last night's clothes. She smelled of stale beer, but otherwise she seemed OK.

"Are you alright?" Lesley asked.

"Of course." Sharon closed the front door behind her. She looked at Elsa, who gave her a smile. "Stop being a copper, Mum. I'm fine. I just stayed out with my mates."

Lesley pulled in a sigh. "In that case, you need to get to college."

"Not till eleven."

"Very well. I need to get to work." She stepped towards her daughter, who withdrew.

"You want a lift, once it's time to go?" Elsa asked Sharon.

Lesley frowned at her: *don't reward the girl.*

Sharon smiled. "That would be great."

"OK." Elsa squeezed Lesley's hand and headed for the kitchen.

Lesley and Sharon stood in the hallway, Sharon shifting from foot to foot.

"I don't want to nag," Lesley said. "But I just—"

"It's OK. I'll tell you next time. Alright?" Sharon trudged to her room, slamming the door behind her.

Elsa reappeared, holding a mug of coffee. She brushed Lesley's arm with her hand. She'd talk to Sharon in the car, see if she could find out where the girl had been. Sometimes Elsa had more success getting her stepdaughter to open up than Lesley did herself.

"Thanks, love." Lesley kissed Elsa's cheek and opened the front door. She lowered her voice. "I messed that up."

"No," Elsa told her. "You did fine."

"Shit, this is hard." Lesley sighed. "I don't want to nag her. But at the same time, I worry."

"You're a detective. You expect the worst to happen. Maybe she was just where she claims she was, out with some mates."

"But what mates?"

"You can't expect her to tell you about everyone she knows. She'll be at university soon. Independent."

Lesley felt the tension intensifying across her back.

She needed to get to work. There was an open case that she hadn't closed yet, and she had to speak to her superintendent.

"OK." She bent to pick up her bag. Her phone rang in her pocket.

"I'm late. That'll be Superintendent Carpenter trying to find out where the hell I am."

Elsa shrugged. Lesley checked her phone: not Carpenter.

"Tina," she snapped as she picked up the call. "I'm on my way, sorry."

"It's not that, boss," Tina replied. "We've got a new case."

Lesley looked at Elsa, her heart sinking.

"What kind of case?"

"The body of a woman has been found overnight in Tyneham, left in one of the abandoned houses. We don't know who she is yet. But they're expecting you over there."

CHAPTER THREE

LESLEY HIT hands-free as she got into her car. Her DS, Dennis Frampton, picked up on the first ring.

"Where are you?" she asked. He would have been in the office since eight; hopefully he was at the crime scene already.

"I'm in the office," he replied. "It's on your way, I was hoping we'd travel together."

She glanced into the rearview mirror. "Fair enough."

She needed to stop worrying about Sharon. The girl was eighteen: in two months' time, she'd be at university.

Thirty minutes later, she was in the car park of Dorset Police HQ in Winfrith. She glanced up at the windows to the team room, and her own office next door to it.

Stanley was in the window, looking down. Lesley leaned back in her seat, waiting, hoping the look on her face communicated the message: *Tell Dennis I'm here.*

The front doors to the building opened and Dennis hurried out. She smiled as he climbed into the passenger seat. "You were quick."

"I was waiting in the foyer. I knew you wouldn't want to hang around."

"Good." She pulled out of the car park and headed towards Wool. "Which way?"

"Take the road for Lulworth, then we can cut off into the ranges."

They sped along country lanes, hedges a blur outside the car. Dennis gripped the sides of his seat as Lesley drove.

"It's alright," she told him. "I was trained to drive a response vehicle back in Birmingham."

He grimaced. "This isn't Birmingham."

He threw his hands up in front of him as a tractor rounded a bend in front of them, heading straight for them.

Lesley took a breath and pumped the brakes. She knew not to slam her foot down hard: she'd learned that fifteen years ago, when the oncoming vehicle had been a getaway car. But this was a dirty great tractor that looked like it might fall apart if she drove into it.

The tractor stopped. Lesley stopped too, waiting for it to get out of their way.

"Bloody thing," she said. "Are they supposed to be that big?"

She turned and flung her arm over the back of Dennis's seat to get a better view through the rear window. She backed the car up until they reached a passing place.

She looked at Dennis as the tractor passed them. His nose was wrinkled.

"Sorry," she said.

He nodded.

"I've got the swear jar out again for you. But this doesn't count."

He raised his eyebrows. "I was expecting you to put it straight back in the filing cabinet."

"But I didn't. It's still there. Waiting."

He gave her a look but said nothing. Lesley smiled and continued driving, controlling her speed this time.

Five minutes later, she reached a turnoff to the right. A padlocked metal gate barred their way, a sign indicating that the road was closed due to 'firing'.

"How do we get through?" Lesley asked.

"They should be expecting us," Dennis said, his phone to his ear. "Tina, did you call the MoD?"

"Is there another way around?" Lesley started to back up.

"Any way we go, it'll be blocked," Dennis said. "But they really should know we're coming."

A vehicle turned a bend ahead of them, beyond the gate. A military truck. Dennis nodded and got out of the car.

A man emerged from the truck, and Lesley watched as he and Dennis spoke. She smiled, imagining Dennis in another life, a captain in the Army or similar. He'd have been good at it.

Dennis got back into the car as another man emerged from the truck with a set of keys, and started to open the gate.

"We're going to have to do that every time we come here?" Lesley asked.

"It protects the crime scene, at least."

"True."

They waited as the man pulled the gate open. Once the gap was wide enough, he stopped and stood next to it, his hand raised in a salute.

Lesley chuckled to herself and started the car. She opened her window as she reached him. "Thanks. Have you let anybody else through today?"

He bent down to look into the car window. "I've only just come on duty, Ma'am. But my captain will have a record."

The other man was standing near the truck. The captain, no doubt. Lesley wondered what he might know about the site, and how he could help them.

She beckoned him over. "When was the site shut to the public?"

"We closed it at 8.30pm yesterday. Ma'am."

Enough of the ma'aming.

"As soon as we'd cleared the area of members of the public," he continued.

"And have any other vehicles been through today?"

"Just two police cars, Ma'am. And yourselves."

"You're keeping a log, I hope."

"We're liaising with PC Mullins."

"Is there another way in?"

"There is, but we're only unlocking this one."

"Good." Gail would approve. "Your name is?"

"Captain Northcott, Ma'am."

"I'll need to have a chat with you later. Find out exactly what happened yesterday. And get an idea of how someone might have gained access."

"Of course."

Thank God for Captain Northcott. Last time she'd had to deal with an external agency, it had been the Prison Service on the Island of Portland. They'd been less cooperative.

"Thanks," she said, closing her window. "Let's get over there, Dennis. Show me the way."

CHAPTER FOUR

"So," Lesley said as they got out of the car. "Any idea where we need to go?"

Dennis pointed towards a row of low buildings with a telephone box in front of them.

"That's the main village," he told her. "The derelict houses are beyond there."

"So, from what we've heard, I imagine that's where she is," Lesley said.

As they approached the houses, Lesley saw a van speeding down the lane towards them.

Dennis muttered under his breath, and Lesley stepped over a wall to get out of the way.

The white van had the Dorset Police insignia on it, and a woman with dark curly hair at the wheel.

It jolted to a halt beside them.

The woman pushed her hair back as she wound the window down. "Lesley," she said, "you beat us."

"Not for lack of trying on your part," Lesley replied. She'd seen Gail Hansford's driving before, and had made a conscious decision never to let the woman give her a lift.

"That wasn't entirely deliberate," Gail replied. "I misjudged the corner."

"Well, I'm glad you didn't hit anything."

"I'll park over there and join you at the crime scene." Gail nodded towards the car park, where two squad cars were already parked. There was no sign of their occupants.

"You know where you're going?" Dennis asked.

"I've been given a *What3words* reference," Gail replied. "Hello, Dennis."

Lesley turned to Dennis. "Why didn't we get a *What3words* reference?"

Gail had her phone in her hand. "Hang on a minute."

"It's OK," Lesley told her. "We'll find it."

Gail shrugged and pocketed her phone, then closed her window.

Lesley and Dennis walked past the ruined buildings, towards a church that appeared to be the only intact building in the village. They turned a corner.

"The church is still in use?" Lesley asked, thinking of Brownsea Island, barely inhabited but still holding church services every Sunday.

Dennis shook his head. "It's a museum of sorts. The main museum's in the schoolroom, but they have exhibits and photos in the church too. I'll show you if you want."

Lesley shook her head. "We've got a murder case to be getting on with."

The schoolhouse was on their left, the door locked. A pathway ran off to the right, with another straight ahead.

She raised a finger to shush the DS and listened for voices.

Somewhere up ahead, two people were talking. Lesley

beckoned. "Come on, Dennis. I think I can figure out where we're going."

She took the path off to the right, glad she'd changed into her walking boots before leaving the car.

The village was quiet, the only sounds the distant chatter of those constables and the birds in the trees around them. Birds Lesley would never be able to name, no matter how long she lived down here.

They reached a derelict building, the path splitting in front of it.

Lesley squinted at it. "Where are they?"

Dennis took the right-hand path. "This way."

"You've been here before?" Lesley asked.

"Pam and I like to do the walk down to Worbarrow Bay."

"Where's that?"

"A couple of miles back in that direction." Dennis jerked his thumb back over his shoulder. "Lovely walk on the right day." He looked at her. "Don't worry. I'm not going to suggest it."

"Good."

The chattering had stopped, but Lesley could hear a grinding noise, now. They rounded the building to find another in front of them, this one blocked off by a fence and a gate.

This was the spot.

Two uniformed officers were securing the gate open. A sign on it told her this had once been the village's rectory. Police tape had been strung across the opening, and two police jackets had been placed on a boulder.

The two constables stopped as they spotted the detectives.

Lesley recognised one of them: PC Mullins. He'd worked with Tina, before she'd moved to the MCIT.

"Ma'am," he said. "Sarge. We've put a tarpaulin up and

taped off the scene, but we don't need to protect it like we usually do, what with the army controlling access. We're hoping the CSIs will find things easier with the fencing out of the way."

Lesley stepped forward. "There's enough room to squeeze through. I wouldn't move it any more than you already have."

PC Mullins flushed. "Ma'am." He exchanged a glance with his colleague.

"Are you the only people here so far?" she asked.

"Yes, Ma'am," the other PC said. "PC McGuigan, Ma'am."

"And you've spoken to Captain...?"

"Captain Northcott," Dennis prompted.

"We have, Ma'am. He'll let us know if any vehicles attempt to gain access. The CSI van is on its way."

She smiled. "It certainly is." What would Gail make of the scene?

She walked towards the fence. A tarpaulin had been erected, covering the space where the roof had once been. The victim was still inside, laid out on a slab of rock.

Poor woman.

"Carry on, Constable," she said. "Leave the fences, now."

"A person would have to climb that fence to gain access," Dennis said. "You've heard how noisy that is."

She nodded. "But I imagine this site is deserted most of the time."

"Not when it's open to the public. It gets pretty busy at weekends. And it won't be open during the week until the end of the month."

"So whoever left her, or killed her there, either found a way to get in when the place is closed, or somehow did it quietly."

Dennis stepped forward. "There's damage to the ground

here." He looked up. "PC Mullins, was it like this when you arrived?"

"We took photos, before we moved anything."

That was something, at least. "Send them to the MCIT inbox," Lesley said. Bloody Uniform. Didn't they know not to mess with a crime scene?

"OK," she said. "Don't touch *anything* until the forensic team get here."

"What do you want us to do?"

"Tell you what, why don't you go back to your cars? You can't do any more damage there."

"You giving people an earful, Lesley?" came a voice.

Lesley turned to see Gail approaching, pulling on her forensic suit.

"Whatever made you think that?"

Gail laughed. "Go easy on them, they're only doing their job. And besides, they've covered the roof over. That looks pretty good to me." She stepped forward and tugged a rope that was holding the tarpaulin in place. "Good work, lads."

"They were disturbing a crime scene," Lesley said.

Gail screwed up her face and waved her hand in dismissal. "That fence isn't about to give us anything useful."

"If there are hairs or fibres, they might have been disturbed. They—"

"Don't worry, Lesley. It's fine," Gail told her.

Lesley gave her friend a look.

"This isn't like you," Gail said.

"Thoroughness *is* like me," Lesley replied.

Gail shrugged.

"Are you going to take a look at the victim?" Dennis asked.

"Of course, I am." Gail walked past Lesley towards the house. She squeezed through the gap in the fence that the constables had made. "Pretty overgrown in here," she said. "Tall grass. There's a pathway that looks like it's been made fairly recently."

"You think the killer went in that way?" Dennis asked.

Gail shrugged. "It's the only route I can see for now." She cocked her head. "I'll go round another way."

She retreated back through the gap in the fencing and walked around the other side of the house. Lesley could see her through gaps in the brickwork as she moved.

"Lesley," Gail said. "You should be here."

Lesley walked around the house to see where Gail had stopped.

There was another spot where two sections of fence joined, the connection secured by a plastic tie. Gail pulled clippers out of her pocket and cut the tie open.

She grabbed the fence and pulled it to one side. She looked it up and down, took out her camera for photos, then looked at Lesley. "I'd appreciate a hand."

Lesley took a pair of forensic gloves from the inside pocket of her waterproof jacket and helped Gail pulled the fence further out of the way.

"Right," Gail breathed heavily. "I knew there was a reason I should have done that yoga practice yesterday."

"You always do yoga?" Lesley asked.

Gail looked at her. "What do you think?"

Lesley smiled.

"Right," Gail continued. "There's less undergrowth over here. I can get through without disturbing the scene, but I'll get Brett to put some plates down."

Lesley hadn't noticed Gail's colleague Brett, standing quietly to the side, observing. He stepped forward with protective plates and placed them in the spots Gail indicated.

At last, they had a route to the victim.

"She's been here a while," Gail said.

Lesley hung back, not wanting to disturb things. "How can you tell?"

"Animal damage." The Crime Scene Manager winced. "Nasty in places. The pathologist will be able to tell you more."

"Anything else?" Lesley asked. Dennis stood beside her, watching Gail through the fence. His hands were in his pockets, his back straight.

"It looks like there was a struggle," Gail said.

Lesley leaned in. She could make out damage to the woman's hands. Her face was obscured from here, hidden by one of the ruined building's walls.

"Her fingernails are damaged," Gail said. "And her clothes have been disturbed."

Lesley nodded.

"Can we come through?" Dennis asked.

"Hang on," Gail said. She moved one of the plates. "You can come in now."

Lesley and Dennis stepped through the gap in the fence, Lesley going first. She trod carefully, her gaze flicking from her feet to the victim.

The woman was in the centre of the house, her features dim with the tarpaulin blocking the sunlight. She lay on her back on a slab of stone, her eyes closed. Three of her fingernails were torn, as Gail had said, and her clothing was ripped in places.

Lesley closed her eyes for a moment. "Poor woman."

She opened her eyes. "Can you check for ID, Gail? Her pockets."

"There's nothing. Pockets are empty."

"What about her clothes?" Lesley asked.

Gail shrugged. "We'll need to check the brand."

Lesley felt Dennis's fingers brush her arm. She turned to him.

His face had paled. He stood motionless, staring at the woman.

Gail looked up. "Dennis, are you alright?"

Lesley reached out and held his arm. "Dennis, what is it?"

Dennis had come close to fainting before. He'd suffered from depression, seen a psychiatrist.

But this crime scene had nothing to do with the death of DCI Mackie, the trigger for Dennis's trauma.

He croaked, then crossed himself. "Another one."

"Another what?" Lesley tightened her grip on his arm. "What is it, Dennis?"

He turned to her, his mouth hanging open. Gail was watching them, her expression puzzled.

"Dennis?" Lesley repeated.

He licked his lips, then closed his eyes.

"I know her," he said.

CHAPTER FIVE

"Do you know if they've arrived yet?" Tina asked.

Mike looked up from his screen at his wife. "The sarge messaged me. He and the boss are there."

"Good," she replied. "I'm looking into the geography of the village. See if I can find any routes in or out while the roads are closed."

Stanley popped his head up to look over his screen opposite Mike's. "It's weird having you two back."

Mike smiled. "It's weird being back."

"You missing that little 'un?"

Tina and Mike's baby, Louis, was in nursery. Mike had dropped him off this morning, leaving him in a room that the nursery assistants had filled with balloons. The boy had gone wild with excitement, laughing and shrieking at the top of his voice. Despite that, Mike felt guilty. And he knew Tina felt it worse.

"Let's not talk about Louis," Tina said. "You'll make me worry."

Stanley shrugged. "What d'you know about Tyneham, then?"

"Not much from this search. My parents took me there when I was a kid."

"I've never been."

"You've never been anywhere," Mike said.

Stanley looked at him. "I know all about it, though. Abandoned in the Second World War, villagers promised that they'd be allowed back, promise broken. Typical government."

Mike laughed. *Typical Stanley.*

"It's closed on weekdays, right now," Tina said. "Open at the weekends. In the summer it's open until sunset."

"They'll be after the grockle trade," Stanley said.

"More like the ranges not being used during the summer break," Mike corrected. "There's not much money to be made from an abandoned village."

"I'm checking the OS maps," Tina said, "trying to work out if there's any way to access the site when the gates are closed."

"The coastal path?" Mike suggested.

Tina nodded. "I don't think they physically close it off. But I guess they must close the path from the coast up to the village."

Mike moved his chair across to look at Tina's screen. She had the Ordnance Survey website up and was looking at a close-up of Worbarrow Bay just south of Tyneham. "If you wanted to get in," he pointed, "you'd go that way."

She nodded. "We'll need to speak to someone from the MoD," she said. "Hang on."

Mike watched as his wife did what she was best at. Tina was brilliant at research, at throwing herself at a problem and digging out whatever they needed to pursue an investigation.

She was brilliant at the people stuff, too. She had a knack for putting witnesses at ease, for making them forget she was a copper. Tina had only been a DC for two years, four years less than him, but Mike could see that she'd end up being promoted to DS before he was.

He shrugged. Part of him was jealous, and another part, a part he was ashamed of, was resentful. But he knew that she loved this job. And he knew that if either of them ended up taking on the majority of the childcare, it would be him.

"OK," Tina said. "I've got a name."

Mike looked over the desk. "Who?"

"Corporal Tim Cole. Went to my school in Lyme Regis. He applied to the police, same time as me. Didn't get in, so he went into the army."

"It's normally the other way round," said Stanley.

Tina shrugged. "Anyway, he went out with my sister when we were teenagers, so hopefully he'll be helpful. He's based at Lulworth Camp."

Stanley cocked his head. "Did you or your sister date everyone we need to talk to?"

She narrowed her eyes. "This is the first time."

"There was the Lyme Bay deaths," Mike reminded her. "The PC there you used to..."

He spotted the look on her face and stopped talking.

"OK," Tina said. "I'll see if I can have a chat with Tim. He might give me some inside info. But we'll need more people at the site."

Mike and Stanley exchanged looks. "We can," they said in unison.

Anything to get out from behind a desk.

She shook her head. "Not until we've got an approximate

time of death. It'll help us work out if she was killed there, or she died somewhere else and was brought there when it was open."

Mike felt himself deflate. "OK."

CHAPTER SIX

LESLEY SAT on a low wall flanking the church in the centre of the village. Dennis was next to her, his hands on his thighs, his breathing slow.

She put a light hand on his shoulder, aware that physical contact made him uneasy.

"OK now?" she asked.

He took in some air and nodded. "I'm fine, boss. Please don't worry about me."

"You almost fainted when you saw the body."

He brushed his palms on his trousers. "I'm fine. As I just said, you don't need to worry about me."

Lesley removed her hand from his shoulder and straightened. "Very well. Are you going to tell me who it is?"

He looked at her. "The body?"

"No, Dennis. The PC putting up the cordon." She sighed. "Yes, the body. Who is it?"

She watched his face for a reaction. Was it a member of an organised crime gang he'd arrested in the past? A suspect in a previous case?

Or something closer to home?

He looked at her. "She's a Detective Constable."

"Shi—" She caught Dennis's expression. "You're sure?"

A nod. "From the Professional Standards Division."

Lesley's chest tightened. "Professional Standards," she muttered.

She looked back towards the crime scene. It was hidden from view, but she could hear Gail talking to her team members.

"What's her name?" she asked.

"DC Dugdale."

"And how do you know her?"

He looked down at his hands. "When I was... when I was arrested, they interviewed me."

"I thought that was the Organised Crime team."

"Not just them. Professional Standards got involved as well. DI Collingwood and DC Dugdale, she was with him." He coughed. "How long has she been there, boss?"

"That's what the pathologist will work out," she replied.

"But we saw the body. The animal damage... she's been there a few days at least."

"Poor woman," she said.

Poor woman, indeed.

"OK." Lesley stood up from her perch on the low wall. "We need to tell Gail what we know. I need to speak to the super."

Dennis stayed sitting on the wall. "I don't think I should be involved in this case."

"Sometimes, Dennis, I want to punch you. You're my second-in-command, and you're the best detective on the team." She ignored his pleading look. "This will be one of our most high-profile cases yet, and I want you on it."

CHAPTER SEVEN

LESLEY LEFT Dennis sitting on the wall by the church, and returned to the crime scene.

The pathologist Matthew Bamford had arrived and was talking to Gail.

"How's Dennis?" Gail asked, turning to her.

"Does he need medical treatment?" Dr Bamford added.

"He'll be fine. Just a bit of a funny turn." She lowered her voice. The two PCs were on the other side of the house. "We've got an ID."

"Who?" Gail looked across at the body.

"Her name was Fran Dugdale. She was a PC, serving in Dorset Police."

Gail sucked in a breath.

"There's more," Lesley told her. "She worked in the Professional Standards Division."

The pathologist was quiet, rooting through his bag. Gail's eyes were wide.

"There'll have to be a press conference, I imagine," Lesley said. But for now…"

"I won't tell anyone," Gail said.

"Nor me." Dr Bamford stood up. "You'll be wanting a time of death, given the location."

"I need to know if she was brought here since Friday, when the ranges were opened up to the public."

"I can't give you a precise time until I've done the full PM. But I'll see what I can get to start with."

"Thanks." Lesley watched him walk towards the body, picking his way over the protective plates. Gail's colleague Brett stood up and moved to let him get closer.

"Poor woman," Gail said. "You think it's related to a case she was working on?"

"I've got no idea. And I don't plan on speculating until we've got some evidence."

"Fair point. We've secured the scene. We can't put a tent up because of that house, but the tarp is doing a pretty good job."

"I'm hoping the pathology team will get her out of here soon. You need her to remain, for recovery of evidence?"

"We've taken all we can from immediately around the body. And Brett's got enough photos to fill a hundred of your old-fashioned boards."

"I'm not using a board on this one," Lesley said. Everything'll be on the system, accessible only to my team."

"Too sensitive. Can't blame you. You think Carpenter'll let you keep the case, now we know who it is?"

"I don't see why not."

"How's Dennis? You're sure he's OK?"

Lesley considered. "He'll be fine. I hope."

"You'll take him off the case, given—"

"I'll do no such thing. He's been pronounced fit for work.

All charges have been dropped, and he can put the whole thing behind him."

"You know it's not as simple as that."

Lesley turned to her friend. "It has to be."

"OK. But there's bound to be shock amongst your colleagues."

Lesley knew that. But working for Professional Standards, DC Dugdale wouldn't have had much connection with officers outside her own department. And little loyalty from anyone she did meet. Most of the officers she would have come into contact with would have been those she was investigating, and their colleagues.

"I need to know more about her background," Lesley said. "See what cases she worked on, who she worked with. How long she was in PSD. And I need to speak to her senior officers."

"Do you know them?" Gail asked.

"Dennis has given me a name," Lesley replied. "But I'll speak to Carpenter first."

She closed her eyes. Chances were she'd be taken off this case. Her last case had been at the lighthouse at Portland Bill, and the Home Office had tried to take it over. The previous one had been at Blue Pool near Wareham, and that one had had Organised Crime walking all over it.

Nothing was ever simple.

"Right," she said, regaining her focus. "I need that time of death."

She strode across the clearing towards the pathologist, leaving Gail behind.

CHAPTER EIGHT

SHARON THREW herself down on her bed, rubbing her hair with a towel. She didn't like being spoken to by her mum like that.

She was an adult now. She could do what she wanted.

Sure, Mum and Elsa wanted the best for her. But couldn't they see that the best was to give her independence? How was she going to cope with being at uni if she spent the year before she went there swaddled in cotton wool?

She lay back and threw the towel across the room. It had been such a good evening, such a good night. And now it was bloody ruined.

Fucking parents.

She grabbed her phone from the bedside table and scrolled through her messages.

There were two from Rick. She smiled, feeling her chest flutter.

Sod Mum.

Sharon read the first one. *Hey, gorgeous. How are you?* She smiled and moved on to the second. *You ignoring me?*

She laughed, then glanced at the door. Elsa was out there, moving around the kitchen. Her stepmum was supposed to be building her new law firm, but she didn't have enough clients to keep her busy. Instead, she drifted around the flat and watched Sharon.

Sharon liked Elsa, but she didn't like being watched.

She started typing: *I'm good. Just taking a shower. How about you?*

The dots bounced at the bottom of the screen: his response.

Imagining you in the shower.

Sharon bit her lip, stifling a grin.

I'm lying on my bed, she replied, *wrapped in a towel.*

It was almost true. Her hair was wrapped in a towel, or it had been until she'd thrown it across the room.

Her body was wrapped in a Peppa Pig dressing gown. But she wasn't about to tell Rick that.

A response came, heart eyes emoji followed by an aubergine. She laughed out loud, then glanced at the door.

I'm going out, she replied. *Want to meet up?*

Sure. Where?

She considered. *The beach in an hour.*

It was close to college. She could get that lift from Elsa, then head to the beach. They were crap at keeping tabs on the students.

Perfect. See you then, gorgeous. Wink emoji.

Sharon threw the phone down onto her bed and stripped off her childish dressing gown. She could be there in well under an hour, but she had to play it cool. She'd use the time to make herself look fantastic.

CHAPTER NINE

LESLEY SCANNED the village as she waited for her call to be put through to Carpenter. The site was quiet – no visitors and no military. She wondered if they'd been told to stand down. And if so, where they were. She hoped there wouldn't be too much military interference in the case.

"DCI Clarke, I assume this is about your Tyneham murder?"

No preamble, as usual. She wondered if Carpenter had ever engaged in small talk.

"It is, Sir."

"Bloody inconsiderate," he said, "sticking a body somewhere we can't get access to without military approval."

"So far we haven't encountered any issues. The place is deserted."

"Good," Carpenter replied. "I don't want the MoD sticking their noses into this."

Lesley frowned. "We've got an ID on the body."

"Good work."

"It's sensitive."

A sigh. "Not another member of the bloody Kelvin family."

That would have been preferable. "I'm afraid not, Sir. Her name's Fran Dugdale. Detective Constable Fran Dugdale."

"Bloody hell." She heard a thump: Carpenter punching something? "One of us."

Lesley scanned the road around her: no one in sight. "She was a Professional Standards detective."

"Jesus Christ on a hedgehog, woman. You do like to dump these things on me, don't you?" A pause. "Tell me the name of her senior officer, if you have it."

"DI Robert Collingwood," Lesley replied.

Silence.

"Sir?"

"Sorry, Lesley. You'll need to leave this with me. Is DI Collingwood somebody you've come across before?"

"Not personally."

"PSD will want to stick their noses into the investigation," he told her. "She's one of theirs."

"But it's a murder. The Major Crimes T—"

"You and I know the correct procedure. But we also know what PSD can be like." He paused. "I'm sorry, Lesley. I may have sent you over there for nothing."

Lesley turned away from the village and walked towards her car. "Her killing could be related to a PSD case. It could even be..."

She wasn't going to say it. Not out loud.

"I think the very last people who should be investigating this case are PSD," she continued.

"Be very careful where you tread, Lesley. PSD officers have to be the most trustworthy and upright officers in the force. By definition."

Hiding in plain sight, Lesley thought. She sighed.

"I'm sure that's supposed to be the case, Sir. But PSD officers will need to be interviewed in the course of the investigation. That needs to be carried out by a team that's independent of the victim."

"I wish it were that simple."

Lesley was at her car now. She leaned against the driver's door, waiting for Carpenter to come to a decision.

"Very well then, DCI Clarke. I'll need to speak to the superintendent in command of Professional Standards. I'll also need to confer with more senior officers. This will be a sensitive case."

"I know that." It wasn't as if Lesley hadn't worked on the death of a police officer before.

"But I know you have experience of this kind of thing, and that as a relatively new member of the Dorset force, you're relatively independent yourself."

Was Carpenter complimenting her? This was new.

"Leave it with me, Lesley. And be careful whose toes you tread on. You and your team have a multifaceted reputation, and it's not all good."

He hung up.

CHAPTER TEN

MEERA SUCKED her finger as she stumbled through the office door. She was late, and to top it all off, she'd just shut her hand in the car door.

It had been one of those mornings; Suzi grouchy and Jill on the brink of grouchiness herself. *I'm jealous of you*, she'd said. *Can't we do what Tina and Mike in your team are doing?*

But Meera wasn't Mike. She wasn't sure she had the skills to be left alone all day with Suzi. And she knew she didn't have the patience.

They'd agreed to swap places when Suzi was one. Meera would go down to three or four days a week and Jill would go back to her old job in Bournemouth CID. It would be fine.

"Sorry, guys," she said as she hurried to her desk. She exchanged glances with Mike, surprised to see him in the office. "Tough morning with Suzi. I'll work late to make up for it." She sat heavily in her chair and cocked her head. "Mike. You're back."

Mike looked at Tina and smiled. "You've got both of us again."

Meera felt her neck tense. "You won't need me, then."

"I don't think it works like that." Tina stood up and put a hand on Mike's shoulder. "The boss seems to want more bodies on the team."

Meera raised an eyebrow. "If that's the case, there'll have to be a formal recruitment process."

"I wouldn't worry," Tina replied. "You've got a head start, haven't you?"

I hope so. Meera hid her frown and opened up her computer. "Did I miss anything?"

Stanley was at the desk next to her. He snorted.

Meera looked up. "What?"

"Only a murder investigation."

"Sorry?"

"Body of a woman found at Tyneham," Tina said.

"The abandoned village? When?"

"Last night. Group of teenagers found her."

"Who's the victim?"

"We don't know yet," Tina said. "There was no ID on her. No purse, no phone."

"So whoever killed her took all that away. She's still got fingerprints, though?"

Tina nodded. "No mutilation, far as we know right now." Her phone rang and she raised a finger: *hang on.*

Meera watched as Tina picked up the call, her neck lengthening. Tina only did that when she was speaking to the DCI.

Tina put her phone down. "We have an ID."

"Who?" Mike asked.

Tina looked around the room. "You're not going to like it."

"Who?" Stanley said.

"DC Fran Dugdale."

Mike let out a whistle. Stanley coughed.

"Anyone know her?" Meera asked.

"She's PSD," Mike said.

"Was," corrected Tina.

"Professional Standards?" Meera said.

"It'll get taken off us," Stanley muttered.

"The boss reckons it might be," Tina told him. "But in the meantime, before the high-ups take us off the case, she wants us to get to work."

Meera nodded. "Doing what?"

"Background research. Find out what cases DC Dugdale worked on, who she might have pissed off."

"She's PSD," said Mike. A shadow fell over his face.

Tina looked at him. "Johnny?" she said, all but whispering the word.

He shook his head. "It didn't go that far."

Meera had no idea who Johnny was. She wasn't about to ask.

"Anything else?" she asked.

"We're to work under the radar," Tina said. "Keep things subtle."

"So no calls to mates in PSD," said Stanley.

"You got any?" Meera asked him.

A shake of the head. "They keep themselves to themselves."

Mike was peering into his screen, his eyes narrowed. "Come on, then," he said. "Let's stop gassing and see what we can find."

CHAPTER ELEVEN

LESLEY TURNED at the sound of a car approaching along the narrow lane that was the only way in and out of the village. It was a dark blue Audi, with new plates.

You didn't take long.

She stayed by her car, looking back towards the village for signs of Dennis. He was still at the crime scene, out of sight.

Good.

The car parked on the road, the driver not bothering to drive as far as the car park. He got out, his face grim. She walked towards him.

"DCI Clarke." The man held out a hand.

Lesley looked down at it. *Play nice.* His handshake was firm, just on the right side of aggressive.

"DI Collingwood," she said. "Have you been informed?"

"I have." He looked away from her, towards the village. "Where is she?"

"There's a rectory beyond the main village," she told him. "Fenced off. She's inside that."

He raised an eyebrow, not turning to look at her. ""All the warning signs. Those houses are dangerous."

"Yes."

He scratched his nose. "So..." He cleared his throat. He hadn't made eye contact with Lesley yet.

"I'll show you," she told him. "The CSM is being strict about disruption to the scene, but I realise—"

He turned, making eye contact with her at last. His eyes were dark, almost black, incongruous against his blonde hair and pale skin. "I'll be the judge of that."

Lesley had been expecting this.

Don't challenge him yet. The longer she could put that conversation off, the longer her team had to get on with their investigations.

"I'll show you the way." She started walking before he had a chance to object.

She could only hope that Dennis would remain calm. The last time the two men had met, they'd been in an interview room.

She passed the phone box and the museum and turned in front of the church. She resisted the urge to look back and check Collingwood was following. Beyond the church and the last of the houses, she took a narrow path until they arrived at the clearing in front of the house where DC Dugdale's body had been found.

The pathology team was in the process of moving the body. Lesley grimaced; Collingwood might give her the creeps, but he deserved to see his colleague in a more respectful context.

She cleared her throat. Gail, who was watching proceedings, turned and frowned as she spotted Collingwood.

"This is DI Collingwood," Lesley said. "DC Dugdale's senior officer."

Dennis, standing next to Gail, turned. His shoulders shifted as his gaze fell on the newcomer. He cast a glance in Lesley's direction, his eyes momentarily filled with something close to panic.

It's alright, Dennis. He's not here for you.

"Oh." Gail approached the pathologist.

Dennis turned back towards the crime scene, his body tense. Collingwood stayed where he was at the edge of the clearing, watching in silence. He hadn't even looked at Dennis.

"Gareth," Gail said, "can we pause this for a moment? The victim's boss is here. I'm sure he'd like a moment."

The pathologist looked past her towards Lesley and Collingwood. "We don't normally let—"

"Our victims aren't normally police officers," Gail reminded him.

Lesley shivered. The last time Gail had dealt with the murder of a police officer, the victim would have been her own predecessor, DCI Mackie. She wondered who had been present at the scene; she'd never asked.

Bamford blinked. "True." The pathologist when Mackie had died had been Henry Whittaker, since retired. *Thank God.*

The pathologist approached his two assistants, who had lowered the stretcher holding DC Dugdale's body to the ground. "Can we pause proceedings for a moment," he said. "Her senior officer wants to pay his respects."

Collingwood walked towards the stretcher on the ground and the group of pathology staff surrounding it.

His gaze flicked down at the body. He flinched, so quickly Lesley wouldn't have noticed it if she hadn't been watching closely.

Dennis was watching closely too, she observed.

"That's not why I'm here," Collingwood said.

Dennis let out a quick sucking sound. Lesley felt her back tense.

"No?" Gail asked.

The DI shook his head. "I'm SIO."

"Sorry?" Lesley said.

He turned to her. "This is a PSD matter. It's inappropriate for regular officers to investigate the death of one of our team."

"But—"

He held up a hand. "Please, DCI Clarke."

Lesley went to stand next to him, close enough that Dennis wouldn't hear.

"DI Collingwood," she said. "This investigation will need to include interviews with members of your team. They may have information that leads to the identification of a suspect."

He looked at her, his eyes hard. He raised both eyebrows, then looked past her at Dennis. He returned his gaze to her face. "I don't think you're really in a position to make a suggestion like that."

How dare he?

"Can I remind you that I'm your senior officer here," she said.

"And I'm PSD. We have precedence."

No you don't, thought Lesley.

Collingwood gave Dennis another brief glance. "Especially when officers who we've had reason to investigate are involved."

"DS Frampton was exonerated, and you know it," she muttered. "That has nothing to do with—"

He cleared his throat and took a few steps away from her, towards Gail and Dr Bamford.

"So," he said, ignoring Lesley, "everybody carry on with what you're doing. You're all experienced in crime scene management. I'll need to attend the post-mortem, so I'll be requiring full details. And if you can share all analyses and investigations you're planning, Gail. We'll need a search, to find evidence of ingress within the house itself, and more generally in the surrounding area. I'll be involving Uniform, and conducting interviews with military officials. Any objections?"

Gail looked from Collingwood to Lesley. Lesley shrugged.

"No," Gail muttered.

"Sorry," Lesley mouthed. Yes, she was a DCI to Collingwood's DI rank. But he was right. He was PSD, and he'd investigated one of her officers.

Much as she hated to admit it, she needed to speak to Carpenter again.

CHAPTER TWELVE

THE DCI barely spoke all the way back to the office. Dennis sat beside her in near silence, wondering what she and Collingwood had said to each other. He'd noticed how close she'd stood to the man, and the fact that both of them kept looking at him.

They were hiding something.

They parked outside Dorset Police HQ at Winfrith, the DCI placing her car across two spaces. Dennis resisted the urge to point this out.

She slammed the driver's door and looked at him across the roof of her car. "I need to speak to Carpenter. You go in and brief the team on what we have so far. Find out what they've managed to uncover about Fran Dugdale."

"You need them to stand down?" She hadn't phoned any of the team en route: Dennis knew she should have. And under normal circumstances, she would have.

She pursed her lips, then sighed. "Tell them to stop all activity until they hear otherwise."No. Carry on. Let me speak to Carpenter."

"Yes, boss."

She rounded the car to walk with him to the office. "And Dennis..."

"Yes?" He carried on walking, avoiding eye contact. "Yes, boss?"

"None of this is your fault, you know. I know Collingwood kept giving you dirty looks back there. But I knew he'd do this. PSD don't like other people getting involved in their business."

"I know."

They stopped at the door. Lesley held it open for him. "Do you?"

Dennis hated it when the boss opened doors for him. She was the boss, and she was a woman. Reluctantly, he passed through. "I do."

But did he? Or did he really believe that Collingwood held a grudge against him? That the man still believed he'd been responsible for Mackie's death?

There was a murder to investigate. The boss had already done the work to get Dennis exonerated for the murder of DCI Mackie. He had to start taking care of himself.

CHAPTER THIRTEEN

CARPENTER WAS BEHIND HIS DESK, working through a pile of papers. He turned them over as Lesley entered. She glanced down at them but knew it would be pointless to ask what they were.

"Sir," she said, stopping in front of his desk.

He leaned back and laced his fingers behind his head. "I heard what happened at Tyneham."

"Which part, Sir?"

The body, the fact it's a PSD officer, or the way Collingwood turned up and tried to boot me off the case?

He smiled, raising an eyebrow. "All of it. And don't worry." He gestured for her to take a seat.

She sat in the centre of the three chairs opposite his desk. "I'm sorry, Sir, but you'll need to enlighten me. What is it I don't need to worry about?"

"It's your case."

"That's not what DI Collingwood seemed to think."

"Why did you let a DI walk all over you, anyway?"

"He's PSD, Sir. You know how it is—"

"Not really. PSD rule the roost in Birmingham, do they?"

"No, Sir." Lesley thought back to the jobs she'd worked with PSD, back when she'd been in Force CID. She'd had an undercover PSD officer in her team for a while: DI Carl Whaley.

"Good," Carpenter said. "In that case you won't let them intimidate you here, either."

"I really do—"

Carpenter waved a hand. "It doesn't matter. What does matter is that this is a major murder investigation, and as such it falls under the remit of the MCIT. You'll need to play nicely with PSD, as I imagine you'll need to speak to poor DC Dugdale's colleagues. I assume you're confident you can do that, given what happened this morning?"

"Of course." Lesley had dealt with far worse than Collingwood.

"Good." He put a hand on his upturned pile of papers. "And don't forget you've got an unsolved case on your hands still."

"David Watson." West Midlands Police had arrested him for drugs crimes, but Lesley knew he'd been involved in a murder on Portland Bill. He'd had a good lawyer who'd managed to get him released. And now her old West Midlands colleagues had no idea where he was.

"That's the one," Carpenter said. "Any progress there?"

"I'm in close contact with West Midlands. They have an alert out for him. If he tries to leave the country, or—"

"He's part of an organised crime gang. If he wanted to leave the country, he'd have done it by now."

"I hope not, Sir. And with respect, the Brum Boys are all but defunct, with their other leaders dead or arrested. I don't think they have the resources to evade Customs checks."

"Very well. But I don't want the Watson case getting lost, now you have this new case to think about."

"No, Sir. I have an extra team member, now that Tina and Mike are both back."

"You still have Meera?"

"Yes." Lesley hesitated, half regretting mentioning her expanded team. Would he take Meera off her?

He sniffed. "Good. Well in that case, you should be able to spare one or two of them to track down this David Watson. If he's involved in organised crime, then I suggest you bring that one to a close as quickly as you can. And make sure you liaise with DI Gough from the Organised Crime unit. They're keeping a close eye on Vera Kelvin, and we have views on how we want things to pan out in that direction."

Vera Kelvin was the mother of Arthur Kelvin, the local organised crime boss who'd been killed by his nephew, his body dumped at the Blue Pool outside Wareham.

"Which are?" Lesley asked.

"Just focus on your cases, Lesley."

She pursed her lips. "Yes, Sir."

Carpenter jerked his head upwards: an instruction. Lesley stood.

"Sir, I also wanted to get your thoughts on Rowan Angus, and how—"

He shook his head. "I want you to leave that one alone."

DI Rowan Angus, Lesley believed, was corrupt. He'd been at three murder scenes, slipping himself into them in a manner that would have been convenient if he wanted to weaken any evidence that he'd been there before. But now, with a PSD officer dead, was it the wrong time to be investigating him?

Or was it exactly the right time?

"As you know, I believe he was involved in the murder of—"

"You heard me." Carpenter put a hand on his papers: a hint.

Lesley nodded. "I'll keep you informed of progress."

"Of course you will. And one other thing."

"Yes?" Lesley bristled. *What now?*

"I suggest you keep DS Frampton away from the Dugdale case. A little bit close to home, really."

It wasn't Carpenter's job to tell her how to allocate individual officers. As long as Dennis was a member of her team, she could deploy him how she thought best.

But she'd been thinking the exact same thing.

"Sir," she said, and headed back towards the team room.

CHAPTER FOURTEEN

LESLEY WAS outside the team room door when her phone rang. She pulled back from the door to stand in the corridor and answer it.

"Sadie," she said.

"Lesley. Are you heading up the investigation into the body they found at Tyneham yesterday?"

You don't miss a trick, Sadie. "How much do you know about that?"

"Not as much as you, I'd imagine. You got an ID yet?"

Lesley hesitated. She'd worked with Sadie Dawes, a reporter from the local BBC, in the past and could trust the woman as well as she could trust anyone from the press.

But she didn't even know if Fran Dugdale's family had been told yet.

"When we have an ID, we'll make a formal announcement," she replied. It wasn't a lie.

"I get it. Next of kin haven't been informed yet."

"Something like that," Lesley replied. "Is that what you're calling about?"

"No. It's about Tim Mackie."

Lesley shifted her weight, huddling into herself to withdraw further from the door. "What about him?"

"I've got more information."

"Presumably information you can't corroborate, or you'd be discussing it on the evening news instead of talking to me."

"Touché. Can we meet?"

"I'm a bit busy, Sadie. As you just said yourself, there's a new murder investigation."

"You'll want to hear about this."

Lesley put a hand on the wall. *Bloody Sadie Dawes.*

"Surely you can tell me whatever it is you have over the phone."

"You're on a police issue phone, right?"

"Of course."

"In that case, I'd rather not."

Lesley rolled her eyes. It wasn't as if anyone listened in on her calls.

"Sadie, you've been watching too many movies. Just tell me what it is you're itching to say."

"Sorry, Lesley. Call me when you've got time, yes?"

"Hang on." Lesley didn't want to leave this hanging.

"Yes?" Sadie's voice had perked up.

"You won't tell me what you've got. But will you at least tell me who you've been talking to?"

"A certain retired officer from another force."

"Phipps?"

"He'd rather I didn't use his name."

"Less of the cloak and dagger, Sadie. Why have you been talking to Phipps again?"

Detective Superintendent Phipps was the Hampshire detective who'd been brought in almost six months ago to reinvestigate Mackie's death. He'd been pulled off the case and retired, all in the space of a few weeks. The case had never been reopened.

"I believe he knows things he's not letting on," Sadie replied.

"And now he's told you those things."

Lesley wished she could reach through the phone and shake Sadie. She looked at the team room door. *I've got a bloody murder investigation to lead. Just get to the fucking point.*

"Tell me what it is you want me to know, Sadie. I have to go."

"Call me when you're less busy."

"That could be a while."

"It won't." Sadie hung up.

Lesley stared at the phone in her hand. Her natural curiosity was urging her to call back, to arrange a meeting. Ever since she'd taken on this job, she'd wanted to know why Mackie had died. After all, if the former head of the MCIT had been murdered, then she might be at risk too.

But she was right. She had a murder investigation to run.

Sadie could wait. It had been two years since this had all started: another week or two wouldn't do any harm.

CHAPTER FIFTEEN

DENNIS WAS STANDING over Tina's desk, looking at what she'd learned about Fran Dugdale, when the DCI entered the team room.

He gave Tina a nod: *stand down.* The team knew that Collingwood wanted them off the case, and they knew that the DCI was discussing it with the super. What none of them knew, including him, was whether the boss had been successful.

In the meantime, they had to be careful.

The DCI walked into the centre of the room and surveyed the team members. For once, everyone was there: Tina, Mike, Stanley and Meera.

"I have news," she said.

"You got the super to give us the case back," Stanley muttered.

The boss looked at him. "You read my mind, Stanley."

Tina smiled and applauded gently. Dennis gave her a frown and she stopped. "Sorry," she whispered.

"It wasn't all that hard, Tina," Lesley said. "It makes perfect sense for MCIT to be running this case."

Dennis looked at her. She was avoiding looking at him.

The DCI clasped her hands together. "OK. It's early days, but we have an ID and we have Forensics and Pathology at the scene. The body has been moved to Poole hospital for the post-mortem, which will be expedited. If the killer left any physical evidence, Gail and her team will find it."

Dennis wished he shared her confidence. The boss seemed to think that Gail Hansford was some kind of miracle worker.

"However, we do need to tread lightly," the boss continued. "There'll be no board in this room, no evidence anywhere other than on the system. We don't know who might decide to come wandering past, or even pay us a visit." She glanced towards the tall windows that looked over the car park. "Or even peer in here with the aid of a pair of binoculars."

"You think they'd be that persistent?" Mike asked.

The DCI shrugged. "I have no idea. I don't know anything about the people we're going to be questioning yet." She looked around the team, again not meeting Dennis's eye. "Do any of you? Has any of you worked with Fran Dugdale in the past, or her colleagues? Mike, Tina, either of you do training with her? Stanley, could you have come across her in your last unit? Meera, have you or DI Scott had any dealings with her?"

A flicker crossed Meera's face. She pulled on a blank expression. "No, boss. Sorry."

Lesley nodded. She looked around the other DCs, her eyebrows raised. "Anyone?"

"No, boss," came a chorus of responses.

Dennis remained silent. He *had* come across Fran Dugdale before. As well as her senior officer, DI Collingwood. He'd been interviewed by the pair of them after his arrest for DCI Mackie's murder.

The DCI knew that. Which was why she wasn't asking him about it.

He took a breath. "Boss," he said. "If we can talk in private..."

She nodded. "You and I will need to discuss tactics, work out how best to allocate resources. We can talk in my office after this."

His hand was on the back of Tina's chair. He gripped it tighter. No one in this room was fooled by her pretence. He wasn't sure if he appreciated her trying to be subtle, or if he'd rather just get it all out into the open.

"Right," the boss said, not waiting for him to speak. "Meera, I want you back at the crime scene. Collingwood will be there, but there's a good chance he doesn't know you're part of this team. Watch him. See if anyone else from his unit turns up. Or if he leaves. Report back. And speak to Gail too, find out what's being uncovered. That's what you're officially there to do."

"As well as being a spy." Meera smiled.

Lesley's eyes flashed. "You said it, not me."

Dennis felt his stomach clench. He didn't like this: the boss insisting on taking cases back from other units, sending officers out to spy on colleagues. It wasn't how she normally operated.

He would raise it when they were alone.

"Mike, Tina, Stanley," the boss continued, "I want you working on background. I'm assuming you've got all you can about DC Dugdale from her official record. I want the reality behind that. What cases was she working on, who was she investigating? Was there anyone in her team who held a grudge against her? Was there anyone she'd investigated or arrested in the past?"

"You think a police officer did this?" Dennis asked.

The DCI swung round to face him. Eye contact: at last. "You sound surprised."

"Well..."

"If DC Dugdale had been a member of the public, we would want to know about her work colleagues, her associates. If she'd been a lawyer, say." She raised both eyebrows, knowing they'd both think of her wife Elsa Short. "Then we'd want to know about her clients. If she'd been one of us, a normal copper, we'd be looking at the people she'd arrested or investigated. This is no different."

"We should speak to her family," Tina said. "Have they been informed?"

The DCI cast around the room. "I don't know. But Tina, seeing as you raised it, can you check that with Uniform? Has a Family Liaison Officer been assigned? Find out what you can, and pay them a visit."

"Boss."

"Good." The DCI paused, gazing at the door out to the corridor. Dennis wondered if there was a problem.

"OK," she said, as if coming out of a reverie. "Everyone get to work. Dennis, you and I need to chat in my office."

He followed her, knowing full well that any talk of 'allocating resources' had already been done. And that she hadn't allocated him to a role.

CHAPTER SIXTEEN

"Dennis, why don't you sit down? You're making me nervous."

Dennis was standing in front of Lesley's desk, shifting from foot to foot.

Sometimes, Dennis...

"Boss." He took the seat in front of her and sniffed.

Lesley leaned back and eyed him. "You met her. What was she like?"

He shook his head. "She barely spoke. I got the distinct impression she was somewhat in thrall to him."

"In thrall? What d'you mean?"

A shrug. "She didn't do anything unless he told her to. She sat quietly, waiting for him to tell her otherwise. She watched him constantly. Waiting for him to give her instructions, I suppose."

"Would you say she was scared of him? What's the culture like in that team?"

Dennis looked at her. "I've no idea. PSD don't fraternise

with other officers." He pulled off his specs and rubbed them on his trousers, then replaced them. "It wouldn't be... wise."

"No. But I've never met DC Dugdale or DI Collingwood, not before today. You have. I'm hoping you can give us some sort of insight."

"I'm sorry, boss. It was a very formal process. And I hope you'll understand when I say that I wasn't exactly... I wasn't looking for information about the two of them and how they worked." He cleared his throat. "I had other things on my mind."

That was the closest Dennis had come to telling her his feelings about being arrested, interviewed and released.

Lesley pushed out a breath. "You were interviewed by Organised Crime, too."

A nod. "DI Gough."

"Was there any interaction between the two teams, as far as you were aware?"

"I have no idea. They don't keep the suspect informed of that kind of thing, boss."

Lesley didn't need Dennis to tell her about PSD protocols. Even Zoe hadn't known much about the way the department operated, and she was now living with Carl Whaley.

"Right," she said. Once again, she had a strong urge to pick Dennis up by the collar of his tweed jacket and shake him.

She looked at his body language. *Why don't you just relax a little?*

He was looking down, one leg crossed over the other, his hands in his lap. The specs were back on his nose, perfectly aligned and clean. His trousers were immaculate, a crease ironed into the front. The tweed jacket looked like it had been recently dry-cleaned.

"Right," she said again. "Well, I can't have you on this case, I'm afraid."

"I suspected as much."

"Carpenter won't wear it and... I don't think it's wise." For one thing, it could tip Dennis's mental health back into a dark place.

He nodded. "What will you have me doing, then?"

"David Watson. He was released without charge, got himself a good lawyer. Edward Startshaw, who represented Trevor Hamm before his arrest."

"That in itself is suspicious."

"It is. Why would a man we suspect of being involved in Hamm's death be represented by his victim's lawyer?"

"You want me to do some digging into that, boss?"

"I do. But the most important thing is to find Watson. He hasn't been seen since his release, and I think he can provide us with information that will help us better understand how and why Hamm died."

"It was a conspiracy. They've all been arrested."

"Not all of them." Lesley didn't mention DI Rowan Angus. "Just see what you can discover, yes?"

A nod.

"Liaise with West Midlands, find out if they have anything new. Then speak to Devon. Some of the Kelvin family are operating from there."

"The other nephew."

"Kyle Kelvin, yes."

Dennis nodded again.

"Dennis." Lesley gritted her teeth. "Stop bloody nodding at me and tell me if you have any suggestions. You're an experienced copper and this kind of thing should be bread and butter for you."

His jaw was clenched: the damn swear jar was back on top of the filing cabinet, where she'd put it after his release. Maybe it was time to put it away again.

"Very well," he said. "As you say, I think Devon is a good starting place. I wasn't involved in the Hamm investigation but when Arthur Kelvin was killed, we didn't really get to the bottom of what was going on there. It could be that there's a link between Kyle Kelvin and the Brum Boys."

"The new gang in Birmingham."

Dennis pursed his lips. "I've looked at their profiles. They're small beer, boss. Not capable of masterminding the murder of Trevor Hamm on their own. If they did it, they must have been working with another gang."

"And now that almost all of them are dead, West Midlands will be worried about that gang moving in to claim their territory."

"Yes, boss."

"That's a good start," she said. "It won't be a problem for you liaising with Zoe?"

"Of course not." He didn't make reference to the fact that she'd already brought Zoe down to Dorset to help her investigate Mackie's death. That Zoe had followed Dennis.

Lesley thought of her phone call from Sadie. Did she have time to follow that up?

No. Not right now.

"Very well," she said. "Keep me updated on progress. And you can take Stanley."

"DC Brown?"

"He came up to Birmingham with me, he met some of the key players. He can assist you, fill you in on what happened while you were off work."

Dennis's cheeks flushed. *Off work.* Under arrest, more like.

"Boss." He glanced back towards the team room, then stood up and left.

Lesley sat back in her chair, her breathing heavy. Why did she always come away from a conversation with DS Dennis Frampton feeling like she'd just run a marathon?

CHAPTER SEVENTEEN

MEERA HAD LIVED in Dorset for thirteen years, but she'd never visited Tyneham. It was one of those activities reserved for grockles, not the kind of thing a local did. And besides, it was only open at the weekends, and she was busy at the weekends.

She took the side road off the B3070 and slowed as she proceeded down the hill. The road was narrow here and her car splashed through puddles on both sides. The rain would mean mud: hopefully shoe or boot prints from whoever had killed Fran Dugdale or left her at the site. She wondered if Forensics would be analysing tyre marks, or if there would be too many for it to be of any use. The place had been open to the public yesterday, after all.

At last the village appeared on her right. She turned a bend and found herself at the edge of a car park that was almost deserted. Two squad cars were parked at the nearest end, along with the CSI van and two unmarked cars she didn't recognise. One of them would be Collingwood's.

Did he know that the super had allocated the case to the

MCIT? Or was she going to have to navigate inter-team politics?

Not with PSD, she hoped.

She parked her car neatly beside one of the squad cars and got out, taking a moment to listen. The site was quiet, the only sound that of a swallow singing. Meera checked her watch: early afternoon. The place must have very few people in it, for the bird to be singing at this time.

She went to the boot of her car and pulled out her walking boots. They were at the bottom of a jumbled pile that included Jill's boots and waterproof jacket, and Suzi's tiny pink all-in-one. Meera smiled, wondering what her family were up to right now.

She sat in the driver's doorway and pulled on her boots, still listening. She could hear voices in the distance: Gail Hansford giving orders. *Good.* It was reassuring to have Gail in charge.

At last she was ready. She secured the car and walked to the first set of buildings.

"Hello?" she called.

No response.

Meera narrowed her eyes. The majority of the buildings were ahead of her, around the church. She could see its open door beyond the phone box and the school museum.

She inhaled, taking in the fresh air and the smell of damp soil, and walked past the church. Muddy tyre tracks led towards a dirt path off to the right. She followed them and then the ridges which seemed to have been made by some kind of wheeled contraption. Maybe a stretcher trolley? They'd have had to use something to get the body over to the car park.

She heard voices again. Gail, and a man. Meera swallowed and proceeded, aware that no one was expecting her.

She arrived in a clearing that was filled with equipment. A man in a forensic suit stood to one side, cataloguing evidence bags and placing them in a pilot case. He turned to her.

"Who are you?"

She flashed her ID. "DC Vedra, MCIT."

"You're one of Lesley Clarke's lot?"

She nodded. "Where's Gail? And DI Collingwood?"

"He's headed off into the woods over there with one of his team."

"Why?"

"Something about a potential way in."

"Shouldn't you guys be checking that?"

A shrug. "I don't think Gail was entirely convinced."

Meera peered past the ruined house in front of them, towards the woods. It wasn't normal procedure for detectives to go tramping all over crime scenes ahead of CSI.

A woman was inside the house. She emerged, pausing when she saw Meera. "You're Meera Vedra," she said. "I know your wife."

"You've worked with Jill?"

"I went to school with her sister."

"Oh." How come Meera hadn't known this?

"You know what it's like round here. We both grew up in Swanage, there aren't exactly a lot of schools to choose from."

True.

"What's going on with the PSD guys?" Meera asked.

"Don't talk to me about them."

"They've got some sort of theory about the woods?"

Gail shook her head. "I know this village. First time I came here was in 1985, on a school trip. I've been here with my son Tim a dozen times or more and I know the layout. Over there is fields and the Army range. No way she was brought in that way."

"What if the Army was involved, in some way? Maybe they had permission to cross the ranges?"

Gail wiped her forehead. She was standing in the doorway to the ruined house, which was little more than a stone archway. "It's a possibility, I suppose. But not a likely one." She picked up a rucksack. "Too dangerous. No, she came in the same way we all did. I'm convinced of it."

Meera said nothing. OK, so she hadn't been here before. But they couldn't rule out the possibility of Army involvement. If the killer was an Army officer...

She made a mental note to call into the office, ask Tina to check for any Army connection. Not that Tina would need reminding.

"Looks like the work of Kelvin's bunch." A man's voice came from beyond the house. Meera took a step to one side and Gail turned towards the sound.

"They're barely operational now, boss. Not since Arthur Kelvin died."

"I wouldn't be so sure."

The voices were growing louder: two men. Meera listened. Gail was doing the same.

"Well, let's not rule it out."

She could see the men now, walking towards them through the woods. She and the two CSIs stood in silence, all listening.

"I'll look into it if you'd like, Sir."

"We can speak to Jim."

The taller of the two men stopped walking as he noticed Meera. "Who are you?"

"DC Vedra, MCIT." She straightened, determined not to be intimidated.

"I told your boss to bugger off."

"With respect, Sir, Superintendent Carpenter has over-ridden that."

"He has, has he? Well, we'll see about that." The man she assumed was Collingwood turned to his companion and bent to speak in his ear. The other man, who was plump with a scar on the back of his hand, glanced at Meera then walked past her towards the car park.

Meera exchanged glances with Gail and her colleague. What was going on?

"So." Collingwood walked towards the ruined house. "What have you been sent here to do, exactly? Spy on us?" He laughed. "That's normally our job. I take it you know about what happened to your DS."

Meera ignored the reference to the sarge. "I'm to liaise with the CSM, Sir. Report back on forensic evidence to my team."

"We've taken samples from inside the house," Gail said. "And from under her fingernails. There was organic matter on her body, and what looked like skin fragments too."

"There was a struggle?" Meera asked, ignoring Collingwood's stare.

"You know it's not my place to speculate on what happened," Gail said. "I'll just give you what I see."

"Of course."

Collingwood was still staring at Meera.

You aren't going to intimidate me like that, mate.

Gail shouldered the rucksack and approached Meera. When she was close to her, she stopped.

"Come back to the van," she said, her voice low. "I'll show you what we've got."

CHAPTER EIGHTEEN

JACINTA AND TONY DUGDALE lived in a low bungalow in Blandford Forum, a few streets away from the river.

Tina pulled up outside, checking the road for signs of anyone else sitting in their car. She wasn't sure who knew about Fran Dugdale's death yet, but once it got out, the press wouldn't take long to get here.

She turned off the engine and took a moment to still the thoughts running around her head. Visiting the parents of a murder victim felt different, now she had a child of her own.

Stop it, she told herself. Fran Dugdale was an adult. A police officer. Not a baby boy who was currently playing with balloons in a nursery in Wareham.

She slid back the cover of her sun- visor mirror and checked her face, then licked her finger and rubbed a bit of mascara from under her eye. No matter how much concealer she used, she couldn't hide the dark circles. Should she apply to reduce her hours further, get more time to sleep?

But Tina was ambitious. She'd been a uniformed PC less than two years ago, and now she was a DC in one of the most prestigious teams in the county. If she carried on like this, she might make DS before long.

Mike might not like being leapfrogged by his wife. Maybe even managed by her.

Mike would have to deal with it.

She suppressed a smile, flipped up the visor and got out of the car. The curtains were open in the Dugdale house, but there was no movement. Fran hadn't lived here – she had her own flat in Dorchester – but she had no partner that they knew of, so her parents were her next of kin.

And Tina was about to shatter their lives forever.

She pressed on the doorbell – a Ring; they would already know she was here. That might be useful for footage, if Fran had been round lately.

The door opened and a heavily-built woman in her late forties wearing a bright pink sweater looked at Tina.

"We don't buy at the door."

Tina looked down at her suit. This was her second best, the grey one. Did it make her look like a saleswoman?

"I'm not selling anything." She held out her ID, which was already in her hand. "I'm from Dorset Police. DC Tina Abbott."

"Oh." The woman paled. "Do you work with Fran? Is everything OK?"

Tina gave as small a smile as she could manage. "Can I come in, please? Is Mr Dugdale home?"

"Tony." A frown. "No, he's not home." The woman blinked at Tina a couple of times, her jaw stiff, then stood back. "Come in."

Jacinta Dugdale was the mother of a copper. She knew what a visit like this might mean.

Best get it over with.

A large living room was at the front of the house. Tina took a seat in a wide leather armchair. Jacinta perched on a sofa beside her.

"Tell me," she said, her breath coming fast. Her fingernails dug into the arm of the sofa.

Tina leaned forward. "It's bad news, I'm afraid. Fran was found at Tyneham village yesterday afternoon. I'm sorry to tell you she's dead."

Jacinta made no sound, no movement. She stayed stock still, her fingers deep in the arm of the sofa. The only sign she'd heard Tina was a single tear escaping from the corner of her eye.

Tina watched her, her own breathing unsteady. She should have brought someone with her. Mike. Or maybe Stanley. That would have been better.

"Is Mr Dugdale around? Would you like me to tell him, or...?"

Jacinta shook her head. "He's gone."

Tina felt a lump in her chest. "Sorry, gone?"

Jacinta blinked. Her gaze on Tina's face intensified. "The bastard left me. Just this morning. He's... I don't bloody know where he is. With *her*."

Ah.

Tina sighed. She'd have to track down another address, before Fran's death could be made public. She'd find the dead DC's dad at his mistress's, by the sounds of it.

"Do you have an address for where he is?"

"Of course I don't. Look, are you sure it's Fran? Only, I'm sure Robert would tell me if anything had happened to her. I haven't heard from him."

"Robert?"

"Robert Collingwood. Her boss."

"DI Collingwood is currently at the crime scene. I'm not sure he—"

"Robert always calls me. He knows I worry about her, living on her own in that grotty flat." Jacinta looked Tina up and down. "Doing the kind of work she does. It's important work, you know. I know most of you must hate her, but she's rooting out the bad apples."

"I'm so sorry, Mrs Dugdale, u—"

"Jacinta." Her shoulders fell. "Jacinta Frost from now on, I suppose."

"I'm sorry, Jacinta."

There was a lot to unpack. Fran's dad had left her mum this morning, and if name changes were being considered, it looked permanent. Had Fran known this was about to happen? Were the two events connected?

"I'm sorry," Tina said, "but it is definitely your daughter. She was identified by two officers who knew her. DI Collingwood, and my own senior officer, DS Frampton."

Jacinta slumped back. "I need to see her."

"We can arrange that."

The woman had her eyes closed. "You can find *him*, though. I'm not bloody talking to him." She squeezed her eyes tighter, and tears ran down her face. "*She'll* be no use to him, with this. But if he thinks he's coming back here, he can whistle."

CHAPTER NINETEEN

DENNIS DIDN'T WANT to do this in the office. He'd briefed Stanley, pulled him off the Fran Dugdale investigation and informed him that he would be working with him on the Watson case. They would be allocated more personnel for the Dugdale case soon, he was sure of it. The high-ups didn't spare resources when it came to investigating the death of one of their own.

Stanley was up in the team room, trawling through HOLMES, looking for references to David Watson and his associates. Dennis was in the car park, sitting in his car.

The phone call he was about to make was a legitimate one. The Dorset force had worked with West Midlands when investigating the murder of Trevor Hamm on Portland Bill, and the involvement of David 'Day' Watson. The DCI had taken Stanley with her up to Birmingham, and they'd spent a day tracking down ne'er-do-wells, most of whom were now dead.

He peered around the car park, phone in hand, aware of how stupid he was being. It wasn't like anyone would hear him. And it wasn't like he was doing anything wrong.

But he hadn't spoken to this woman since she'd spent time following him, brought in by the boss to investigate DCI Mackie's death without anyone knowing. Something the boss still didn't appear to have been reprimanded for, to Dennis's surprise.

He dialled.

She picked up on the second ring.

"DS Frampton."

"You've stored my number," he said.

"Sorry if that's thrown you," DI Zoe Finch replied. "What can I do for you?"

"I'm trying to track down David Watson."

"I thought that was solved. West Midlands arrested him."

"He was given a suspended sentence. You only arrested him for drugs offences."

Silence.

"DI Finch?"

"You say *you*. I wasn't involved in that arrest. When was he released?"

"A week ago. He's not been seen since."

"He's breached the terms of his sentence."

Dennis swallowed. "I would have thought that inevitable."

"True. But you can't blame my team for sentencing decisions."

Dennis wrinkled his nose. "I'm calling to see if you're looking for him too. If you've heard anything about his whereabouts."

"Whereabouts?"

Was that laughter in her voice?

"I'm sorry, DS Frampton," she said, "you've taken me by surprise. I had no idea that Day Watson wasn't in custody, or that he'd disappeared."

"So you don't know where he is."

"No. And I'm afraid the West Midlands case regarding him is closed. I—"

"I do know that, Ma'am. He was never charged with aiding and abetting Trevor Hamm's murder, though."

"And you want to find him so you can arrest him for that."

"We do."

"If I hear anything about him, Dennis – you don't mind me calling you Dennis, I hope – I'll make sure to tell you."

"I expect you will. But I wanted to be thorough."

"I'm sure you do. I've heard good things about you, from Lesley."

Dennis doubted that. Why would the woman have followed him, if she thought he was trustworthy?

"Right. Well, I'd be grateful if you decide to actively look for him. We can pool resources and—"

"Sheila might be looking for him. That's DS Griffin. I can give you her contact details."

Dennis wrote down the number she gave him. "DS Griffin is in your Organised Crime unit, is that correct?"

"She is. I'm surprised you didn't call her first."

Dennis might have done some research, found DS Griffin's name another way. But he'd wanted to hear the sound of Zoe Finch's voice again. To show her he was still working in the MCIT, and no longer under suspicion.

"I owe you an apology, Dennis. DS Frampton."

"I'm sure that's not necessary."

"It wasn't Lesley who told me to watch you. She's always believed you to be beyond reproach."

Beyond reproach? "I don't think—"

"It was entirely my idea to focus on you," DI Finch said.

"And I hear that any suspicions I may have had were proven wrong."

Dennis felt sweat break out on his brow. How many people knew?

"Well, yes," he replied.

"If it means anything, I'm glad to hear it. You seemed trustworthy to me. I'm glad you were exonerated."

"This call isn't about me, it's about—"

"Yes, I know. Day Watson. And if we hear anything about him, I promise you'll be the first to know. I assume you're leading on this, while Lesley focuses on the murder case at Tyneham."

"You've heard about that?"

"It's a tourist spot. There are no pictures of it yet, what with the Army not letting the press in and drones being banned, but it's certainly been reported. Wish her luck with it, will you?"

Dennis knew that DI Finch had a partner who worked in PSD. Would she have any insights that might help?

It wasn't his place to ask.

"Thank you, DI Finch. I'll keep you apprised as well, should we track David Watson down."

"Good. Call Sheila. She might know something I'm not aware of."

"Thank you. I will."

He hung up, cursing the fact that he was sweating and breathing heavily.

CHAPTER TWENTY

STANLEY PICKED UP THE PHONE. Mike was in with the DCI, no doubt talking about the murder case, Tina was out informing the next of kin, and the sarge had disappeared. The ringing phone was on Tina's desk, but he was the only one here to take it.

"MCIT, DS Brown speaking."

"Stanley, it's Meera."

"You need to talk to the boss?"

"Her phone's engaged."

He looked up and through the glass separating the team room from the DCI's office. "Yep. She's on the phone."

"I guessed as much. Can you pass on a message?"

"Course. What's happening?"

"I've been talking with Gail and her team. There was skin under the victim's fingernails and bruising to her arms. Definite signs of a struggle. She's gone to the morgue now, so someone's going to have to get over there and observe the PM."

"You're already out. Why don't you do it?"

"I thought someone else might want the chance."

He smiled. "I've been pulled off the case. Back on the Hamm murder."

"Tracking down Day Watson?"

"That's the one. Is that all you need me to tell the boss, this stuff about evidence of a struggle?"

"Tell her that DI Collingwood's being an arse, too."

"Don't say that in front of the sarge."

"If the sarge was in the office, he'd have picked up. So I'm guessing you're on your own."

"There's clearly a reason you're a detective, Meera. What kind of an arse is he being?"

"I'm not sure how many kinds of arse there are, mate, but he's trying to prevent me from getting close to the scene. It's Gail's scene to manage, but he's acting like he's in charge."

"You really want me to tell the boss that? It's not exactly a surprise."

A pause. "Good point. OK, tell her he's been disappearing into the woods with his colleague, DS Strunk. I heard them talking about Arthur Kelvin."

"Why would they care about Arthur Kelvin?" Stanley leaned back in his chair, glancing over towards the DCI's office. She was still on the phone.

"They might have been investigating links between dodgy coppers and organised crime. Maybe Fran was working on a case, got her into trouble with Kelvin's lot."

"Day Watson." Stanley clenched a fist on his desk. "Did they name any names?"

"Just Kelvin. He's dead, though."

"His nephews aren't." Both Darren and Kyle Kelvin were in prison for murder: in Kyle's case, it was the murder of his uncle.

"No. Look, Gail needs me, I've got to go. Can you pass on the message about the PM? And about—"

"Don't worry, Meera. The sarge and me are working on Watson, trying to track him down. If it's linked, we'll work it out."

"OK. But don't forget to tell the boss, will you?"

"Course not."

Stanley put his phone down. He needed to speak to the sarge.

CHAPTER TWENTY-ONE

LESLEY'S PHONE rang as she drove through East Lulworth towards the crime scene. This wasn't a part of Dorset she'd visited before, probably because much of it was closed to traffic most of the time. The roads were quiet, the public aware that they couldn't get through to the east of the county this way, and it made her wonder what it must have been like for the locals, forced out of here during the Second World War.

She picked up without looking at the phone display, her eyes on the road as she steered to the side to avoid a farm vehicle coming the other way and taking up far more than its share of road.

"Bloody farmers," she muttered as the call kicked in.

"Bloody what?"

Lesley glanced down at the phone: it was Carpenter.

"Nothing, Sir. Just trying not to hit half of South Dorset's farm machinery."

"Always a challenge. I have news."

"Promising news, I hope."

"PSD have been told to leave this case alone. It's all yours, DCI Clarke."

She pumped the steering wheel with her fist. "That *is* good news. Thank you, Sir."

"It wasn't my decision. But I had a word with Chief Superintendent Price, who agreed that it's inappropriate for any unit to investigate the death of one of their own."

"My team will need to interview members of PSD."

"Of course they will. But you know what I said. I've had my PA check your team's files, and they're all fine to conduct those interviews with the exception of DS Frampton."

Lesley was relieved Dennis wasn't sitting in the passenger seat, as he so often was. "Dennis is working on the Day Watson case, Sir. He's following up with the West Midlands force, and he'll be speaking to the remaining members of the Kelvin family."

"Good luck to him."

Lesley smiled. The turnoff for the village was coming up on her right. She slowed and took it, checking carefully in the distance in case anything was coming towards her. Maybe even Collingwood leaving the crime scene.

"Anything else, Sir? I'm about to arrive at the crime scene."

"I'm sure you don't need me to tell you how sensitive this case is. I'll be announcing a press conference in the morning. Better to give them what we want them to know rather than have them speculating."

"Absolutely. Will you need me at that?"

"You're SIO, Lesley."

"I'll be there."

"Carla will give you the when and where. And meanwhile..."

"Sir?"

"I imagine you don't like him very much after what happened to your DS, but take care not to go pissing DI Collingwood off more than you have to, will you? He's a powerful man, despite his rank, and I know what you can be like."

The village was coming up ahead. Lesley slowed to pass it, and turned into the car park.

She stopped the car and looked at the phone in its holder. "What can I be like, Sir?"

A laugh. "I think you know, DCI Clarke. Just let me know if you make any progress. And tread carefully."

He hung up. Lesley resisted an urge to stick her tongue out at the phone and got out of the car.

CHAPTER TWENTY-TWO

"STANLEY," said the sarge, approaching his desk with a smile that at least seemed to be genuine. "Shall we formulate our plan of action?"

Stanley looked at Tina, who shrugged, then back at the sarge.

"Er... yeah. I s'pose so."

The smile broadened. As the sarge drew closer, Stanley realised it didn't extend to the man's eyes.

"OK." The sarge looked back towards the DCI's office. "Let's go in there." He scratched his chin. "In fact, no. Let's take over the bank of desks in the corner."

The team room was large, a blank space overlooking the car park. At one end was a bank of desks without any permanent inhabitants. When a major case was on, it filled with Uniform and temporary investigators. Right now, it was empty.

"There won't be new people moving in there to help with the Dugdale case?" Stanley asked.

A shrug. "If there are, we can shift back. It might be good

for you and me to set up base away from the rest of the team, though."

"Fair enough." Stanley grabbed his rucksack and laptop and moved across to the area the sarge had indicated. The DS followed, carrying only a notepad.

The sarge waited for Stanley to pick a seat, then took the chair beside him. Stanley glanced back at the rest of the team again, feeling uneasy. The sarge was being weird.

"Right, Stanley," the sarge said. "I hope you don't mind being dragged away from the murder case."

Stanley shook his head. "Makes sense for me to work with you on this. I was in Birmingham, after all."

"Exactly." Another insincere smile. "Can you fill me in on what happened while you were there?"

Stanley licked his lips. "I made notes."

The sarge nodded: *go ahead*.

Stanley opened his laptop and brought up the file where he had typed up his hand-written notes from the Sunday he'd spent travelling to the West Midlands with the DCI, and driving around with her old colleagues.

"OK," he said, scanning the notes. It was amazing how quickly you could forget the details. "So we went up to the West Midlands on Sunday, May the twenty-first. We reported at Harborne Police Station, where we met the boss's old colleague DI Finch."

"What was she like?"

Stanley frowned. "Like?"

Another nod. "Did she seem competent?"

"Oh. Yes, yes she did. Knew local criminal activity inside out. Seemed to have been investigating organised crime for a while, despite the fact she wasn't in the Organised Crime unit.

That was Sheila Griffin. DS Griffin, sorry. We met her at her house."

The sarge raised an eyebrow. "Her house?"

"It was a Sunday, sarge."

"True. Where *was* her house?"

Stanley checked his notes and read out the address in Halesowen.

The sarge listened as if it might mean something to him. But the geography of the West Midlands had been a mystery to Stanley. Not to mention all those bloody motorways and dual carriageways.

"So you went to David Watson's mum's house, is that right?"

"Yeah. We went to tell her about his brother dying. She reckoned the brother – Samuel, Zee, she called him – was in Gran Canaria."

"But he was on Portland Bill."

Stanley nodded, remembering that the sarge hadn't been around for any of this. He felt his face heat up. "Yeah. He was involved in breaking Trevor Hamm out, then killing him. Then he was murdered himself."

"And David?"

"David – Day – was part of the gang that broke Hamm out with Zee. They were trying to take over his territory in Birmingham, wanted him dead so he couldn't control things from prison."

"Was he at his mum's?"

"I never clapped eyes on the bloke, sarge. His mum didn't know where he was and it was Sheila Griffin's lot who eventually tracked him down."

The sarge nodded. "Did anyone have any hypotheses as to where he was?"

"Hypotheses, sarge?"

"Theories. Where did you think he might be?"

Stanley shrugged. "Not sure. Sheila didn't mention anything to us, but she must have found him eventually."

"At his mum's." The sarge opened his notebook. "I've checked the arrest sheet."

"If he was arrested, why are we looking for him now?"

The sarge looked up. "Because he was given a suspended sentence for drugs possession, not arrested for conspiracy to murder, and he absconded without reporting to his probation officer."

"Ah. Right. So, we got any hypothe— any theories?"

The sarge smiled, his eyes glinting this time. "Not yet. I was hoping you might help with that."

"I've been thinking about Arthur Kelvin's lot."

The sarge's eyebrows lifted. "You have?"

Stanley scratched his chin. "There's a vacuum here in Dorset, with Kelvin dead and half his family missing. I've been wondering if the Brum Boys – that's the Watson gang – came down here not just to finish off Hamm, but to fill that hole, too."

"Pretty ambitious."

"I reckon they had eyes bigger than their bellies, sarge."

The sarge laughed. Stanley smiled.

"Arthur Kelvin's nephew Kyle was working in Devon," he said. "So maybe Day is down there."

The sarge put a hand on his shoulder. "I've been thinking the exact same thing."

Stanley felt the heat rise further up his cheeks. "That's good."

"OK," the sarge said. "So we have two lines of enquiry we need to follow. The first is whoever Kyle Kelvin was working with in Devon. There's a chance Watson's working for the same people now."

Stanley nodded.

"And the other is Vera Kelvin. She's the only member of the family who's still around."

"She's an old woman."

"Have you met her?"

"No, sarge."

The sarge's cheek twitched. "She's a force to be reckoned with. She'll be causing trouble until the second she's in her grave, I can assure you."

Stanley paused, remembering something.

The sarge eyed him. "You're wishing you were on the Dugdale case."

"No, sarge. But there is something else. Meera heard something at Tyneham. She asked me to pass it on."

"To the DCI?"

"Yes. But it might be relevant to us."

The sarge leaned back in his chair and pushed his glasses up his nose. "Go on."

"She heard Collingwood talking to someone, a PSD colleague. They were talking about the Kelvin family, speculating."

"Speculating on what?"

"He seemed to think Kelvin might have something to do with Fran Dugdale's death."

"Was she investigating the Kelvins before her death?"

"We can't find any evidence of that on the system. But..."

"But PSD's investigations might not all be available to us." The sarge straightened in his chair. "Very well. I'll make sure the DCI knows, and we can see what we can sniff out about

PSD possibly investigating officers who were working for the Kelvins." He paled.

"Sarge? You alright?"

The sarge wrinkled his nose. "I'm fine. Just..." He shook himself out and stood up.

Stanley glanced back toward the team desks. He knew that the sarge had been interviewed by PSD, but he didn't know if it had been Fran Dugdale doing the interviewing. And it wasn't his place to ask.

But could the fact that PSD had been talking to the sarge have anything to do with Fran Dugdale's death?

CHAPTER TWENTY-THREE

SHARON SAT on the sea wall at Boscombe, her knees huddled against her chest. There was a stiff breeze today, despite it being July, and she wished she'd worn something sturdier.

But she was meeting Rick, and she wanted to look good.

She checked her watch again: sixteen minutes late.

He wasn't coming.

She huddled deeper into herself and considered her options.

There was a café behind her, under the cliffs. She could go in there, get a Coke, watch to see if he arrived.

She could stay here like a lemon, waiting for a boyfriend who might never come. Freeze her arse off and look like a windswept mess by the time he arrived.

Or she could go home.

She didn't much relish the idea of looking like a force nine gale had swept over her when Rick arrived.

And she wasn't giving up yet.

The café it was.

She picked herself up, brushing sand off her top, and trudged towards the buildings that bordered the beach. A few hardy souls were out on the sand, attempting to build sandcastles and wrestle with windbreaks. It wasn't the school holidays yet, so the real idiots who came out here in any weather hadn't arrived, but there would always be a few holidaymakers with smaller children anxious to make the best of their time by the seaside.

She arrived at the café to find it full. All of the inside tables were taken and there was only one outside, with just one chair and the table leg sitting squarely in a puddle.

Sharon grimaced.

The queue inside was ten deep.

It wasn't worth it, just for a Coke.

She cast around for somewhere else to shelter. There was the pier, of course, but that was miles away across the sand. Or at least, it felt like miles.

She checked her watch. Thirty minutes late.

He wasn't coming.

Give up, idiot.

It had been good while it lasted. He'd flattered her, made her feel good. Told her she had great legs, and admired the dimple next to her mouth when she smiled. They hadn't talked all that much, but he'd been a hell of a kisser.

She let out a deep sigh and pulled her thin jacket tighter around her. Her phone pinged.

Sorry, sexy. Got caught up at work. See you tomorrow, maybe.

He'd just got a job at Monkey World, cleaning out the enclosures. Shitty work, he'd told her: literally. But it paid the bills. She couldn't imagine him with animals.

Tomorrow.

Maybe.

It was something.

Sharon smiled, feeling her back straighten. And headed back for home.

CHAPTER TWENTY-FOUR

COLLINGWOOD WAS STILL at the crime scene. Either he hadn't received word that he was supposed to be standing down, or he had but didn't care.

Lesley had a sense it might be the latter.

She walked into the clearing in front of the abandoned house and pulled on a smile.

"DI Collingwood, good to see you again."

He was at the edge of the clearing, as close as he could get to the house without disturbing the CSIs. He turned.

There was a flicker on his face, a suggestion of disdain. Then he controlled it.

"DCI Clarke." He held his hands up. "Don't worry, I won't get in your way."

"Glad to hear it." Lesley walked to stand next to him. "Is there anything you can tell me? Anything that's been discovered while I've been away?"

After a moment, he turned to look at her. "You really need me to do your job for you?"

Lesley felt her skin prickle. *I'm your bloody senior officer, you—*

"They found evidence of a struggle," he said. "But then, you'll know that, seeing as you sent your spy." He gestured to indicate Meera, standing on the other side of the house.

Meera gave Lesley a small wave. Lesley returned it.

"True," she said. "I didn't want to lose any momentum."

Dumb explanation. And she didn't need to explain herself.

"Anyway," she said, holding out a hand, "it's been good to meet you. I'll be in touch."

He looked down at her hand for a couple of seconds, then took it. His handshake was limp. "You'll be wanting to interview my team members."

"For background on DC Dugdale. If you could provide details of what she was working on in recent days and weeks. Anyone she was investigating. We can't rule out the—"

"You know I can't do that."

She clenched a fist. "You're going to have to."

"PSD investigations are confidential." He leaned closer to her. "You of all people should be aware of that, given you brought an undercover PSD man into your own team."

How did he know that?

"Imagine how criminals feel about you," he continued. "That's how other police officers feel about us."

"Not the honest ones."

A laugh. "You'd be surprised."

Lesley beckoned to Meera, who started to pick her way around the site. "Anyway, DI Collingwood," she said. "I really need to ask you to—"

"I know." He brushed his right hand on his trouser leg as if he'd sullied it by shaking her hand.

Arsehole.

He gave her a nod. "I'll see you again." He turned and left the clearing, unaware that she longed to shout the word at his back.

CHAPTER TWENTY-FIVE

"DS Frampton," the woman said." I was wondering when I might hear from you."

Dennis was sitting at the bank of desks in the team room, the one he and Stanley had commandeered. So far no one else had arrived to help with the Dugdale case.

"DS Griffin," he replied. "Thanks for taking this call. This is DC Brown, he's working with me on—"

"Hello, Stanley," she said, giving a little wave into the camera. "How's things? Glad to be away from all our motorways?"

Stanley, sitting next to Dennis and also peering into the screen, gave a shrug. "Something like that."

She smiled and shifted her gaze, presumably looking at Dennis on the screen. As her camera was somewhere above her screen, it was difficult for Dennis to tell.

Video calls. He hated them. But she'd insisted.

He glanced at the notes he'd made while talking to Stanley earlier. "DC Brown has filled me in on his and our DCI's trip to Birmingham. I gather you went with them to the house of David Watson's mother."

"That wasn't me. That was Zoe. DI Finch. It was my day off."

"Ah."

"They all came round here to pick my brains, though. Stanley got rather fond of my Freddie too, didn't you?"

Dennis frowned. Stanley must have seen it, on the screen, and turned to look at him. "Her dog, sarge."

Dennis felt his brow furrow even more. What had this trip to Birmingham been, a fun day out?

"DI Finch suggested I speak to you about David Watson, in case you've had any reports of his whereabouts."

"You don't need to shout, DS Frampton." DS Griffin leaned forward, possibly to turn down the volume.

Dennis felt his skin tingle. "Sorry. Is that better?"

"Perfect."

He felt Stanley's weight shift next to him and turned to the DC. *You'd better not be laughing at me, son.*

Stanley was sitting very still, his lips clamped together.

I'm not that much of a dinosaur.

"I thought you'd be looking for the other guy," said DS Griffin. "There was an extra set of prints at your crime scene, multiple crime scenes, from what I can remember."

Dennis turned back to the screen. "Pardon?"

"The boss told us they weren't relevant, sarge," Stanley said.

Dennis looked at him. *Why didn't you tell me?*

He turned back to the screen. "I gather DCI Clarke looked into that and it was deemed irrelevant."

DS Griffin nodded. "That's what Zoe said. Turned out it

was one of yours and he had reason to be there. Not to mention that he used to be married to one of your victims."

Dennis felt his chest tightening. He blinked, wishing he could ask Stanley what on earth DS Griffin was talking about without looking stupid.

"Of course," he said, trying to sound calm. "I'll be checking all that with my DCI."

DS Griffin nodded. "I'm sure you will. She runs a tight ship, does Lesley."

DCI Clarke to you, he thought. Why was everyone so familiar?

"Anyway," she said. "I'm afraid we don't know any more about Day Watson than you do, but I'll be sure to tell you if he turns up. I know Devon are looking for him too, though."

"Devon?"

"Their Organised Crime lot heard mention of his name while they were working on an investigation. You'll have to speak to them, though, I'm not at liberty to—"

"I understand. Thank you, DS Griffin." Dennis reached for the mouse and clicked the End Call button, feeling his skin prickle.

He turned to Stanley. "What's this about another suspect?"

Stanley frowned. "There was no other suspect."

"DS Griffin just said there was another set of prints at the scene. Someone who was married to a victim."

"Dawn Stephens,'," Stanley said. "She was the one who let them into the lighthouse. She died too, at her house. But her ex was a copper, only at the scene cos he was part of the investigation."

Dennis looked at the DC. "A copper?"

Stanley nodded. "DI Rowan Angus, Sarge. The DCI met

him a couple of times, said he was pretty slimy. But like I say, he had good reason to be there, so we didn't follow it up."

CHAPTER TWENTY-SIX

MIKE WAS BORED.

Was it always going to be like this?

The DCI taking other members of the team out with her, leaving him behind.

He knew he wasn't the most dynamic of coppers. He knew he didn't have Tina's way with witnesses, or Stanley's knack for asking what seemed like a stupid question but actually uncovered the truth about an investigation. And he wasn't new and keen like Meera.

But he wanted to make DS one day, and he wasn't going to do that sitting here trawling through HR files.

This was the third time he'd checked Fran Dugdale's file. He'd searched for her on HOLMES and drawn a blank, and her personnel file was as uninteresting as it was possible to be.

There had to be something.

Someone had killed the woman, and while there were some crimes that didn't have a motive beyond mindless violence, he had a feeling this wasn't one of them. You wouldn't kill a PSD officer and leave her in a place like Tyneham without planning it out in advance.

And planning meant motive.

Tina was with the family. She'd rung in to say that there was tension at Fran's mum's home, that it looked like her dad had moved out and gone to live with his mistress. They didn't have a name or a number for the mistress yet, so no one knew if that might be connected to Fran's death.

She was a PSD officer, for God's sake. It had to be something to do with that.

Mike leaned in and peered at the screen.

What else was there to check?

Fran was based out of the PSD offices in Bournemouth.

Should he go there, look at her desk, her workstation?

He hadn't been given the OK to do that by the boss. But this was a murder case. If it was a member of the public, they wouldn't think twice.

It would give him an opportunity to get out of the office while still working on the assignment he'd been given.

"I'm going to head over to the PSD offices, T," he told his wife, who was staring into her screen. Stanley was with the sarge at the other bank of desks.

Tina looked up. "You're interviewing her colleagues? I'll come with you."

He shook his head. "Someone has to stay here. And I'm not talking to anyone yet, I'm waiting till the boss tells us to do that."

"It's frustrating."

He perched on her desk and grabbed her hand. One upside to being left in the office was that it was just the two of them here. If you ignored Stanley and the sarge, at least.

"I know," he said. "I want to look at her desk. See if there's anything in it that might help us get to grips with what she was working on."

"Good idea." Tina hesitated. "Tell me what you find, will you?"

He squeezed her hand, wondering how Louis was getting on at nursery. "Yeah."

Thirty minutes later he was in the reception area of the PSD offices. He'd never been here, something he was grateful for. The building made him feel uneasy.

A woman emerged from a lift and approached him, unsmiling. "You're Mike Legg."

He held up his ID.

She nodded. "I'm Agnieska. DC Wójcik, more formally. You want to look at Fran's desk, is that right?"

"We're trying to get to grips with what she was working on, in case it's related to her death." He hesitated. "Sorry, by the way."

She raised an eyebrow. "You're sorry you're here?"

"No. For Fran... can't be easy having a colleague die."

She looked at him. "Why didn't you just ask what she was working on?"

"Because..." He didn't have an answer for that.

He looked at her. She gazed back at him, her expression blank. *Poker face.* He imagined PSD would be good at that.

"I will," he said. "But first, I want to take a look."

There would be someone up there already, removing anything useful. But that would be tampering with evidence, and if anyone knew how big a deal that was, it was PSD.

She shrugged. "Well, if you want to know any more, I'm not going anywhere."

"Thanks." He wanted to confer with the boss before interviewing anyone here. It was the kind of thing that required preparation.

Tina would have just gone ahead and interviewed this DC Wójcik, without a plan and without feeling the need to get the boss's input.

But he wasn't Tina, and he shouldn't try to be. Sometimes being cautious was more appropriate.

He followed DC Wójcik into the lift, and they emerged on the second floor. The office she led him to was small, only two desks.

"It's just the two of you in here?"

She waved a hand as if taking in the expansiveness of the pokey office. "DI Collingwood has the bigger office next door. And Nathan and Jay work out of Dorchester."

"OK." Mike grabbed his notebook from his pocket and wrote down the names. "Which is her desk?"

"The one closest to you."

The desk in front of him was tidy, with hardly anything on the surface. The desk by the window, which presumably belonged to the woman staring at him right now, was covered in paperwork, pens, notebooks and evidence bags. Her jacket had been slung over the back of the chair in such a way that he half-expected it to fall off at any moment, and three mugs sat on the desk. He was sure one of them was full of mould.

"Was Fran always this tidy?"

"Yeah. She hates – hated – the state of my desk. She'd nag me to tidy up almost every day. Often when she's out or on holiday I spread out, start using her desk too." Agnieska's gaze flicked between the two desks. "But now, it seems..."

It does.

"OK," he said. "I can do this more easily alone."

"Sorry, I can't let you do that."

He looked up at her. "No?"

"I've been told not to leave you in here without supervision." A smile, the first he'd seen. "Sorry."

Mike sighed. He wasn't exactly surprised. "Alright, then. In that case, you get on with your work and I'll do what I need to."

He sat down at Fran's desk. Should he call the CSIs in, treat this like a crime scene?

Don't be daft. It was just her desk.

He tugged on a pair of forensic gloves and pulled open the top drawer. It was neatly arranged, compartments containing stationery, business cards and notepads. A pile of post-it notes. Nothing that gave the appearance of having been used.

He rooted around, checking for anything more interesting underneath the stationery supply. Nothing.

He opened the second drawer, and was surprised.

In here were clothes. An entire outfit: shirt, skirt, underwear, tights. It was all clean and smelled of washing powder.

"Why did Fran keep a change of clothes in her desk?"

DC Wójcik looked up. "A what?"

"A change of clothes. There's a full outfit in here. Everything except a jacket."

She shook her head. "No idea."

"OK." Mike examined inside the drawer, under the clothes, looking for more. There was a box of tampons and a packet of paracetamol. Right at the bottom was a t-shirt, from the police training college in Chantmarle. Oversized, the kind of thing he might have expected Fran to sleep in. He looked around the office.

"When you're working on a demanding case, do people bed down here?"

"I don't. I think Fran did, once or twice."

That would explain it. "Often?"

"About once a month, maybe. Just when things were pressurised."

"How far away did she live?"

"She had a flat in Dorchester."

Mike nodded. That was an hour's drive, even with the traffic in your favour. He could understand why an officer working long hours might choose to stay in the office overnight.

"Where did she sleep?"

"There's a sofa in Collingwood's office. I think she used that."

Mike bit back his next question.

But Collingwood's office? A junior colleague, and a woman at that, sleeping in there? Even if it wasn't frequent, it felt off.

"Did anyone else sleep here? Did you?"

"I only live in Ferndown. So no."

"Right."

Mike pulled at the bottom drawer. It didn't open.

He bent down to look at it: locked.

He opened the top drawer again, searching for a key.

No key.

"Is there a master key somewhere? I need to get into this drawer."

Agnieska looked up. "I'm trying to work, you know."

"Sorry." *You could always go somewhere else, like I asked.*

She sighed. "Here." She opened her own drawer, which was as chaotic as the surface of the desk, and pulled out a small silver key. "Try mine."

He slid the key into the lock of Fran's drawer. It didn't turn. *Damn.*

Either there was something in there that might help them

solve Fran's murder, or there was nothing more than a pair of pyjamas or a sponge bag.

Either way, he wasn't about to destroy her desk trying to get in. He'd speak to the CSIs: they'd have something he could use.

"Try this." DC Wójcik was next to him, holding out another key.

"Where did you get that?"

"In her coat, over there." She indicated a row of hooks by the door. Mike fought an urge to punch himself.

"How long's that been there?" he asked.

A shrug. "Since March, something like that. She never wore it."

"OK. Thanks." He took it off her and put the key in the lock. It moved.

Yes.

"Thanks," he repeated. He didn't want her watching as he opened this.

"No problem." She didn't move.

"Sorry, Agnieska, but I have to do this without a witness. We'll have to ask you what you know about Fran as part of the investigation, and this mi—"

"I understand." She withdrew and sat at her own desk, her body at an angle towards him but her eyes on the monitor.

Mike slid out of Fran's chair and crouched on the floor. He put one hand on the desk drawer and used the other to open it.

All but holding his breath, he pulled the drawer open.

It contained one single spiral bound notebook.

Mike reached into his pocket and grabbed an evidence bag. If Fran had decided to hide a notebook on its own like this, then he wasn't going to take any chances with it.

He laid the bag on the desk. The DC looked round, frowning at the sight of the bag, but said nothing.

Mike reached into the drawer and pulled out the notebook. He placed it inside the bag, and put the bag in his inside pocket. The notebook was small, just A6 size. Not a standard police notebook.

He looked across at DC Wójcik, whose foot was twitching.

You're dying to know what this is.

He ran his fingers around the drawer to find it empty. He pushed it closed and locked it, pocketing the key.

He stood and walked to Fran's jacket. He rooted in the pockets, but all he found was a tube of mints.

"I'll give you a call when we need to take a witness statement," he said.

Agnieska glanced round, her gaze flicking to his pocket. She'd be on the phone to Colllingwood as soon as he left the room. "OK."

Mike left the room and headed for the lift. He wanted to know what was in the notebook, but he'd wait until he reached the privacy of his car.

CHAPTER TWENTY-SEVEN

DENNIS AND STANLEY sat at the bank of desks, across from the rest of the team. Dennis hadn't thought it necessary to move all of his belongings from his own desk just a few yards away, but he'd brought the essentials: a couple of pads, some pens, his phone.

Stanley was trawling through press reports on Trevor Hamm's murder and the arrests they'd made. Dennis was making calls.

He wanted to call the DCI, ask her about Rowan Angus. He knew the man: he'd been a DS in the CID branch where Dennis had been starting out.

Why hadn't the DCI mentioned him?

She was busy at the crime scene, and the Dugdale case was more urgent. It could wait.

Still, it was eating him up.

His next job was to phone DI Gough from the Organised Crime unit. Jim Gough had turned up in Sandbanks just as Dennis was about to arrest Kyle Kelvin, and insisted that he should make the arrest instead. The boss had told Dennis to play nice.

And then, of course, Gough had arrested Dennis. But Dennis had been cleared of any involvement in DCI Mackie's death, and released. His counsellor had told him he should hold his head high when encountering the officers involved in that excruciating period of his life.

He was innocent. He had nothing to worry about.

It didn't feel like that.

"Dennis," Gough said as soon as he picked up the phone.

So he had Dennis's number programmed in, too.

"DI Gough," Dennis said, his voice stiff, "I'm calling in connection with the Trevor Hamm case."

"Now there you do surprise me."

Dennis ignored the veiled reference to the fact that when Hamm had died, he himself had been suspended, under suspicion of killing his former boss.

"One of the gang members involved is missing," he said. "We're looking for him."

"Are you?"

"A David Watson. Does the name mean anything to you?"

Silence.

"DI Gough?"

"It does, yes."

"And?"

"Dennis, why is the MCIT investigating a member of an organised crime gang?"

"He was also involved in a murder. That's—"

"You do realise that by storming around alerting people like Day Watson to the fact we're looking for them, you jeopardise our operations?"

Gough had referred to Watson as *Day*. He wouldn't have done that if he didn't know plenty about Brum Boys.

"Do you have any leads as to where Watson might be?"

"Dennis, tell your DCI to leave this one to us, yes?"

"He's wanted for conspiracy to murder."

"He's wanted for plenty. And West Midlands arrested him."

"For drug related activity. He received a suspended sentence." Dennis could feel the hairs on the back of his neck standing up. He should have got Stanley to make this call.

But that would have been cowardice. And Dennis was no coward.

"Is he in the county? Has he perhaps taken over Arthur Kelvin's operation?" he asked.

"Look, DS Frampton. All I'm willing to tell you is that we're not looking for David Watson in Dorset. We're working on an interforce operation to bring him and some others in, and I'd appreciate it if you'd stand down. If you're capable of that."

Dennis wrinkled his nose. *If you're capable.*

"I'll speak to my DCI," he said. He knew that Superintendent Carpenter had told her to look for David Watson. But he also knew that he didn't want to get involved in inter-team politics.

"Good lad." Gough hung up.

Dennis put the phone down, his palms damp.

CHAPTER TWENTY-EIGHT

MIKE SAT down at his desk, the notebook burning a hole in his pocket.

"You OK?" Tina asked. "You look like you've seen a ghost."

"It's odd, looking through the desk of a dead woman who was using it just a couple of days ago."

She nodded. "Especially when it's another copper."

"Yeah." He pulled the notebook out, still in its evidence bag, and placed it on the desk. "She was hiding this."

"What is it?" Tina stood up and walked to stand behind him.

He shrugged. "A notebook."

She gave his shoulder a punch. "You know that's not what I mean. What's in it?"

"I don't know yet. I found it in a locked drawer in her desk. It was the only thing there."

"But you got hold of the key."

"It was in her coat pocket."

"She left her coat at the office? Did you get that, too?"

"I've sealed off the office and put a call in to CSI."

"You think her office is a crime scene?"

"I think there might be evidence there. If nothing else, we can get her DNA from the coat."

"They'll get that from her body."

He turned to look up at his wife. "Yeah." He wasn't thinking straight. He was tired from being up at 3am with Louis, and despite himself he was finding it weird being back at work with Tina.

"OK," she said. "Are we going to take a look at this notebook, then?"

"Maybe we should wait for the boss."

"She's at the crime scene. She wouldn't want us to hang around."

Mike gazed at the notebook in its evidence bag. "OK." He pulled on a pair of gloves and pulled it out of the bag. He placed the book down on the bag and started to leaf through it.

The first twenty pages or so were blank.

"Bugger," he said. "It's nothing."

"She wouldn't hide a notebook she hadn't written in. Keep going."

Mike continued leafing through. After a dozen or so more pages, he found one that had been written on. He felt his heart rate pick up.

"You're right," he said.

She gave his shoulder a squeeze. "I always am, love."

Mike raised an eyebrow but said nothing. He scanned the first page of text.

"OK," he said.

He could hear Tina's breathing, close to his ear. It had slowed.

"Are you thinking what I'm thinking?" he said.

"Maybe. Turn over."

He flipped the page. There was more. Pages of notes. Bullet points, dates, names.

Evidence.

"Shit," Tina said.

"You think it's related to her death?"

"No idea. But she was keeping it secret."

"And there's no way *he'll* have told anyone."

Tina straightened. "You need to call the boss."

Mike knew that. He grabbed his phone.

CHAPTER TWENTY-NINE

LESLEY WAS in the clearing by the house. Collingwood had long since left, and now she was observing Gail and her colleague Brett picking over the scene, checking for anything Fran Dugdale's killer might have left.

"Do we have a time for the post-mortem yet?" she asked Meera.

"Not sure, but it looks like it's not going to be till tomorrow."

"Call Pathology, will you? I want you to attend."

"You don't want me here?" Meera looked disappointed.

"Collingwood's buggered off and Gail knows what she's doing. We don't need to stay here any longer today. You can head over tomorrow morning and see what's going on, before the PM."

"OK." Meera walked off, her phone to her ear.

Lesley's phone rang: Dennis.

"Dennis," she said. "Got anything to report?"

"I've been talking to DI Gough from Organised Crime."

Lesley glanced over at Meera, and lowered her voice. "That can't have been easy."

"Just doing my job, boss."

"Did he give you anything useful."

"He told us to back off. Even told me to pass the message on to you. But he knew David Watson. He even referred to the man as Day."

"So he's investigating him. Why?"

"He said it was an inter-force operation."

Lesley turned away from the crime scene. "Devon, maybe."

"He didn't say."

"OK. Anything else?"

"Yes."

Lesley waited.

"Dennis?"

'Sorry, boss. Yes, there is something else."

"Go on then."

"I spoke to DS Griffin from West Midlands. Stanley and I did a video call with her."

"Sheila. What did she have to say?"

"She couldn't help us with Watson. But..."

She sighed. "But what, Dennis?"

"She gave me another name."

"Which was...?"

"Rowan Angus. A DI in Blandford CID."

Lesley felt her shoulders dip. "Ah."

"Is there something I need to know, boss? I worked with the man."

"You did?"

"Five years ago." Dennis's voice was clipped.

"He was at all the crime scenes," she said. "We found his prints."

"He's a member of CID. DS Griffin said he was investigating."

"Yes."

Lesley walked back towards the car. She'd been so busy
investigating Fran Dugdale's death that she hadn't had time to
pursue this.

Even Carpenter had encouraged her. In his oblique, never-
take-the-blame way.

"How well did you know Rowan Angus, Dennis?"

"Is he a suspect? Because if he's corrupt, then—"

"How well did you know him?"

"He was a good officer. He was a DS when I was a DC."

"He's younger than you."

"Yes." Dennis sounded pinched.

"OK, Dennis."

After everything that had happened to Dennis in recent
months, this was the last thing she wanted to get him involved
in.

"Like Sheila said," she continued, "Angus had a reason to
be at the scenes. I saw him at two of them. It's nothing to worry
about."

A pause. "Very well."

Change the subject, Lesley thought.

"OK, I want you to follow up the Devon lead. Kyle Kelvin
was working down there before we arrested him. Find Vera
Kelvin and speak to her."

Vera Kelvin was the mother of Arthur Kelvin and the
matriarch of the family. She was also a force to be reckoned
with.

"I'm not sure..."

"Dennis, if you don't feel able to work on this case due to
your personal history with the family, just say so."

"No, boss. It's not that."

"Then what's the problem?"

She heard an intake of breath at the other end of the line.

"Where does Vera live now?" she asked.

"As far as I know, she's at the Sandbanks house."

"The one that was owned by Arthur Kelvin."

"It's actually owned by one of his companies," Dennis said.

"Convenient. Get over there, see if you can speak to her."

Silence.

Lesley sighed.

Dennis, I got you released after you were falsely arrested for murder. Now I need you to get over yourself.

"Or do you want to send Stanley?" she asked.

"No." His voice was tight. "We'll go together."

"Good." Lesley checked the time. "Do it on your way home for the evening. I'll see you in the office, first thing."

"Yes, boss."

"Good." Her phone was buzzing. "I need to take another call."

She switched calls.

"Mike, what's new?"

"We've found a notebook that Fran Dugdale was hiding, boss."

"A notebook? Where?"

"She had it in a locked drawer in her desk."

"Where are you now? At the PSD offices?"

"No. I'm back at Winfrith, with Tina."

"OK. So what's in this notebook?"

"The first thirty or so pages are blank but then it—"

"I'm assuming you found something, or you wouldn't have called me. What's in there?"

"Sorry, boss."

Lesley heard Tina's voice in the background. She tapped her thigh with her fingertips. *Get to the point, Mike.*

"She's written down places, events, dates. It's an evidence log."

"An evidence log for what?"

"It's not entirely clear. But there's a set of initials that's repeated again and again."

"What initials?"

"RC."

Lesley frowned. "RC?"

"I'm wondering if it might be Robert Collingwood."

Lesley felt her breath catch in her throat. "What kind of evidence is it, Mike? If it is Collingwood, what was she recording him doing?"

"It's not entirely clear. But there are references to the beach at Sandbanks, some to the Blue Pool. Numbers relating to something being handed over."

"Money?"

"I'm not sure, boss. It's not marked as currency."

"OK." Lesley bit down on her bottom lip. "Make sure this notebook's properly accounted for and stored in evidence. We have to make sure we do everything properly."

"Yes, boss."

"It's gone six. You two get back to your little boy. I want to see this notebook in the morning."

"Yes, boss. Hang on."

"Hang on for what, Mike?"

"Tina's got something."

"What kind of something?"

"There's another date. It's got RC written against it, and... oh."

"Who else?"

"It's dated last week, boss. And it's got Superintendent Carpenter's name on it."

CHAPTER THIRTY

MEERA TURNED her key in the lock and opened the door to the cosy seventeenth-century cottage in Winterbourne Abbas.

This place had been Jill's idea: she'd grown up in a modern housing estate in Swanage and loved the thought of owning a bit of history.

Meera wasn't so sure. She'd grown up in Wiltshire, in a Victorian terrace overlooking cottages like this, and she'd seen how much work they were.

She'd been proven right. As she opened the front door the smell of damp assaulted her nostrils. The building didn't have a damp proof course, at least not a working one, and the rain of the past few days had taken its toll.

"Jill?" she called as she hung her coat on a hook in the narrow hallway.

"In here," Jill's voice came from the kitchen.

Meera walked through to find Jill and Suzi sitting at the tiny table in the corner of the kitchen. Suzi was working her way through a bowl of pasta in tomato sauce, most of which seemed to have ended up in her hair. Jill had her fingers laced around a cup of coffee.

Meera bent to kiss her wife on the top of the head. "How was your day?"

Jill turned to her. "Good. I got a job offer."

"You did?" Meera checked the water level in the kettle and flicked it on, then leaned against the wall next to Jill. This room was only big enough for two chairs.

Jill nodded, then picked up a piece of pasta that had landed on the table next to Suzi's plate and placed it back in her bowl. "I saw you, you little monkey, trying to hide the pasta."

Suzi giggled.

"Eat it all, Susu," Jill said.

Suzi grimaced, an exaggerated expression of the kind only a child would make, but went back to eating her pasta.

Jill blew hair away from her face. Her hair was wavy and blonde, and always got in her eyes. "I just wish she'd bloody eat the stuff," she muttered.

Meera gave her a sympathetic smile. "The job?" she reminded her.

"Oh. Yeah, that. It's for when I'm back to full time, in six months or so."

"You going to tell me what it is, or are you going to keep me guessing?"

The kettle flicked off. Meera took the two paces it required to cross their kitchen and poured water into a mug for tea.

"Sorry. I'll be like you. Investigating murders."

Meera turned. "You're joining MCIT?"

There was a gap in the unit's structure: no DI. It made sense to fill it, but the idea of working with her wife...

Jill smiled. "Don't worry. I'm not going to be your boss."

"Good." They'd agreed years ago that they'd avoid

applying for jobs that meant managing each other. Jill had been the one who'd climbed the ranks, so Meera had always dreaded the prospect of being subordinate to her wife. "So what is it, then?"

"New unit. Cold cases."

"Cold cases? Why are they focusing on that?"

"Apparently there's been political pressure."

"Will you take it?"

"I need to find out more, including who I'll be working for. But yes, it sounds interesting."

Meera returned to her spot next to the table. She put down her mug and stroked her wife's shoulder. "Good for you."

Jill turned to Suzi, motioning for her to eat. She turned back to Meera. "Anyway, how about you? How's your murder case going?"

Meera flicked her gaze towards Suzi. "I don't like talking about it, in front of her."

Suzi looked up. "Pata."

Meera smiled at her. *Pasta.* "All on one spoon, you clever girl."

Suzi giggled.

"Eat it, though," Meera said. "That's what it's for." She reached over and stroked her daughter's arm. She wanted to give her a hug, but was waiting until she had a chance to clean up the pasta sauce.

"Tell me in words she won't understand," Jill said. "Do you know who it is?"

Meera nodded. "She's PSD."

Jill's eyes widened. "Really? Who?"

"Fran Dugdale. You know her?"

"No."

"You know many PSD?"

Jill returned another piece of pasta back to Suzi's plate. "No. Thank God."

"Yeah."

"So what have they got you doing?"

"I was at the crime scene, spying on Fran's boss. DI Collingwood, you ever come across him?"

"Sorry."

"But he's gone now, high-ups have told him it's ours. So I'm not sure what I'm s'posed to be doing."

Jill touched Meera's arm. "I'm sure whatever you're doing is important."

"It doesn't feel like that. And now Tina and Mike are both back, I'm not sure they need me there."

Jill grabbed Meera's hand. "They do, love. You're ten times better than Mike Legg."

"Not Tina Abbott, though."

A shrug. "She's good. But stick in there. What have they got you on tomorrow?"

"Back at the crime scene. The CSIs were packing up when I left, and the DCI told me to check in on them in the morning."

"Why?"

"Not sure."

Jill licked her lips. She had that look in her eye, the one she got when she was planning something.

"OK," she said. "In that case, you get there early. Familiarise yourself with the scene, without doing any damage of course. See if there's anything you can spot that no one else has identified yet. Make yourself useful."

"Surely that's the CSIs' job?"

"It doesn't do any harm to have an extra set of eyes. And if they've got you down there, you might as well make yourself useful." Jill's blue eyes brightened. "I know."

"What?"

"It's at Tyneham, right? Middle of Lulworth Ranges?"

"It is."

"Who lets you in? It's closed on weekdays."

How did Jill know all this, when Meera had only learned it this morning? "An army Corporal. Name of Tim Cole."

"You talk to him. The CSIs won't be doing that, it's not their job. Find out what you can from him about the site. Look for connections, gaps in the information. You'll find something, love. They'll realise they can't do without you."

Meera nodded, unconvinced.

CHAPTER THIRTY-ONE

"How long's this going to take, Sarge?" Stanley asked as they crawled through Poole. They'd been sitting in near-stationary traffic for twenty minutes.

Dennis pushed back his irritation. "As long as it needs, Stanley." He glanced at the DC. "You've got somewhere you need to be?"

Stanley blushed. "It's six months since me and Julie started going out. We're going to The Old Granary."

"That's nice. I didn't know you had a girlfriend."

"She works at the Blue Pool. I met her when we were working on a case there."

"Arthur Kelvin's death."

A nod.

"Apt, I suppose," Dennis said.

Stanley flushed even redder. "I hope you don't mind, Sarge. She was friendly, I—"

Dennis reached out to put a hand on the DC's arm. "It's perfectly fine, Stanley. She wasn't a witness." He hesitated. "Was she?"

"She wasn't." Stanley's arm was tense; Dennis withdrew his hand. "She made us sandwiches, when me and the CSIs were at the site."

"Well I'm glad for you then." The traffic was moving again, and they were approaching Poole Harbour. "We're nearly there now."

Stanley looked at his watch but said nothing. It was almost 6pm, and Dennis would need to return the DC to the office before either of them could go home.

On your way home, the boss had said. As if Sandbanks was on anyone's way home.

At last they reached Shore Road. Dennis parked on the double yellow lines outside the Kelvin house.

Stanley looked down at the road as he got out of the car. "You sure we'll be alright here?"

Dennis didn't relish the idea of wasting time finding a parking space back in the Shore Road car park, and walking all the way back up here. Stanley had checked his watch six more times since telling him about his date, and it was starting to grate.

"We'll be fine. We're police."

Stanley shrugged. "S'pose so."

S'pose so? Did he think he wasn't a genuine copper, because he wasn't driving a squad car? Dennis realised he didn't know much about Stanley's history before the DC had joined this team. Had he driven a squad car, or had he gone straight into CID after training?

The Kelvin house was barred by a tall gate, an intercom system on the wall next to it. Dennis pressed the button and stood back to get in view of the camera.

"Hello?" A woman's voice.

Dennis took a step forward and held up his ID. "DS

Frampton of Dorset Police. I'd like to speak to Mrs Kelvin, please."

"Mrs Kelvin?"

"Vera Kelvin. Is she at home?"

"Sorry. One moment."

Dennis exchanged looks with Stanley and waited, tapping his foot. Stanley had rolled up the sleeve of his jacket for a better view of his watch.

Calm down, son. We'll be done when we're done.

"Hello? DS Frampton?" A man's voice this time. "Wait a moment, we'll let you through." Something clicked and the narrow door next to the main gate shifted a little. Dennis pushed on it and it opened.

"Come on, Stanley."

The driveway was familiar, the house too. He'd visited enough times to speak to Arthur Kelvin, and then it had been a crime scene after the man's wife had died.

But the man walking towards them down the slope of the board driveway was not familiar. He wore pale cream trousers and a blue striped shirt, had a broad smile in a tanned face, and did not look like anyone's idea of an organised crime boss.

He held out his hand as he neared them. "DS Frampton?"

"That's me." Dennis gestured towards Stanley. "And this is DC Brown."

"Officers." The man looked between them. "I'm pleased to meet you, but I'm afraid I can't help."

The accent was American.

Dennis felt his stomach dip.

"Why's that?" he asked.

"My wife and I moved in here just six weeks ago. We bought the place from a company, Purbeck Holdings?"

One of the many businesses Kelvin had run across the region.

"I don't suppose you were given a forwarding address for the previous owners?"

A laugh. "I'm afraid not, Officer. And they must have set up redirection for their mail, as we haven't received anything for them." He held out his hands in an apologetic gesture. "Awfully sorry I can't help."

"Thanks for your time," Dennis said.

"Do you mind providing the name of their conveyancing solicitor?" Stanley asked.

Good question. Dennis, who'd been turning away, turned back to the man.

"That I remember. I spoke to the woman once, terrifying, she was. Aurelia Cross."

Dennis knew Aurelia Cross.

And so did the boss.

Stanley wrote the name in his notebook. "And your name is...?"

Dennis raised an eyebrow, looking at Stanley. Was the DC getting better, or was he losing his touch?

"Alvin Hymes, Detective. And my wife is Marissa Hymes."

"Thanks, Mr Hymes. We appreciate your help."

CHAPTER THIRTY-TWO

"HELLO!" Lesley dropped her keys in the bowl on the hall table and slipped off her shoes as she listened for signs that the flat was inhabited.

There was a sound coming from the living room: sniffing?

She walked through to see Elsa and Sharon on the sofa. Elsa had an arm round Sharon who was red-faced and shaking.

Lesley hurried to the sofa and sank down next to her daughter, placing a hand on her knee. Sharon flinched.

"Sharon, love. What's up?"

She looked at Elsa across the top of her daughter's head. Elsa shook her head and shrugged.

Lesley bent to bring her face closer to Sharon's. "You can tell me, sweetheart. Is it something that happened at college?"

She rested the urge to ask if Sharon's dad had upset her. He had a new girlfriend and had started making excuses for the weekends when Sharon was due to go up to Birmingham.

Sharon shook her head. "It's nothing."

"It doesn't seem like nothing."

Sharon looked up and into Lesley's eyes. "You wouldn't understand."

"Sharon love, I'm fifty-two. I'm sure whatever it is you're going through, I—"

"That's it, see? It's always about you."

"That's not what I—"

Sharon pushed Lesley aside and stood up. "I'm going to my room."

She stormed out and slammed her bedroom door.

Lesley sank back into the sofa. "What was that about?"

"Sorry, sweetie." Elsa shifted across and put a hand on Lesley's knee. "She wouldn't tell me either."

"Shit." Lesley stood up and walked to Sharon's bedroom door. She knocked, gently.

"Sharon, love. Can I come in?"

"No."

"Can I get you anything, then? Cup of tea? Bowl of cereal? Some chocolate? I find chocolate helps."

"Leave me alone."

Lesley leaned her head on the door. "OK, love. But if you want to talk, I'm right here."

Silence.

CHAPTER THIRTY-THREE

"I'm not sure about this." Meera was on the phone to Jill, driving towards Tyneham. "Maybe I should go into the office."

"It's fine," Jill replied. "You're doing the right thing."

"The place won't even be open yet."

"You called that corporal, didn't you?"

"I did."

"And he knows to expect you. So the gate will be open, and once you're through the gate there's nothing else in your way."

"You make me sound awful."

"You're not awful, love. You're just doing your job."

"Maybe I should go to the office. There's going to be a briefing."

"You've been asked to go to the scene, haven't you? And you'll be at the office in time for the briefing. It's only seven am."

Meera sighed. Jill was right.

She was at the gate. Sure enough, an Army truck was waiting for her.

"You're early," Corporal Cole said as he unlocked the gate for her.

She smiled. "No rest for the wicked."

"I guess not," he replied. "Any idea when you'll be finished here?"

Meera shook her head. This wasn't like a normal crime scene. Usually there was a homeowner wanting their space back, or a business wanting to open up again. This time, it was the MoD wanting to fire guns across the countryside.

"Sorry, mate," she said.

He cocked his head. "We're all twiddling our thumbs. Can't come near the place with you lot here, too risky."

"Sorry," she said again.

He was about to get back into his truck. She approached it. "Can I ask you a few questions?"

He turned back to her. "Sure. As long as the answers aren't classified."

"Oh."

He laughed. "It's OK. It doesn't work like that, I'm just a corporal. Fire away."

"OK." She licked her lips. "I know this is the main access road to the village, but are there any others?"

"No roads, no. You're thinking your killer might have snuck in another way?"

"Maybe. You're sure there's no other way across to the village?"

"The ranges are fenced off, but the fences aren't exactly high. It's here at the edge of the ranges that things are more secure. And there's the path down to Worbarrow Bay."

"Worbarrow Bay?" She'd never heard of it.

"A mile and a half from the village, links up to the coastal path. There're fences alongside the paths. But if you were determined, you could get through them."

"Has anyone checked to see if the fences have been damaged?"

"That's one of the first things we did after we found out what had happened. Sorry, no sign of damage."

Damn.

"OK. Thanks." Meera considered. "Could you drive a 4x4 across the ranges maybe, get access that way?"

He looked past his truck, over the low hills beyond. "You'd have to be pretty determined. And it would leave tracks. The ground's soft."

"And is that something you check for?"

"Far as I know, nothing was spotted around the fences. So a 4x4 wouldn't have got through them. But..."

"But what?"

"I suppose you could drive down to the village when it's open and then conceal a vehicle. We'd... No. It would be spotted."

She looked at him. "Drones?"

"Sorry, Detective. That's all I can help you with. But I'd say it's pretty unlikely someone would gain access any way other than via this road without us either spotting them at the time or noticing the damage afterwards."

Meera nodded, feeling frustrated. She'd tried, at least. And she wanted to check the path to the coast.

"Thanks."

He gave her a salute and climbed back into his truck. Meera gave him a wave in return, then went to her car.

She hadn't asked him if anyone else was here yet. The CSIs didn't tend to start this early, but it would have been helpful to know.

Only one way to find out.

A few minutes later, she was in the car park. There were no other cars.

Was that good?

Meera sat in her car for a few moments, then got out, breathing in the cool morning air. The sky was clear today, and it would be hot later.

She closed the car door, as quietly as she could to avoid disturbing the wildlife, and walked to the village. The place was eery at this time in the morning, the reality of its abandoned status even starker than usual.

She walked past the church, along the path and through to the house where Fran Dugdale had been found.

She froze.

Up ahead, in the trees beyond the house, she could see movement.

A deer?

No. No deer would venture into this part of Dorset. Not with all the shooting.

She pulled back to conceal herself behind a wall, and watched.

There was a person in the woods.

Meera glanced back towards the car park. It had been empty. There had been no cars parked along by the houses.

Damn. She should have asked Corporal Cole if anyone else had been through. She'd check later.

She held her breath. Whoever was up there hadn't seen her. They were still in the woods, moving around.

They hadn't seen her. She had to hope they wouldn't have heard her car.

But what the hell were they doing? And how had they gained access?

CHAPTER THIRTY-FOUR

LESLEY KNOCKED on Carpenter's door. She'd checked with his PA and knew he was in. Even so, her heart was racing.

"Come in."

She took a deep breath and pushed the door open.

"Lesley." He looked puzzled. "You're back. Is everything alright?"

"I need to speak to you about something."

He was standing in the centre of the office, a mug of coffee in hand. He motioned towards the two armchairs in the corner. "Let's sit."

Lesley nodded and hurried towards the closest of the two chairs, aware that she still hadn't looked him in the eye.

She sat down, bending forward so her gaze was on her knees. She rubbed them with her hands.

"You look perturbed," Carpenter said.

Lesley looked up. "We've found some notes that Fran Dugdale made."

He cocked his head. "Notes?"

"DC Legg went to her office and found a notebook locked up in her desk."

He nodded. "The cases she was working on might be relevant to her death."

Lesley pursed her lips. She drew out her phone: photos of the notebook. It wasn't a police issue one, but one the DC had presumably bought herself.

"Have you spoken to her senior officer?" Carpenter asked.

She looked up at last. "Are you suggesting I should?"

A pause. "That depends."

"On what, Sir?"

He sighed and stood up. "On what she was investigating. Will you just get to the point please, DCI Clarke?"

"Sorry, Sir." Lesley twisted to follow him as he walked back towards his desk. "The notes aren't about a case. They're about a formal complaint."

He stilled.

"Your name is in her notes, Sir."

Carpenter turned. "Do you have a copy?" He held out a hand.

Lesley tapped her phone to bring it to life and brought up the photos from Fran's notebook. She held her phone out, but Carpenter didn't take it.

"Describe what she says about the complaint," he told her.

"Her notes are in some kind of shorthand, so I can't be clear on the details. But three weeks ago she says she submitted a formal complaint about RC."

"RC."

"Robert Collingwood."

"She uses his full name?"

"No. But she also refers to him in the context of her work

and the investigations she's part of. It's pretty clear he's the person she's referring to."

Carpenter returned to the chairs and faced her. "And you say she also mentions me."

Lesley flicked through to another photo. Mike was on his way into the office. She'd told him to put the notebook into evidence storage; now she wished she had it in her hand. And it wouldn't hurt, she thought, if she could understand half of what was in it. Most of the entries were in code, or shorthand. Gail had promised to get someone to look at it, see if they could make sense of it. But that would take time.

"She says she had an interview with AC, Sir."

"AC."

"She writes that he's investigating her complaint. She describes her annoyance at not being permitted to bring a Federation rep with her." Lesley looked up. "Are you AC, Sir?"

He gave her a long look. "I am."

"And is the complaint about DI Collingwood?"

Another long look. Lesley waited.

"It is," Carpenter said at last. "But you'll understand that I can't tell you the detail of it."

"No." Lesley felt her stomach clench. "Why wasn't Fran allowed a rep?"

"Regulations allow for Federation representation when an officer has been accused of misconduct and is being inter-viewed under the Misconduct Regulations. DC Dugdale was a witness. She was accused of nothing and therefore did not need representation."

"Did she ask to have a rep with her?"

Carpenter leaned back and surveyed her. "She did not."

"She didn't ask you, in the interview which she refers to in her notebook?"

Another sigh. "She didn't. This isn't what you're making it sound like, you know."

Lesley rubbed her forehead. "Sir, I need to know if there's any possibility this complaint might be relevant to the investigation into Fran Dugdale's death."

"If you're asking me if Robert Collingwood killed her in revenge for her raising a complaint against him, then the answer is not to be so absurd."

"So it's not relevant?"

Carpenter said nothing.

Lesley's phone buzzed in her pocket. *Go away.*

"You'd better pick that up," Carpenter said. "It might be a lead."

"It can wait, Sir."

"Pick it up."

He was trying to distract her.

Lesley pulled out her phone. It was a message from Sadie: *Fran Dugdale spoke to Phipps.*

Lesley put her fist to her mouth.

"DCI Clarke, you've turned pale."

She looked up. "When you interviewed Fran, did she say anything about Detective Superintendent Phipps?"

"Who?"

"The detective from Hampshire who was brought in to investigate DCI Mackie's death."

Carpenter looked puzzled. "No. I don't see why—"

"Was Fran's complaint about corruption, Sir?" She'd assumed it was a harassment complaint.

"I've already told you, I can't—"

"If Collingwood has something to do with her death, we can't cover it up. It would—"

Carpenter stood up. He took Lesley's phone from her hand

and flicked through the photos, shaking his head. "I need you to bring me the original notebook, please, and not show this to any other members of your team."

"That's—"

"It's an internal matter, Lesley. It doesn't relate to a case DC Dugdale was working on, and it isn't appropriate to drag her name through the mud."

"I don't think it's *her* name that's at risk of being dragged through the mud, Sir."

He raised an eyebrow. "You're treading on thin ice, Lesley. I thought this wasn't how you worked. West Midlands assured me that—"

Lesley stood up to look at him. He was six inches taller than her, but she wasn't going to let that daunt her. "Sir. In West Midlands I helped to bring down a network of corrupt police officers and the organised criminals they were working with. In Dorset I have been instrumental in closing down operations by the Kelvin family a—"

"Mainly because they all seem to keep killing each other."

She licked her lips, taking in Carpenter's firm expression. He didn't know about the call from Sadie. She still had an avenue of inquiry.

Very well.

"Sir." She turned towards the door. "I'll bring you the notebook when I have it, so that there's no danger of the chain of evidence being compromised."

"Thank you."

Lesley was at the door. She put her hand on the door handle and felt Carpenter move behind her.

She flinched. He was right behind her, all but breathing down her neck.

She shuddered.

Could she challenge him, tell him to back off?

He leaned in. She felt the hairs on the back of her neck prickle.

"Take a copy, Lesley."

Lesley felt her jaw drop open. She was about to speak, but then thought better of it.

Why was he whispering like this?

She turned the door handle.

"Sir," she muttered.

"And keep digging," he added, still under his breath. He stepped back, clearing his throat. "I hope you've got the message, DCI Clarke. I'll see you when you have that piece of evidence for me."

CHAPTER THIRTY-FIVE

LESLEY DIDN'T KNOW if she could focus sufficiently to run the briefing.

As she walked back to the team room her mind raced, turning over what had happened in Carpenter's office.

He'd said one thing out loud, and then whispered something entirely different to her.

Did he think his office was bugged?

If so, did that mean hers was too?

As Lesley entered the team room she found herself looking up at the wall, checking the corners and the motion sensors that sat across from the door. They were all over the building, part of the security system.

There were cameras and motion sensors throughout Dorset Police HQ. Everyone ignored them, and she'd never heard of them being used.

And besides, the cameras didn't record sound.

So was there a recording device somewhere in Carpenter's office? One that he believed to be there but hadn't found, or had chosen not to remove for fear of alerting whoever might have planted it?

Dennis stood up from his desk. Lesley shivered.

"You alright, boss?"

"Fine," she said, noticing Stanley watching her too. "Do you know when Mike and Meera will be here?"

"Mike's just parking, with Tina," Dennis replied. "Meera went to the crime scene early to check on progress with the forensics."

"Have you heard anything from her?"

"Not yet. Would you like me to give her a call?"

"Please." Lesley eyed the door, waiting for Mike and Tina. Mike had brought the notebook back to the office yesterday, but she didn't know where it had been filed.

The door opened just as Dennis put his phone down. "No response. I've left her a message."

Lesley nodded. "Morning," she said to Tina and Mike as they approached their desks.

"Morning," they replied in unison.

"Let's have everyone in my office."

The team exchanged glances as Lesley turned to enter her office. She cast her gaze around as she did so, taking in the light fittings and the fire sensors. If Carpenter was bugged, then she would be too.

Stop it. You're being paranoid.

No one entered this room from outside the building. Not even PSD.

Not as far as she was aware, anyway.

CHAPTER THIRTY-SIX

DENNIS FOLLOWED the DCI into her office, wondering why she kept turning and looking into the team room. She seemed on edge, her movements jerky.

She turned to the team as Dennis took one of the seats in front of her desk. Stanley closed the door while Tina sat next to Dennis and Mike leaned against the empty board.

"Has anyone from outside the team been into the office in the last few days?" she asked.

Dennis frowned. "Anyone specific, boss?"

Lesley shook her head. "Anyone other than us. And Meera, of course."

"There were a few of the Traffic team using the other set of desks last week," Tina said, "but that happens all the time."

"How long were they here for? Did they access my office at all?"

"No chance," Tina said. "No one comes into this room without your say-so."

"Except the cleaners," Stanley added.

Dennis looked at Tina, who shrugged. He frowned. "Should I speak to Mrs Holland?"

"Who's she?" the DCI asked.

He looked at her. "Building manager. She'll be in charge of the cleaners."

The boss shook her head. "I'm not worried about the cleaners."

He pushed his glasses up his nose. "Can I ask what it is you are worried about?"

She glanced up at the ceiling. What was troubling her?

"Nothing, Dennis. Don't trouble yourself about it." She took a breath and placed her clasped hands on the desk. "Let's review where we're at with both cases."

"Surely we can do that separately."

She shook her head. "I want us to continue working as a team."

Dennis frowned. Did she think the cases were connected?

He took a breath. "Very well. Why don't we start with the Dugdale case?" He wanted to know what progress the other side of the team was making. That poor young woman.

The DCI's phone buzzed in her pocket, but she ignored it.

"You're right, Dennis." She gave him an apprising look. No doubt wondering if he was up to being in the room while they discussed the death of the woman who'd interviewed him about DCI Mackie's death.

He was.

But something was holding the DCI back.

"Tina, why don't you start?" Dennis asked. "You've been looking into DC Dugdale's background, is that right?"

Tina nodded. "I can't find anything untoward in her files. She lives alone, no partner, no close friends as far as I can tell.

And there's nothing in the case notes from her current work that indicates any particular conflict."

"There's always conflict, with PSD," Stanley said.

"Not necessarily," the boss said. "Mike, tell us about the notebook."

Mike stepped forward. Dennis turned to look at him.

"Fran kept a notebook in her desk. It contained personal notes about issues she was having with a colleague."

He looked at the DCI who gave him a nod.

"She made a formal complaint about DI Collingwood," he continued. "And..."

Another look at the boss. She hesitated, then nodded.

"She had spoken to Superintendent Carpenter about it," Mike continued.

Stanley sucked in a breath. Tina glanced at Mike, who shrugged.

"Superintendent Carpenter was dealing with the complaint?" Dennis asked.

The boss raised an eyebrow at him. "I thought you weren't involving yourself with this case."

"Sorry."

She smiled. "It's OK, Dennis. You're in the room. And I'm not sure Carpenter can tell us who does and doesn't work on which case right now."

Dennis shifted in his seat. What did she mean?

She stood up and rounded the desk, perching on an edge of it right next to Tina. "I want to know more about this complaint," she said. "Fran's notes are in some kind of short-hand. Gail's team will try to decipher it, but I'd like one of you working with them."

"I'll do it," Mike said.

"Thanks," the DCI replied. Her phone buzzed again.

"Do you need to get that?" Dennis asked.

She looked at him, then down at her pocket. She pulled the phone back, looked at it, then replaced it.

"Anything relevant?" he asked.

She ignored the question. "We've got the post-mortem to attend as well," she said, "and the father to track down."

"I looked him up," Tina said. "His name's Tony Dugdale."

"Any idea where he's living now?"

"I've got a work address. He's a manager at a chain hotel in Bournemouth."

"That's where he might be staying, then. If we can't find the girlfriend, it's a possibility."

"That's what I thought, boss."

"OK. Mike, you're working with the CSIs. Tina, you go to the hotel and see if you can speak to the father."

"No problem." Tina grimaced.

"You sure you're alright handling a second grieving parent on your own?"

"I'll be fine. The FLO's already with the mum."

"Good. We'll need to brief them."

"On it."

The boss smiled at Tina. "I'll ask Meera to go to the post-mortem. Is Meera still at the crime scene?"

"She didn't answer when I called," Dennis reminded her.

"I wasn't expecting her to still be there."

"I can try her again, get an update," volunteered Tina.

"Do that, please. I want her back here. She can attend the press conference with me and then go on to the PM."

"Press conference?" Stanley asked.

"The super wants to quash any speculation of this being internal before it starts."

Stanley nodded. The boss turned to Dennis. "What progress are you making with David Watson?"

"Not much, I'm afraid. We went to the Kelvin house and it's been sold, and no one at West Midlands knows where Watson is. We spoke to DS Griffin, who suggested another name." He watched the DCI's face, not wanting to name DI Angus in public. "I'm not sure that will help us, though."

"What about Devon?" she asked. "Have you followed up with them?"

"That's our next port of call."

"Good." The DCI straightened up. "OK. Mike, you're on the notebook with CSI. Tina, get hold of Meera if you can, then find Fran's father, see if he can tell us anything about possible grudges, people she might have annoyed."

Dennis raised a hand. The boss glared at him. "It's not school, Dennis."

"Sorry, boss. Is there a possibility Fran was involved in an investigation connected to organised crime?"

"We don't have anything on file that suggests that. But yes, given she was investigating bent coppers, there's a very good chance of that. What are you suggesting?"

"Well, it's unlikely another officer would murder a member of PSD, even if they were afraid for their career and reputation. But if an officer was involved with a gang, maybe providing them with information—"

"I know how it works, Dennis."

"— then maybe the criminals killed DC Dugdale to protect the identity of their accomplices."

"It's a reach."

"Just a suggestion."

"We don't have any evidence that leads us to organised crime right now. And I prefer to go where the evidence takes me. But I will bear your hypothesis in mind. And I suggest you watch less *Line of Duty*."

Dennis felt his skin heat up. He never watched police shows, and the boss knew it.

"Just carry on with your own case, Dennis. Tell me if Devon gives you anything useful. And don't worry about our Fran. Right now, I'm focused on the estranged father angle. I want to know if there's any chance that an argument about him leaving her mother for another woman might have turned nasty."

Dennis frowned. Fran Dugdale had been left at an abandoned village miles away from where she lived. That didn't sound like a domestic to him.

But it wasn't his case. He had his own case to deal with.

CHAPTER THIRTY-SEVEN

MEERA HAD BEEN SITTING in the middle of a clump of bushes for what felt like hours, cursing the sharp branches that pierced her jacket and wishing she'd thought more carefully about her position before she sat down.

Her right leg ached and her left arm was going to be red-raw by the time she finally stood up.

But at least she hadn't been spotted.

No one else had arrived at the village yet. No CSIs, no Uniform. Maybe they'd all finished.

But the person she'd spotted on the other side of the clearing was still here.

They were moving around in the bushes opposite her, digging through the undergrowth.

The person had their back to her, and she hadn't yet seen their face. From the height, she would have guessed it was a man. Slim, tall, wearing a dark coat.

That could be just about any man in Dorset.

Meera shifted her weight a little and a twig snapped.

Shit.

She stilled, waiting for the man to turn and spot her. Her heart was racing.

Who was he? How had he got to the village, given that there were no cars in the car park? And what had he found in the woods?

Whatever it was, the CSIs had missed it.

None of it made sense.

Her phone rang.

Her mouth dry, Meera fumbled in her pocket and switched it off without looking at it.

Too late.

The man stopped moving. He stood still for a moment, like an animal sniffing the air.

Then, slowly, he turned around.

Meera felt an urge to close her eyes.

Idiot. It's not like he won't see you if you can't see him.

The man scanned the woods, barely moving. Clutching something in his hand, he looked towards the house that separated them.

Straight at her.

Meera held her breath.

She was wearing a green jacket. She was hidden in the middle of a thicket of bushes.

For the first time, she was glad of the branches and leaves that crowded in on her and scratched her skin.

He hadn't seen her.

But she'd seen him.

And now she knew who he was.

CHAPTER THIRTY-EIGHT

THE TEAM FILED out of the boss's office. Lesley spotted Dennis and Stanley exchanging glances. Dennis gave the DC a nod and Stanley left the room, heading for their new desks.

She checked her phone: there was a message from Matthew Bamford, the pathologist, about the post-mortem. When she looked back up, Dennis was still there, watching her as the door closed.

"Everything alright?" she asked.

"There was something else."

"Something you didn't want to discuss with me in front of the others."

Dennis nodded.

"Is this to do with the fact you met Fran Dugdale and Robert Collingwood? Is there something you can tell me about their relationship?"

"Sorry, boss. DC Dugdale barely spoke during our... meeting."

She sighed. "And there was me hoping you'd have some kind of insight. What is it, then?"

"It's about the Kelvins."

"They're not exactly a secret."

"This isn't about me, boss. It's about you."

She sat down, irritated. "Which means it's about my wife. What have you discovered?"

Elsa was a lawyer. She'd previously represented the Kelvins. Dennis hadn't made much secret of the fact that he'd never approved of Lesley being connected to organised crime in this way, however loosely, but there was nothing he could do about it.

"When we visited the Kelvin house," he said, "we spoke to the new owner."

"Who told you it had been sold."

"Yes. DC Green thought to ask who the Kelvins' solicitor was, for the sale."

Lesley smiled. "Don't tell me."

"It was—"

"Aurelia Cross." She chuckled. "That's no surprise, Dennis. She acted for Arthur Kelvin while he was alive, her firm covered all his legitimate activities as well as the more shady ones."

"I thought..."

"You thought wrong, Dennis." She went to the door and opened it. "If you want to follow this up with Aurelia, then do so. She might be able to tell you where Vera Kelvin is living now. But I doubt that she'll be willing to."

"I wasn't planning on speaking to her."

"Good. It would be a waste of time. That woman hates us, and she'd no sooner give us information than she'd eat a lemon." She frowned. "Come to think of it, she often looks like she's eaten a lemon."

"Stanley will be checking Land Registry records along with

Companies House," Dennis said. "Hopefully we can match them up, find a new address."

"Vera Kelvin will be a director of whichever company they used to buy the new house."

"She will."

Lesley smiled, her hand still on the door. "Good work, Dennis." She looked out. "And Stanley."

He nodded and walked past her through the door.

"And Dennis?" she said.

"Boss?"

"You don't need to be secretive about evidence that leads us to my wife's old law firm, you know. Elsa's got herself away from all that now."

He nodded, not looking entirely convinced.

CHAPTER THIRTY-NINE

THE SUPER WAS ALREADY in the press room when Lesley entered. He sat at the centre of the front table, adjusting his tie and checking his breath against the back of his hand.

She cleared her throat, causing a tech at the back of the room to straighten up in surprise.

Carpenter shoved his hand back into his pocket, looking embarrassed.

Lesley approached the top table. "Sir. You're early."

"Doesn't do any harm to be prepared."

She glanced past him to see a screen was being set up, the image on it shifting from a photo of Fran Dugdale to those of the crime scene and a display with the public phone number.

"What do you need me to do?" she asked.

"Just sit next to me and look competent."

"You don't want me to discuss details of the case? If a member of the public saw someone accessing the village—"

He shook his head. "I'll cover all that. This is too sensitive. But they need to know there's an experienced SIO on the case. I'll run through your history, reassure people that you know what you're doing." He cocked his head. "You are confident you're going to catch this bastard, aren't you?"

She eyed him. "Sir, what you said to me in your office. Is there—"

The door behind them opened: the press officer, letting the journalists and camera operators in. Lesley sighed.

She leaned in closer to Carpenter. "Is there anything else I need to know, Sir? Anything that can help me find out who killed DC Dugdale?"

"Let's focus on the press conference, shall we DCI Clarke?" He stood up, walking away from her and shaking hands.

Twenty minutes later, the press conference was done. Carpenter had stuck to his plan, barely allowing Lesley to speak but waxing lyrical about her history of arrests, including some she'd made in the West Midlands. She'd sat next to him in silence, twisting her hands in her lap. She hated this kind of thing.

She checked her watch. The post-mortem would be starting soon, and she hadn't briefed Meera yet.

She pulled out her phone and dialled the DC.

No answer.

"Meera, it's DCI Clarke. I need you to attend the post-mortem for Fran Dugdale." She gave the location and time, in just under an hour, then hung up.

"Lesley."

Lesley looked up to see Sadie Dawes standing in front of her. She gave the journalist a reluctant smile.

"Sadie. I noticed you staring at me from the second row."

"I didn't think I was staring."

"I hate to think how it must feel for someone you actually are staring at. You wanted to speak to me."

"Yes." Sadie looked behind her. "Can we go somewhere more private?"

Lesley considered. The team were busy with their allotted roles, and would call if they needed her. Carpenter was deep in conversation with Chief Superintendent Price.

"OK."

"I'll meet you in the beer garden of the Seven Stars, fifteen minutes."

"You sure we can't do this here?"

Sadie raised her eyebrows. "Absolutely sure."

"Very well." Lesley sighed.

This had better be relevant to the case she was supposed to be working on, and not just the one she'd delegated to Dennis.

CHAPTER FORTY

MEERA HELD her breath as the man left the clearing the house sat in, heading for the main village and the car park beyond.

Had she missed a car, parked at the edge of the car park or in an overflow parking area?

No. The place had been deserted. She'd stopped to breathe in the air and listen to the birds.

So how had he got here?

The same way Fran's killer had got in, perhaps.

Her hand flew to her mouth.

He couldn't be...?

When she was sure he couldn't see or hear her, she scrambled out from her hiding place. She ran towards the village, careful to keep her footsteps silent. The wind was rustling nearby trees and she hoped it would muffle any sound she made.

She stopped as she approached the schoolhouse, knowing that when she passed it, she would be visible to anyone in the car park and beyond.

Taking a few deep breaths, Meera scuttled over to the wall of the schoolhouse and leaned against it, her senses on fire.

She could hear a car.

Damn.

Was it coming, or going? Was it leaving already?

She looked past the schoolhouse to the road leading into the village. A van was approaching.

It wasn't a CSI van.

The van was small and white, with dents to the rear wheel arch. In the front was a young man.

She pulled back against the wall of the schoolhouse.

She hadn't checked if Gail was due here today. Could she have brought in some kind of expert who drove a battered white van?

Meera pulled out her notebook and wrote down the registration number: a 2018 registration.

Definitely not police issue.

She listened as the van drove into the car park then stopped. She peered round the wall of the schoolhouse to see the door opening and a man climbing out.

Her hand trembling, she held up her phone and fired off photos. He was a distance away and the zoom on her phone was terrible, but someone at the office might be able to identify him.

The man closed the van door and walked away from her, towards the path down to Worbarrow Bay.

If he was working on the case, he would have walked in her direction.

And he didn't look like a morning walker. There were no hiking boots, no dog.

Instead, he wore freshly washed jeans and a white bomber jacket.

Not clothes anyone would wear for a morning walk down to the coast.

So where was he going? And where was the other man?

She pulled her phone out of her pocket. It had rung while she'd been in the thicket: the DCI.

Meera didn't like making the DCI wait.

She checked her voicemail: a message about the post-mortem.

Damn.

She checked her watch: forty minutes till it began.

But she didn't want to leave the crime scene.

She peered round the edge of the wall again.

The man in the bomber jacket was about to disappear along the path to the coast.

She ran to the telephone box outside the houses in front of her, stopping behind it to catch her breath and check she hadn't been seen.

She peered out: the man was gone. And there was no sign of the first man.

Her car sat in the car park, opposite the white van. They'd have wondered whose it was. They'd be looking for her.

She ran again, stopping when she reached her car. She leaned against it and scanned the area.

No one.

She fired off some photos of the van, approaching it to get shots of the inside through the windows in the back. It was full of boxes.

She needed to let the boss know where she was, and that she wouldn't be able to make the PM.

She crouched down behind the van and pulled out her phone. Her breath came in ragged gasps.

I'm at the crime scene, she typed.

She hesitated, thinking.

Two men here, she continued. *A man in a decorator's white van.* She typed in the registration number. *And DI Collingwood, who arrived before me. No sign of his car.*

DI Collingwood had been the man in the clearing.

But the boss'had said he was off the case. So why was he sneaking around in the woods?

The woods.

Meera hit send. She typed another email, this time to Gail: *Look in the woods behind the house. I think there might be evidence.*

Gail would think she was being weird. But she didn't have time to make phone calls, or to explain.

She had to follow the second man. If he was meeting Collingwood, then she needed to know why.

CHAPTER FORTY-ONE

THE PUB WAS CLOSED.

Lesley pulled up in the car park to find Sadie standing outside its main door, her hands up to the glass and her expression one of irritation. Sadie looked round at the sound of Lesley's car and walked towards it. Lesley opened her window.

"Sorry," she said, "I thought most pubs opened for breakfast these days."

Lesley smiled. "Not in Wool. But you said the beer garden."

"It's a bit exposed." Sadie frowned at the scattering of tables on the grass between the pub and the road and back at Lesley's car. "Can I get in?"

"Of course."

Sadie rounded the car and got in the passenger seat, while Lesley closed her window. There was a swarm of wasps somewhere nearby, and a few of them had already tried to get in.

"What's up, Sadie?" she said. "Why all the secrecy?"

"I didn't want your superintendent to see me talking to you."

"So you bring me to a car park a couple of miles from Police HQ and expect no one to notice."

Sadie blushed. "Sorry."

"Just tell me what's going on, before we find ourselves in an underground car park in Washington DC."

Sadie frowned.

"Watergate. Deep Throat. Surely you...?"

But Sadie looked none the wiser.

Blimey. How young is she?

And how could a journalist like Sadie not have heard of Watergate?

"I told you I've been talking to Phipps."

"Again."

"I wasn't satisfied with what he told me last time."

"You didn't tell me what he told you."

Sadie looked at Lesley. "He's had another call, since I last spoke to him."

"Did you stalk him this time?"

A frown. "I don't stalk people."

Lesley let it go. Strictly speaking, Sadie didn't stalk anyone. But she could be damned tenacious.

"Another call?" she asked.

"From Fran Dugdale."

"Did he tell you anything about this call?"

"Only that she was scared. He was worried about her, thought I should alert someone."

Why you? Lesley thought. "Did he say why she was scared?"

"She knew something."

"Something she told him about, I hope. Something he then told you about."

Sadie looked down at her lap. "No."

Lesley squeezed the steering wheel tight. "Sadie, don't tell me you've dragged me out here to tell me about a phone call that doesn't give me anything useful."

Sadie looked up at Lesley. "Not quite."

"Go on."

"She told him she'd been investigating a detective. She wouldn't name them. But she believed it was connected to Tim Mackie's death."

"And she said all this to Phipps?"

A nod.

"Why? He retired. They closed the investigation into Mackie's death."

Sadie shrugged. "Maybe with him being from another force, she thought he was safe."

Lesley's phone buzzed. She ignored it: *one minute*. "Did he tell anyone else about this, apart from you?"

"I asked him. He wouldn't answer that question."

"OK. So when did you speak to him? Was this after Fran's death, or before?"

"Last Thursday."

"Before." Lesley stared at her. If Sadie had said something sooner, would Fran Dugdale still be alive? But who would she have spoken to? She was only speaking to Lesley now because it was Lesley who was investigating Fran's death.

Lesley looked away, out of the front window. A flock of seagulls had gathered in the corner of the car park and seemed to be tearing apart some scraps of food they'd found. "Do you think he'll speak to you again? Tell you more, now he knows Fran's dead?"

"He might. But surely this is something you should follow up. You're investigating Fran's death, after all."

"I am."

Sadie was right. Lesley hadn't spoken to Phipps since he'd been pulled off the Mackie investigation, had avoided talking to him when he was working on it. But he'd spoken to a woman whose death she was investigating, and only three days before her death.

"You can't report on this," she said, "not while the case is ongoing."

"Why d'you think I came to you?"

Lesley nodded. *Good.*

"Anything you uncover before Fran's killer is tried, you can't report."

"Lesley, I do know the law."

Not when you trespassed on Brownsea Island and filmed my suspect, you didn't. Maybe Sadie had calmed down since then.

"I'm glad to hear it," she said.

Sadie twisted her lips together. "I'm going to speak to her senior officer. If he gives me anything that confirms what Fran was doing, I'll..." She paused. "I'll tell you first."

"Thanks. By her senior officer, you mean..."

"DI Collingwood."

Lesley looked into Sadie's eyes. Should she tell her that Collingwood had been sniffing around the crime scene, that she didn't trust him?

No. When it came to Collingwood, it was best to let the journalist reach her own conclusions.

CHAPTER FORTY-TWO

FRAN'S FATHER was the concierge at a large chain hotel set back from the seafront in Bournemouth. Tina parked in the street alongside it and walked round the building to the front, ignoring the clifftop view and scrolling through the hotel website on her phone.

"Oi. Watch out."

She looked up to see she'd narrowly avoided walking into a woman with a pushchair.

"Sorry." She slid her phone into the inside pocket of her jacket. "I was miles away."

"Too right you were."

The truth was, Tina was tired. She'd been on middle-of-the-night duty last night and Louis had woken twice. She was running around the county speaking to family members and briefing FLOs and it was all she could manage just to stay upright.

She reached the hotel entrance and sniffed in the sea air. It was tinged with the smell of hot dogs from a stand just down the path towards the town centre. Seagulls wheeled overhead and their shrieks filled her ears.

Bloody seagulls. She was glad she lived inland where they weren't such a menace. They'd brought Louis to Bournemouth beach a couple of weekends ago and he'd watched one of them attack a bag of chips someone had dropped on the ground. Not exactly David Attenborough material.

She pushed open the doors to the hotel and strode inside, blinking a few times in an attempt to remove the tiredness from her eyes.

It didn't work.

She brought up her hand to hide a yawn.

Get a grip, Tina.

If she was going to cope with juggling work and a young child, then she had to find a way to get more sleep. Maybe a nap as soon as she got in from work?

But there was always washing to be done and Louis needed his tea, then there was bath time and by the time that was done she needed an hour in front of the telly just to feel like a human being and not just a baby-tending automaton.

It would get better. Her sister Sam, whose youngest was almost two now, had reassured her.

She scanned the hotel lobby. It was lighter than she'd expected, with pale furnishings complementing the views from the large windows. She was sure she'd been here for a family lunch years ago and didn't remember it being so airy.

There was no sign of a concierge desk. She approached the reception desk and held up her ID without drawing attention to it. The young blonde woman behind the counter looked at it, flinched, then looked at Tina.

"Can I help you?"

Tina gave her a reassuring smile. "I'd like to speak to Tony Dugdale, please."

"Oh." The woman's face fell.

"Is he here?"

The woman rubbed her cheek. "Oh, he's here alright."

Was this the mistress that Jacinta Dugdale had talked about? She was barely older than Fran. No wonder Jacinta wasn't happy.

"If you could tell me where he is, I'd be grateful. Is there somewhere private I can speak to him?"

"You might as well go to his room." The woman pointed to the right. "Room 103, ground floor."

"He's staying here?"

"Ground floor is staff quarters. They're letting him stay here. For a while." The woman's nostrils flared.

If this wasn't Tony's new partner, then Tina was a monkey's uncle.

She walked away from the desk, following signs to the bedrooms. It didn't take her long to find room 103.

She knocked, her ID still in her hand.

The door flew open.

"Ruth, I'm sorry. I didn't mean to... Oh."

A man stood in the doorway, his initial expression of excitement replaced with one of disappointment.

The woman behind the reception desk had worn a badge with the name *Ruth* printed in large gold lettering. So Tina had been right.

"Mr Dugdale?" she said.

"Yes. Are you from Head Office?"

"No." Tina held up her ID. "DC Tina Abbott, Dorset Police."

The disappointed look on his face shifted to dread. "What

is it? Is it Jacinta? Has she done something stupid?" He looked away. "Oh, fucking hell. Stupid woman."

"Can I come in? Or is there somewhere else private we can talk?"

"You can come in."

Tina peered past him. She didn't feel comfortable about going into this man's bedroom to break the news to him that his daughter had died.

But she'd been to worse places. Much worse.

"Thanks." She followed him into the room.

Tony's bedroom had the same layout as the light, bright bedrooms on the hotel website, but looked like it hadn't been decorated in about thirty years. The wallpaper had a browning floral pattern, the carpet was brown with an abstract swirly design and the curtains were so thin she wondered if there was any point in them being there.

There were two folding chairs by the window. She gestured for Tony to take one, and took the other herself.

She swallowed. "It's bad news I'm afraid, Mr Dugdale. Your daughter, Fran. Her body was found in Tyneham village on Sunday." She watched his face as his eyes widened, then filled with tears. "I'm sorry to tell you we believe her death was suspicious."

He wiped away tears. "Suspicious?"

"We believe someone murdered your daughter."

"She's a police detective."

"I know."

Tony blinked at her. "Satvinder. Have you told him?"

"Sorry, who's Satvinder?"

"Her fiancé." Tony took in a shaky breath. "He'll be devastated."

Fiancé, what fiancé?

"Fran lived alone," Tina said, "is that right?"

"She's got a flat in Dorchester. They're buying a house together, for after the wedding." He smiled. "My daughter's the old-fashioned type."

Was, thought Tina. And why hadn't Fran's mother mentioned that her daughter was engaged?

"Can you tell me where Satvinder lives?"

"Er..." Tony scanned the room, his movements jerky, then stood up and went to a bag on the bed. He brought out a phone and scrolled through it.

"Weymouth." He held out the phone.

"Thanks." Tina wrote down the address. "Do you want to sit down again?" She was worried he might keel over. "Is there anyone here who can stay with you? And we'll assign you a Family Liaison Officer."

"Ruth." He put his head in his hands. "Ruth. *Shit*. No. I'll be fine."

"I'll tell your wife that we've spoken to you."

"You've seen her already?" He lowered his hands.

"This morning."

"Of course. God, I've been such an arse." He looked at Tina through red-rimmed eyes. "Tell her I'll come back. We need to pull together."

Tina drew back. From the way the man's wife had spoken about him, she wasn't sure he'd be welcomed into the house. "I think that's something you need to tell her yourself."

"Yes. Of course, yes."

The relationship breakdown between Fran's parents was unfortunate, but Tina couldn't see how it might be connected to her death. And both parents had seemed genuinely shocked.

Tina leaned towards him. "Is there anyone you can think of who might have wanted to hurt your daughter?"

He shook his head. "No. Of course not."

"Her work in PSD. Maybe she—"

"PSD. What's that?"

"Professional Standards. They police the police."

"She was being investigated?"

"Fran was a member of PSD. Her job was to—"

"She's a detective. Was." His face slumped.

"Mr Dugdale, what did you know about your daughter's job?"

"She's – was – a detective. CID. That's right, isn't it?"

So Fran hadn't told her dad about her work. Did that mean she was ashamed?

"Can you think of anyone who might have wanted to hurt her?"

"No one. No one at all. Fran was quiet, she didn't have a lot of friends. But she was loyal, steadfast. Not the kind of girl anyone would hold a grudge against."

Tony Dugdale clearly didn't know much about his daughter's life, although from what Tina had heard so far, he seemed to know her character.

She stood up. "Thanks for your time, Mr Dugdale. The liaison officer will be wi—"

He shook his head. "That won't be necessary. I'm going back to the house."

Tina smiled. She wasn't sure that would work out, but hoped it did.

"Just a moment," he said, holding out a hand as she stood in the doorway. "Her necklace. Have you...?"

She frowned. "Necklace?"

"Satvinder bought it for her. Gold, with a ruby at the centre. Well, a garnet probably. She never took it off. He'll want it. Or if he doesn't, me and her mum would."

Tina nodded. "We'll look for it, Sir. It might be evidence, though."

He nodded, and she turned for the door, thinking over the photos of Fran's body.

What necklace?

CHAPTER FORTY-THREE

THE MAN WAS by the barns outside Tyneham, on the turnoff from the path down to Worbarrow Bay.

Meera held back as she saw him walk inside, positioning herself behind a hedge.

He had his back to her and was talking into his phone in a low voice, standing just inside the barn's doorway. The barn was filled with old farming equipment, surrounded by information boards telling visitors about the way of life here before the village had been abandoned.

"Turn around," she muttered. He still wore the jeans and white bomber jacket; there was no doubt it was the same man. But she couldn't make out his face.

She caught movement from the corner of her eye and tuned to see another man approaching the barn, from the direction of the path.

Collingwood.

His car couldn't be down there. The only access was via the coastal path, and the nearest that came to a road was five miles away at Kimmeridge.

Collingwood drove an Audi. She'd seen it the day before when she'd argued with him about their mutual presence at the crime scene. If she could find it and take photographs, that might be evidence.

But evidence of what?

Collingwood entered the barn. The other man turned to greet him, and Meera finally saw his face.

Her breath caught in her throat.

She shifted her weight, moving downwards so they wouldn't spot her. She was behind a pile of wood now, and couldn't tell if they'd noticed her.

If Collingwood saw her, he'd recognise her. The other man wouldn't. Only Stanley and the boss had encountered him, when they'd been investigating Trevor Hamm's death at Portland Bill.

She grabbed her phone, then stopped.

Who to contact?

Stanley.

She brought up her history of messages to him and started typing.

I'm at Tyneham. Collingwood's here, doing something in the woods. Don't know what yet. I followed him and he's meeting someone you're looking for. He's just given him something.

She glanced up, checking that the two men hadn't seen her. She had a sudden, awful vision of them watching her as she typed.

They were still in the barn.

She added the name before hitting Send.

David Watson. Collingwood is here with Day Watson.

CHAPTER FORTY-FOUR

LESLEY STOOD in the Dorset Police HQ car park, waiting for Tina's car to arrive. When it did, she jumped in.

"Thanks, boss," said Tina as Lesley strapped herself in. "We can go in your car, if you'd prefer?"

"Yours is already warm. And I can think better as a passenger."

"The sarge says you—"

Lesley gave Tina a look and Tina stopped talking. They both knew that the reason Lesley drove when she was with Dennis was that if Dennis drove, they'd never reach their destination. At least, not without Lesley losing her patience.

She sat back as Tina headed into Wool, turning right towards the sea before the level crossing. A train had passed as they approached, and the traffic was starting up again.

"Tell me what you know about Satvinder Gill," she told Tina.

Tina nodded. "Fran's dad told me they got engaged three months ago. They've been an item for the last four years."

"That's a long time."

A shrug. "Not everyone puts the cart before the horse like me."

Lesley gave her a tap on the arm. "It worked out alright for you, though."

Tina flinched. "Of course it did. Wouldn't have things any other way." The DC had discovered she was pregnant while they'd been working on a case in Lyme Regis. Marriage to Mike had come soon after that, but they seemed to be happy. Lesley hoped to God the day wouldn't come when Tina and Mike weren't happy together. She didn't want to have to choose between them.

"He's not police?" she asked.

"Not as far as I know. I got Mike to check him out while you were waiting for me."

"Mike told me he works at a trendy café on Weymouth Harbour."

"Wheelers, boss." Tina glanced in her rearview mirror as she passed an open top bus that was wending its way slowly along the road towards Durdle Door. "That's where I'm hoping we'll find him."

"We don't know if he's been told about his fiancée dying."

"No." Tina frowned. "We need to ask him about a necklace, though."

"A necklace?"

"Fran's dad said Satvinder gave it to her. She never took it off." She turned to Lesley. "She wasn't wearing it, was she?"

Lesley shook her head. "I don't recall a necklace. We'll need to check with Gail."

Tina nodded. The bus turned off.

Lesley sighed. Tina had already done this twice. "I'll break the news."

Tina glanced at her. "You're sure?"

"Of course I'm sure. You've had to tell both the parents."

Lesley's phone rang.

"Dennis, what's up?"

"Stanley's had a message from Meera."

She frowned. Stanley and Meera were working on separate cases. "Go on."

"She's at Tyneham still, but she's been keeping an eye on DI Collingwood, by the sound of it."

"Have you spoken to her?"

"That might compromise her."

"OK. So what's this news?"

"He's been looking for things in the woods, apparently. And he appears to be having a clandestine meeting with David Watson."

Lesley shook her head. There was something about the way Dennis said *clandestine meeting* that sounded so wrong.

"Boss?"

"Sorry, Dennis. You're sure it's Day Watson?"

"Meera would have seen his photo when she was working on the Hamm case. I've exchanged messages with her now, and she's certain."

"OK. Tell her to sit tight. Call for uniformed backup; Day Watson could be dangerous."

"Do we request an armed unit?"

Lesley gazed out of the windscreen. They were approaching East Lulworth now, passing the first sign warning of the firing ranges.

How long would it take for an armed unit to get to Tyneham? They'd need to be briefed and travel from Dorchester or Bournemouth.

"No," she said. "Get a regular response unit in. And Dennis..."

"Yes, boss?"

"You and Stanley hang back, yes? I don't want any heroics."

CHAPTER FORTY-FIVE

WHEELERS WAS INDEED a trendy coffee shop on Weymouth Harbour. Lesley hadn't been aware this sort of place existed in Weymouth: she'd assumed it was all fish and chips and ice cream kiosks.

She and Tina entered to find the place full of punters sheltering from the same shower that had caught them while they were walking from the Cosens Quay Car Park. A young Asian man was behind the counter, chatting to people in the queue and churning out coffees like it was an assembly line.

They approached him, and he looked up from the pattern he was making on the top of a latte.

"Can I help you?" He looked between Lesley and Tina, probably wondering what their relationship was and why they'd jumped the queue. A woman standing next to Lesley muttered "at the back", and Lesley flashed her a smile.

She leaned across the counter. "Are you Satvinder Gill?"

He stopped mid-pattern, the milk almost slopping onto the saucer. "Yes. Why?" He glanced back at a door behind him.

She smiled. "My name's DCI Lesley Clarke, Dorset Police. Is there somewhere private we can speak?"

He all but dropped the cup, letting it clatter onto the surface. "I'm busy right now." He indicated the queue with his free hand.

"Is there anyone else who can take over?" Tina asked.

"What's the hold-up?" asked a man at the back of the queue.

"Sorry, mate." Satvinder glanced at the man, blinking rapidly. "Bit of an emergency. Jaz?" He called across the counter.

A boy who looked barely old enough to be out of school, let alone working in a coffee shop, was cleaning tables. He looked up. "Yeah?"

"Sorry, mate, but can you take over for a minute?"

"Err..."

"Just do the easy stuff. I won't be long." Satvinder looked at Lesley again. "I... yeah. Just do the easy stuff."

Jaz was standing next to the counter now, a tray of dirty cups and plates in his hands. "You're sure?"

"I'm sure." Satvinder flashed the boy a smile. Lesley and Tina exchanged glances. There was no way this young man had been told that his fiancée was dead.

"Thanks," Lesley said. "We won't keep you too long."

He shrugged. "Hope not." He jerked his head to beckon them towards the door behind the counter, then disappeared through it. Lesley and Tina followed him into a store room. It was piled high with boxes of coffee and cartons of plant milks of all descriptions. A tiny table sat in one corner, with a chair squeezed in beside it and a laptop open. Satvinder lowered himself into the chair, careful not to disturb a pile of napkins next to him.

"What's this about?" he asked. "We're all up to date on our VAT returns. Jaz is a refugee but he's legal, I did all the paperwork—"

"This isn't about your business," Lesley said.

"*Is* it your business?" Tina asked, looking around the stock room.

"Yeah. I'm hoping to open another one in Lyme Regis, but it's competitive there... but you don't need to know about this, do you? What's this about?"

His tone had hardened. The friendly openness he'd adopted with his customers had been replaced with distrust.

"It's bad news, I'm afraid," Lesley said. "About your fiancée, Fran."

Satvinder's arm jerked. "Fran? Is she OK?"

"I'm very sorry, Mr Gill. But she's dead."

The colour drained from his face. "What? No. I saw her on Saturday. She's..." He gripped the table.

Tina took a step towards him. "Do you need a doctor? You look faint."

He shook his head. "No." He looked up at Lesley, his eyes bloodshot. "How?"

"She was found at Tyneham Village, on Sunday."

"Sunday? Today's Tuesday."

"We didn't know she was engaged until just over an hour ago. We came straight here after talking to her father."

"Tony." Satvinder licked his lips, the colour slowly returning to his face. "Is he OK?"

Lesley gave a gentle smile. "He's shocked, too."

A nod. "And her mum? Does her mum know?"

Lesley noted that he'd referred to Tony by name but not Jacinta.

"She'll be fine. Did you know that Fran's parents had split up?"

"What? No. That's... no. She didn't say anything about that." His breathing was shallow.

"You sure you don't need a doctor?" Tina asked.

"A coffee would be good. Lots of sugar."

"Good idea." Lesley raised her eyebrows at Tina, who stepped out into the main coffee shop.

Lesley crouched down, finding it easier to move now there were just two of them in the small space. Satvinder had a hand on his knee, his fingernails gripping the fabric of his black trousers.

"We believe Fran was murdered," she said, her voice low. "Do you know of anyone who might have wanted to hurt her?"

"Murdered?"

"Yes. Again, I'm so sorry."

Satvinder blinked. "Someone who might have...?" He raised a hand to his cheek and rubbed the skin.

"Anyone at all who Fran might have talked about. Someone she'd investigated, maybe. Someone connected to a case."

"She investigated coppers. You really think one of your own killed her?"

"We don't think anything right now." Lesley knew that her team would need to interview Fran's team in PSD, and soon. Carpenter was still making the arrangements.

He pushed out two quick breaths and leaned forward. *Where's that coffee?* Lesley thought.

"There was..." He shook his head.

"Yes?"

"No. It's daft."

"Nothing is daft."

He looked at her. "I don't think this person killed her."

"No. But there was someone who might have wished her harm?"

"I don't know. Not harm, maybe. But... but ill will."

Lesley nodded, encouraging him. "Can you tell me who?"

The door opened behind her. *Bad timing.*

"Here you are." Tina put the coffee on the table, pushing the laptop aside to fit it on. She stepped back.

"Can you tell me who?" Lesley repeated.

Satvinder sipped the coffee, his eyes darting around.

Was he scared?

"Whatever you tell me," she said, "they won't know it came from you. But we need to find out who killed Fran."

He gulped down a mouthful of coffee. "Can I see her?"

"Of course you can." The post-mortem would be under way soon, and she didn't have anyone there. Not with Meera at Tyneham.

Damn.

"Did she have... was she wearing...?" He wiped his eyes.

"A necklace?" Lesley suggested.

He looked up and nodded. "I gave it to her."

"We don't have it. But as soon as we find it and have finished with it, you'll have it back."

"Thanks." A sniff. "She'd..."

"She'd what?"

Satvinder looked at her. "The necklace. She'd... nothing." He shook his head.

"Satvinder," Lesley said, keeping her voice low, "can you tell me who might have wished Fran harm?"

She needed to hurry. But she also needed to give this man the time he needed to tell her what was troubling him.

He looked at her. "She made a complaint."

Lesley nodded. "She told you?"

"Her boss. DI Collingwood. She thought he was..." He shook his head and drank the coffee.

Lesley waited. Behind her, Tina shifted from foot to foot.

She turned to the DC. "Can you call Mike, ask him to get to the PM?" she muttered.

Tina glanced at Satvinder. "You're sure?"

"Sure." Lesley had a feeling Satvinder would be more likely to open up if there were fewer people in the room.

"OK." Tina left the store room.

Lesley twisted her head from side to side. Crouching like this meant she was holding her neck at an odd angle, and she was going to pay for it later.

"She made a complaint against DI Collingwood," she prompted.

"She thought he'd... No. I... I told her it was absurd."

"Please. Just tell me. It's for me and my team to judge if it's absurd or not."

"OK." He gulped in a few quick breaths. "She thought he'd had..."

Lesley looked at him, desperate to speak. She waited.

He put down the cup and rubbed his cheek again. "She thought DI Collingwood was working with organised crime." Another gulp of air. His skin was fading again.

"Did she have evidence?"

"I don't know. She must have done, to make a complaint."

"When you say organised crime..."

"I don't know any names. Fran didn't want to tell me. But..." He stared at her.

"But what?"

"She thought..."

Lesley tried to ignore the fact that her neck was screaming

at her now. She could hear voices outside: Tina talking to the young barista, Jaz.

Don't come in.

"What did she think, Satvinder?" she muttered, her voice barely more than a whisper.

He looked at her. "This is mad."

"Just tell me."

"OK." He ran a hand through his hair. "I didn't listen much, thought she was being melodramatic. When you work in the job Fran does, you see this kind of thing everywhere."

Lesley nodded. He was rambling. Was he going to tell her?

"What did she think?" she repeated.

"Her boss. Collingwood."

A pause. His gaze darted around Lesley's face.

"She thought... she thought he'd killed someone. A DCI."

CHAPTER FORTY-SIX

ONE SQUAD CAR and a police van were already at Tyneham Village when Dennis and Stanley arrived.

Dennis felt his heart sink. He hated it when he was last on the scene.

"Right," he said. "You stay here, I'll go and speak to the officer in charge."

He got out of his car and walked towards the vehicles just as a woman emerged from the squad car.

He gave her a nod. "PS Dewberry."

"Dennis. We haven't been here long, if that's what you're wondering."

He looked around the car park. Other than the three police vehicles, including his own, it was empty.

"No sign of your DC Vedra," Sergeant Dewberry said.

Dennis frowned. "Maybe there's another car park."

Dewberry shook her head. "The only places you can leave a car are on the road coming in, and right here."

"Did you see her car coming the other way as you arrived?"

"If I'd seen her, I'd have told you."

Dennis felt his skin prickle. He took out his phone and dialled Meera.

Voicemail.

He put a hand to his neck, feeling a chill run down it.

Meera, where are you?

He typed out a text message to her: *DC Brown and I are at Tyneham. Please report your whereabouts asap.*

Stanley was emerging from the car. Dennis waved him back inside. *It's not safe.*

He turned to PS Dewberry. "Any sign of the two men she was following?"

"None."

"She reported a decorator'swhite van."

"We haven't seen it."

"Have you—"

"I've phoned it in, Dennis. Along with DC Vedra's car. If either of them are spotted, we'll know."

"I want to check the barn."

Dewberry nodded. "Is that where they were when she was watching them?"

"It is."

Dennis turned and gestured for Stanley to get out of the car. He didn't like this. David Watson hadn't been seen for weeks. Now he'd turned up at an unrelated crime scene, talking to a PSD officer...

But then he'd disappeared again. Along with one of their own team.

"Stanley," he said as the DC approached. "Apparently there's no sign of Meera, or the men she was following."

"DI Collingwood?"

Dennis shook his head.

Stanley turned back towards the car. "We should go

looking for her, Sarge."

"Where exactly do you suggest we start?" Dennis could feel his heart rate rising. "No. We stay here. Uniform are looking for her." He hesitated. "I'll need to tell the boss."

"What d'you want me to do?"

"Go to the barn where she was watching them. The house too, where they found DC Dugdale. Why aren't FSI here?"

"They finished yesterday, Sarge. The crime scene's been fully investigated."

Dennis looked past the DC towards the village and the house where DC Dugdale had been found.

Poor woman.

She'd been quiet in his interview. Almost like she wasn't even present.

Was that normal, for her and Collingwood? Was it how they operated?

Or was she scared of him?

He drummed his fingertips against the side of his head. Watson meeting Collingwood.

Think, man.

Why would the two of them be meeting? Could Watson be a witness for PSD, providing evidence against a corrupt officer who'd been working with one of the gangs?

Or was there more to it?

Either way, they had to find Meera.

Dennis watched Stanley walk towards the barn. He dialled the DCI.

No answer.

"Boss," he said. "I'm at Tyneham. There's no sign of Meera. Nor of the men she was following. Uniform have got an alert on their vehicles and we're looking for anything that might tell us where they've gone."

He hung up.

The boss was visiting members of DC Dugdale's family, along with Tina. She'd have turned her phone off, not wanting to take calls when breaking bad news to a member of the public.

He was on his own.

CHAPTER FORTY-SEVEN

"SAY THAT AGAIN," Lesley said. Tina had entered and was standing behind her, barely moving.

Satvinder looked at Lesley. "I told her she was being paranoid. He's a copper, right? He can't have killed someone."

"No." She rubbed her temples, thoughts crowding in on her. "Tell me what you said again. And tell me exactly what Fran told you."

"Her boss, DI Collingwood." His gaze flicked to the door, as if he expected the man to come bursting in. "She thought he killed another copper."

"And the name of the other copper was...?"

"Sorry, I don't remember. It was a DCI, I think. I'd forgotten that, too, but it came back to me when you told me your name. Your rank."

"She didn't give you a name?"

"She might have done. But... well, I thought she was being ridiculous."

Lesley wanted to suggest a name. She certainly had a name in mind. Right at the forefront of her mind, screaming at her.

But that would be a leading question. And she needed to be careful.

"Satvinder, I'm very sorry to ask you this, but would you be prepared to come into a police station and tell me what you know on video?"

He frowned. "Am I under suspicion?"

"No." She gave him what she hoped was a reassuring smile. "And I'm really sorry to ask you to do this right now. I know we've... well, you'll be in shock, about Fran. But—"

"Have you set a wedding date?" Tina asked.

Lesley looked over her shoulder. She frowned at the DC.

Satvinder nodded. "Next July."

Next July? That was a long way off.

Lesley and Elsa had waited ten months between Lesley's proposal and the wedding. And that was only because they'd had to wait for Lesley's divorce to be finalised. But every couple had their own unique circumstances, she supposed.

"Is there anyone we can call, who can come with you?" Tina asked. "You might want support."

"My mum." Satvinder put his head in his hands. "She'll be gutted. She loves Fran." He looked up, his eyes wet. "What do you need me to do? Will it help you find who did this to her?"

"It might," said Lesley. And it might also lead them to DCI Mackie's killer.

And that was something she couldn't afford to ask questions about here, in the back room of a coffee shop where there was no official record of the conversation.

"We can go to Weymouth police station," Tina said. "It won't take long." She looked from Satvinder to Lesley. "I'll give them a call."

"Thanks." Lesley stood up, glad to finally stretch her aching muscles. Tina gave her a meaningful look.

She looked back at Fran Dugdale's fiancé, who was sobbing into his hands.

Poor man.

Taking him to a police station, interrogating him about not only his girlfriend's death, but possibly that of Tim Mackie...

It was cruel.

But it was necessary.

CHAPTER FORTY-EIGHT

MEERA WAS careful to hang back, aware that these lanes were quiet and the men in front could spot her if she got too close. Every time the van rounded a bend she felt her pulse rise, worried it might not be there when she turned the same bend after it.

She had to rely on the fact that there were few turnoffs or driveways, hoping they'd still be there even if she couldn't see them.

It wasn't like the van was difficult to spot. Battered and rusting with that dent on the rear wheel arch, she wasn't going to miss it each time it reappeared.

They were heading towards Wareham, over the ranges. The area had been closed off since Fran's body had been found, and it was eerily quiet. She was aware that if the two men in the van realised she was behind them, there would be nobody to help her.

She'd turned her phone off when she'd been watching them, and hadn't had a chance to turn it on again to ask for help.

She should.

But right now she was too focused on keeping a good distance from the van, making sure she didn't lose it, and avoiding ploughing into a hedge.

At last they reached the gate at the eastern entrance to the ranges. She hung back as the van took the right turn onto Grange Hill without waiting. After a moment, Meera drove on and took the same turn.

There were no other cars on the road. Nothing she could put between her and them. And they'd have noticed her car in the car park at Tyneham.

She was putting herself at risk.

After just over a mile, the van turned right.

Meera cursed herself. This road led to Kimmeridge, and to Kimmeridge Bay beyond it. A narrow, quiet lane. It was unlikely there would be any cars she could put between her and the men she was following.

She could hang back, assume that was where they were going.

But there was a turnoff to the left, where the farmer had erected a sign telling people to ignore their satnav and not take the turn. It led back to the road she'd left, and to Corfe Castle via Church Knowle.

They could be going anywhere.

They could be aware she was behind them. They could be throwing her off the trail.

She pulled over and turned on her phone.

"Meera. Where are you?" The sarge sounded worried.

"I'm on the road to Kimmeridge just south of the junction with Grange Hill. Following a white van with the two men in it."

"You left the village without alerting anyone. We've got a

whole team of uniformed officers here ready to arrest David Watson."

"I'm really sorry, Sarge. I didn't want to turn my phone on in case they heard me."

"'If you're on the Kimmeridge road, where are they?"

"Somewhere ahead of me. I'm hoping they're heading for the sea."

"Right. You keep following, but maintain a safe distance. Keep your phone switched on and phone me if anything changes. I'll alert Uniform and have cars sent to Kimmeridge and to Corfe."

Meera felt her breathing slow.

"Be quick, Sarge. If they're heading to Corfe they could go anywhere from there."

"I know that. But Uniform know the roads. We can outpace them."

She nodded. It was reassuring to have the DS supporting her.

"Keep on them, Meera. Try not to lose them."

"Sarge." Meera hung up and started driving.

CHAPTER FORTY-NINE

"Thanks, Chris." Tina nodded at the civilian on the front desk at Weymouth police station as she and the boss led Satvinder Gill through to an interview room.

"No problem, Tina. Good to see you back. How's that little 'un doing?"

"He's fine." She felt a pang of guilt. This murder case meant long hours, and she and Mike were having to juggle. She wished she lived closer to her mum in Lyme Regis. "Mike's back at work."

"I heard. Good on him. Can I get you a cuppa?"

The DCI was already in the interview room, Satvinder opposite her. Tina poked her head in.

"Satvinder, can we get you a drink?"

He frowned. "Coffee, please. Plenty of milk."

She turned back to Chris. "Two coffees, one of them black. Stick some sugar in the one with milk, he's had a nasty shock. And a tea for me." She touched his arm. "Cheers."

"No problem." Chris walked away, leaving Tina to slip into the interview room and take a seat. She moved the chair so it wasn't right next to the DCI; she didn't want Satvinder feeling like he was under interrogation.

"Thanks for doing this, Satvinder," the boss said. "I realise it's not the nicest thing to do when you've just learned your fiancée's died."

He drew in a shaky breath. "I want to help."

"And we appreciate it." She leaned in, clasping her hands together on the desk. "Now, do you mind if we record this? You're not under any suspicion, it's just so we've got a record of anything you tell us."

A shrug. "It's fine." He glanced at the recording machine.

The boss indicated for Tina to turn it on.

"Thanks. For the recording, I'm DCI Lesley Clarke, Major Crimes Investigation Team." She looked at Tina.

"DC Tina Abbott, also Major Crimes Investigation Team."

Satvinder was watching them. He cleared his throat. "Satvinder Gill. Fran Dugdale's fiancé." His expression dropped. "Former fiancé."

Tina wanted to reach across the table and give his arm a squeeze. But every time she'd gone near him on the way here, he'd shrunk back. Instead, she gave him a sympathetic smile.

"We've asked you to speak to us," the boss began, "because your fiancée DC Dugdale spoke to you about suspicions she had about another officer. Is that right?"

"Er... yes, it's right."

"She told you she'd raised a formal complaint."

A nod.

"I'm sorry, Mr Gill, but the tape won't pick up your gestures. You'll have to speak."

"Oh. Of course, sorry. Yes. She did tell me she'd done that." He eyed the machine, looking wary.

The DCI gave him a smile. "Can you remember what Fran told you about the content of that complaint?"

"She..." he rubbed his nose. "She didn't trust her boss. He'd been involving other officers in their work, officers who weren't members of PSD."

"Like who?" Tina asked.

The DCI shot her a look. Tina shrugged: *sorry*.

The boss turned back to Satvinder. "Did she say which officers?"

"A DI Angus was one. I can't remember any others."

The boss's face had tuned pale. Tina looked at her, puzzled.

"DI Angus?" the DCI repeated.

"Yes. Sorry, is that right?"

"Nothing's right or wrong, Satvinder. It's just what you remember."

"Yeah. Right, sorry."

"It's OK." Tina leaned towards him. "You don't have to apologise for anything. We really appreciate your help."

He gave her a sad smile. She resisted the urge to reach for his hand.

"Did Fran give you DI Angus's full name?" the DCI asked.

"No. Sorry."

Tina looked at the boss. Surely there wasn't more than one DI Angus in Dorset Police. Certainly not more than one the MCIT had had recent dealings with.

Still, you couldn't be too sure. Tina noted the name in her pad. She'd check it on the system later.

"Did Fran say what DI Angus was doing, exactly?" the boss asked. "You say he was getting involved in PSD investigations."

"She didn't know. She just saw him talking to her boss, heard mention of a case or two."

"Any specific cases?"

"She mentioned DS Frampton."

Tina shifted in her chair, unable to control herself. The DCI had tensed.

"DS Frampton," the boss repeated.

"I assume Fran was investigating him." A pause. "Look, I know Fran wasn't supposed to talk to me about this kind of thing. It's all confidential and that. But it wasn't the cases she talked about. She was frustrated. She thought her boss wasn't doing his job properly. That he'd had DS Frampton arrested deliberately."

"Deliberately?" The boss's voice was little more than a whisper.

Satvinder took a deep breath, meeting her gaze. Tina wondered what he would say if he knew their connection to DS Frampton.

"Yes," he said. "She reckoned he had the DS arrested to cover up his own involvement in a murder."

The boss's hand was on the table now, clenched in a fist. "Whose murder?"

Satvinder slumped in his chair. "That's what I was talking about, earlier. I don't know the name, sorry. But it was a DCI. Like you."

CHAPTER FIFTY

MIKE WASN'T unusual in disliking post-mortems. But at least this victim hadn't spent two weeks submerged in water, or been given a drug that made her skin swell up. This victim had spent forty-eight hours being subjected to no more than what the assorted insects of Tyneham Village were capable of, it seemed.

"It's a puzzle," Dr Bamford said. "She's definitely dead, but I can't find a cause. Not yet."

Mike stepped forward from his position at the back of the room. "Not yet?"

Bamford looked up. "I'll find one. Don't you worry. It's just not immediately obvious."

"Have you looked for poisons?"

"I've sent various samples off for a toxicology analysis, and analysed what I can right here." He shook his head and wiped his face with the back of his glove, then grimaced. "I'll get this lot off, then we can talk."

Mike nodded and followed the pathologist. Gareth Bamford had come across from Devon after his predecessor, the chronically lazy Henry Whittaker, had retired. The DCI had worked with him on the Lyme Regis case, the one during which Mike had met Tina's family.

They peeled off their protective gear, changed into normal shoes, and went into Bamford's office. It was clean and tidy, the only sign of occupation a family photo on the desk. Gareth touched it as he sat down.

"So have you got anything at all?" Mike asked. "It *is* poison, I assume."

"It must be. There's no sign of trauma, no bruising – not significant anyway – and no—"

"Not significant?"

"I showed you the bruising on the back of her hand. She hit something, or someone. A while before she died. And there's some damage to her fingernails. But not that much."

"How much is not that much?"

"There's skin under her nails, quite a lot of it. If she'd put up a fierce fight, you can expect a nail or two to break, or at least spilt. There's some damage to the nails, but to be honest it could have just been caused by her biting them."

"So if there wasn't a fight, how did the skin get there?"

"Maybe she just didn't inflict that much damage. Maybe..." the doctor cocked his head. "I'm not sure. I'll give it some thought."

"And none of that would have killed her."

"No." Bamford leaned back and sighed. "Sorry, mate. Whoever did this was either very clever, or very lucky."

"You've got the skin from under the fingernails, though," Mike said. "We can find the killer from that."

Gareth raised an eyebrow. "Without a cause of death, there's no way of confirming that the owner of that skin is her killer. Or even confirming DC Dugdale's death as murder."

Mike leaned forward. "What?"

"You heard me. We need a cause of death to be able to show that it was suspicious. Otherwise it could have been natural causes. The coroner won't like it."

"But she was found abandoned inside a ruined house, miles from anywhere. She clearly had a fight with someone before she died. And she was a—"

Bamford had his hands up. "You don't need to tell me all that, Mike. But the reality is, that without a cause of death being pronounced, a good lawyer will get anyone you arrest exonerated." He eyed Mike. "You know that."

Mike sighed. "The DCI's not going to like this."

A faint smile played on the doctor's lips. "I have to admit, I'm glad it's you here and not her."

"Thanks." Mike stood up. "When you do come up with a cause of death, you'll let me know, won't you?"

"The very instant. I promise."

CHAPTER FIFTY-ONE

MEERA PULLED UP ON A VERGE. She'd driven down to the sea at Kimmeridge Bay, then backed up and taken the narrow lanes to Corfe Castle via Church Knowle. She'd even taken the road up to Stoborough.

But the van was gone.

While she'd been on the phone to the sarge, assuming, naively, that she wouldn't lose her quarry on these roads, they'd evaded her.

She slammed her palm into the steering wheel. *Fuck*.

They must have known she was behind them. They'd have seen her car at Tyneham. Collingwood might have recognised it: he'd certainly have been able to check it was a police vehicle just by making a phone call.

And they'd got away from her.

A car passed her, driving carefully and giving her a wide berth: the sarge.

Meera dipped her head, wishing she could hide from him.

She'd got him all the way out here. She'd called out two squad cars, both of which had failed to find the van.

And all for nothing.

What did she have?

She flicked on her phone.

Fifteen photographs. Five of Collingwood in the woods, looking for something, it seemed. A couple of him on the path, taken from behind so you couldn't tell who the hell it was. And more of the van.

She'd run the plates. But it was just a van. Whoever owned it, if they were smart, would be using false plates anyway.

And if they weren't now, they certainly would be by morning.

The sarge's car returned, going in the opposite direction. He wound down the window and she did the same.

"There's a passing place a couple of hundred yards that way," he said. "I'll park there and walk back."

Meera shook her head. Her car was halfway up a verge, parked at an angle which was almost dangerous. Not the way an officer who'd had response vehicle training should park.

"It's OK, sarge. Meet me in the car park in Kimmeridge."

He looked behind him. "I'll have to reverse."

"Can't you...? It's OK. We can go back to the office."

"You're sure?"

Meera nodded.

"Only, there are uniformed officers out here. Are they still looking for the van?"

She closed her eyes. "I'll call it in. Tell them to stop."

The sarge leaned out of his window, his face almost level with her door. "Don't give up, Meera. You saw a police officer and a known gang member. You've got photographic evidence."

"Not really." Meera remembered something. "Wait, though."

"Yes?"

"I... I might have got a photo of whatever it was I think he gave to Day Watson."

"He gave him something?"

She nodded. "In all the confusion, I forgot. But he did. Maybe that was what he was doing. Removing evidence. He passed it to Day."

Dennis gave her a pat on the back. "Watson might still have it. The registration number of that van is on the system and I'm sure we'll find it." He sniffed. "You and I can go back to HQ and regroup."

Regroup. That wasn't a word she'd ever imagined the sarge using.

"OK," she said.

"And don't let it get you down. It's not done. Not yet."

CHAPTER FIFTY-TWO

LESLEY WAS WALKING into her office as Dennis and Meera clattered into the team room, Meera looking dejected.

"What's up?" she asked Dennis.

He shook his head. "The van."

"You lost it?"

He raised his eyebrows. Meera looked up. "Sorry, boss."

"Not your fault." Lesley gripped the doorframe. "We've got the plates, it'll turn up. We've got a lot to catch up on, I'd like you all in my office."

Dennis looked at Stanley and back to Lesley. "Including us?"

"Including you." Lesley glanced at the door. "It's looking increasingly like our two cases are connected."

But the question was, had Carpenter known that when he'd told her to take Dennis off the Dugdale case?

They all shuffled into her office, mutters of 'after you' and 'excuse me'. *Stop being so bloody polite*, she thought. They had two cases to solve and they'd just lost a major advantage in one of them, if not both.

When they were all inside she turned to Meera. "Tell us what happened."

"I got to the crime scene early, I wanted to check if there was any more evidence from CSI that might be useful."

"They've finished," Tina said. "They're back in Dorchester collating evidence."

"I know that now." Meera sounded impatient. She looked back at Lesley. "I was by the Rectory, the building where Fran's body was found."

"And you saw Collingwood there," Lesley interrupted.

"I wasn't sure who it was at first."

"Hang on," Mike said. "DI Collingwood? Fran's boss?"

Meera looked at him. "There isn't another Collingwood, is there?"

He gave her a scowl.

Meera was clearly rattled. She needed to rein that in if she was going to be able to deal with her colleagues. Cases went badly, sometimes. Leads disappeared. She couldn't let that throw her.

Meera clenched a fist and looked at Lesley. "I watched him. He was doing something in the woods. I sent a message to Gail asking her to take a look and see if he'd left something, but if they've finished..."

Lesley nodded. "Once this is done, I want you back there. Take a look at where he was."

Meera's shoulders slumped, but she nodded yes. "I followed him back to the car park but his car wasn't there."

"Where was it?" asked Stanley.

Lesley stifled a laugh. *Trust Stanley to ask the obvious question.* She raised her eyebrows at Meera.

"I still don't know how he got there," Meera said. "I've checked maps of the area and there are only two ways in. The official road, the one the tourists use. And the emergency vehicle road, that they let the squad cars use when Fran was found."

"Did you check both of those?"

Meera shook her head. "I was following Collingwood and his associate when I left, I didn't have time. But the gate to the emergency road's been locked."

Lesley pursed her lips. "Double check it, when you go back."

"Collingwood's car will be on the emergency road," Dennis said. "Watson may have taken him back there, after you lost them."

Meera looked at Dennis. She ran a hand through her hair. "Sorry, Sarge."

"You did your best."

Meera looked around at the group. Lesley watched her body language: did she think they were being unfair on her?

"You uncovered a crucial piece of evidence," Lesley said. "Don't be hard on yourself."

At least, it might turn out to be a crucial piece of evidence.

Meera nodded. "Tell us about the van," Lesley said.

Meera looked round the team, her expression wary. "I heard a vehicle approaching and saw it enter the car park. A van. A white van." She pulled out her phone and read out a registration number. "Collingwood met the driver by the barns outside the village. The two of them had a conversation, then went back to the car park and got in the van. I followed them along the lanes towards Kimmeridge." A pause. "But then I lost them."

"There's a number of turn-offs along those lanes," Dennis said. "Farmyards they could have gone into."

"I still lost them. There were no other cars on the road."

"You had to hang back," Lesley said. "You didn't want them spotting you. And that meant losing sight of them."

"I suppose so." Meera leaned against the wall. "I've spoken to Uniform though, got them to alert me if the van turns up."

"Good. Thanks." Lesley turned to Tina. "Tina, you and I spoke to Fran's father and fiancé."

Tina straightened up. "Yes, boss."

"Why don't you tell the team what we discovered?"

Tina frowned. "Everything, boss?"

"Everything pertinent to Fran's death."

The frown deepened. "OK. We spoke to Tony first, well I did. That's Fran's dad. He's living in a staff bedroom at a chain hotel in Bournemouth. He and Fran's mum have split up. I thought it might be relevant at first, but I saw the reactions of both parents. They're devastated."

"Why did they split up?" Meera asked.

"Nothing to do with Fran, if that's what you're thinking. In fact, her dad didn't even know she worked in PSD. He had an affair with a colleague, Fran's mum kicked him out. Nothing out of the ordinary."

"Her father gave you the details of Fran's fiancé," Lesley prompted.

"Yes. Satvinder Gill. The DCI and I went to see him. He told us more about the complaint you uncovered, Mike." She glanced at Lesley. "The one against DI Collingwood."

Meera straightened from her position leaning against the wall. "Always Collingwood."

"We don't have enough yet to tell us he killed her," Lesley reminded her.

"No?" Mike said. He raised a hand, counting on his fingers. "First, Fran made a formal complaint about him. He would have been pissed off—"

Dennis cleared his throat.

"Sorry, Sarge," Mike muttered. He continued counting. "Two, Meera saw him meeting a known gang member at Tyneham. A man who's on the run, wanted in connection with a murder investigation. I know Collingwood's PSD, and they have their own way of doing things, but surely meeting a witness in secret like that—"

"There's whatever he was doing at the crime scene, too," Stanley added.

"There is," agreed Mike. "And third, we've got Satvinder corroborating the fact that Fran was suspicious of Collingwood."

"That's the same as your point one," Dennis said. "The complaint."

"Not when you hear what she was suspicious about." Tina looked at Lesley. "Boss?"

Lesley looked at Dennis. "Fran believed that Collingwood arranged for your arrest in order to cover his own tracks. According to her fiancé."

Dennis looked perplexed. "According to her fiancé."

"She reckoned he killed Mackie," Tina blurted.

Lesley watched as the colour drained from Dennis's face. He reached out, feeling for the arm of the chair he was sitting in.

Bad call. She should have told him this in private.

"Are you OK, Dennis?"

He blinked at her. "All you have is hearsay. Fran believed something, and she's not alive to tell us about it. Even if she was, it's nothing without evidence."

"Collingwood was meeting with Watson," Meera said. "That's something."

Dennis looked at her. "Members of PSD investigate officers

who have connections to organised crime. In the course of running an investigation, he may need to speak to a junior gang member."

"Watson isn't all that junior," Stanley said. "He was part of the gang that killed Trevor Hamm. He's on the run. He's wanted for murder."

Dennis shook his head. "And meeting a witness like that in a secluded spot is exactly what an astute officer would do." He turned to Lesley. "I can see what you're trying to prove here, but we don't have the evidence." He scratched this forehead. "If you don't mind me suggesting what you should be doing, boss, I think we're looking in the wrong direction."

"You do?" Lesley asked.

He nodded. "Our job here isn't to find out how DCI Mackie died." The colour was slowly returning to his cheeks. "We've been given two cases. We need to establish who killed Fran Dugdale, and we need to bring David Watson in. I suggest we focus on those two things."

Don't you want to know who killed your old friend?

"You're right," Lesley said.

"And we don't even have a cause of death," Mike added.

Lesley turned to him. "Sorry, Mike. The post-mortem. How did it go?"

"CSI have tissue from beneath her nails. That's positive. It might give us something. But Dr Bamford can't work out how she actually died. It must be some kind of poison, but he hasn't discovered it yet."

"And without a cause of death, we can't even prove murder," Dennis muttered.

Lesley felt her shoulders dip.

"We need to ignore that, for the time being," she said. "Remember how Fran was found. People don't end up in an abandoned building like that if they died of natural causes. Even if she did die naturally, somebody acted illegally in disposing of her body like that."

Nods and murmurs around the team. Tina's phone rang.

"Can I?" she asked Lesley.

"Of course."

They all watched as Tina took the call, speaking into her phone in a low voice. She gasped, spoke again, then hung up.

"They've had a match from the samples," she said. "The skin under Fran's nails."

"They've got a name?" Mike asked her.

Tina looked at him, excitement in her eyes. She switched her gaze to Lesley. "It's one of ours."

Dennis's mouth fell open. Stanley stood up.

"Who?" Lesley asked, keeping her voice level.

"A detective in Blandford CID," Tina said. "DI Rowan Angus."

CHAPTER FIFTY-THREE

"OK, EVERYONE," Lesley said. "Don't get ahead of yourselves."

"His skin was under her fingernails," Tina said. "Surely—"

Lesley put up a hand. "He's a CID detective. Blandford is no distance from Tyneham."

"Actually, it's over twenty miles," Dennis said.

She frowned at him. "Do we know if he was at the scene at all? Local CID might have attended before we got there."

People shook their heads. And even if he had been on the scene, it wouldn't account for his skin turning up under DC Dugdale's nails.

"The post-mortem, though," said Mike. "It was odd."

"Odd how?" Dennis asked.

"Well, firstly there's the fact that Gareth – Dr Bamford – can't work out the cause of death. But then there's the lack of evidence of a struggle."

"I thought she had skin under her nails," Lesley said.

"Rowan Angus's skin," added Tina.

Mike nodded. "She did. But that's all. Bamford says the

bruising on her hands is earlier, not immediately prior to her death. And that the damage to her nails isn't excessive."

"But the skin..." said Tina.

Lesley held up a hand. "It makes that unsafe, in evidential terms." She looked at Mike. "Is there more? Fibres?"

He shrugged.

"OK. We need to know that. We need to determine if he had a legitimate reason to be near Fran's body, and if he was at the scene. The log—"

"I'll check it, boss," said Mike.

"Thanks, Mike."

"We should interview him," suggested Stanley.

"Not yet. I want to find out more about Collingwood and what he was doing in Tyneham this morning."

"You want to interview Collingwood?" Stanley asked.

"No. I want to know what he was doing in those woods."

"He was holding something," Meera said. "I reckon he gave it to Watson."

Lesley nodded. "I also want to track down David Watson's van. We have more cause to be speaking to him, and we can ask him about his connection to DI Collingwood."

"And possibly DI Angus," Dennis suggested. "There was a link in the Hamm case."

Lesley nodded. Rowan Angus had turned up at each of the crime scenes when they'd been investigating the death of Midlands crime boss Trevor Hamm at Portland Lighthouse. He'd managed to convince everyone that he had a legitimate reason to be at each location, but his DNA and shoe prints had been found. It still niggled at her.

"Right." Lesley pulled in a sharp breath. "Firstly, I want none of you talking about our suspicions or hypotheses to anyone outside of this room. We need to tread exceptionally carefully from now on. If there's a suspicion that officers from Dorset Police are involved in this crime, then PSD will get involved."

"Who are the exact people we're suspicious of," added Stanley.

Lesley glanced at him. "And the less we can voice that kind of thinking, the better. You never know who might be listening." She scanned the room, remembering Carpenter's behaviour in his office the previous day.

She considered. What did she have? Nothing concrete.

They needed to find evidence. Not conjecture, not hearsay. Evidence.

"OK, everyone. Here's what you're going to do. Meera, head back to Tyneham, see if there's anything he left behind, any traces of him being in the woods. Go now."

"Boss." Meera hurried out of the room.

"Mike, I want you on the physical evidence taken from Fran's body. Speak to Gail, find out if there's anything else. And go to Fran's house, see if you can find any sign of a struggle there."

"She had a flat in Dorchester," Tina said.

"That'll be near Gail's lab. Good." Lesley turned to Dennis. "I want you and Stanley to stay focused on tracking down Watson. Run all the checks you can on that van, find out if it has a history of involvement in crime. Keep on Traffic until they find it. It's got to be somewhere."

"What if they've changed the plates, boss?" Stanley said.

"If they know what they're doing," she replied, "and I believe they do, that's their next move. But they might not have had a chance to do it yet. Let's hope that's the case."

"No problem, boss," Dennis said. "We're working on finding where Vera Kelvin is living now too, in case—"

"Vera Kelvin isn't going to talk to you."

"Someone working for her might, though," said Stanley. "She'll have domestic staff."

Lesley raised an eyebrow. "You need to be careful, you could be putting them at risk. It can take months to groom a witness like that."

"Normally a job Organised Crime would do," said Dennis. A muscle under his right eye twitched.

"We don't have months," Lesley said. "And I don't want Organised Crime involved." She didn't want *anyone* else involved. "Do what you can," she said. "Find Watson."

"Will do," Dennis said.

Lesley glanced at her watch. "Right," she said. "If there's any developments, call me. I want to know about Watson, the flat, the lab, the scene, Even Vera Kelvin, if she decides to speak. Find out what you can, then go home."

"What d'you want me doing?" Tina asked.

Lesley turned to the DC. "Sorry, Tina. I haven't forgotten you. Can you work on background again? I know we've already looked into Fran's career and her personal life but I feel there are other people she might have spoken to. Is she linked to DI Angus, for starters? Go to her flat with Mike, see if you can find a diary or anything like that. Talk to her fiancé and her parents again. I want to know everything there is to know about Fran. I want to establish whether she's someone we can trust."

"Even in death?"

"Even in death."

CHAPTER FIFTY-FOUR

LESLEY EMERGED FROM HER OFFICE, pleased to see that most of the team were already gone, out pursuing leads.

She wasn't sure which case she should be focusing on. Fran Dugdale's death was the one she'd been allocated, the one on which she was SIO. But now that Meera had seen David Watson at the crime scene, there was no longer any doubt that the two cases were linked.

And then there was Tim Mackie's death...

She'd been wanting to know how Mackie had died ever since Gail had shown her the spot where he'd gone off the cliffs, back when she'd been investigating the death of Elsa's colleague. That had been... how long? Almost two years ago.

The closer they got to Mackie's killer, the more at risk she and her team were. She couldn't afford to waste time.

She needed to speak to Carpenter. Maybe Sadie. Possibly Detective Superintendent Phipps, if he would take her call.

The team room door opened and Meera entered. She looked at Lesley, her eyes alight.

"You can't have been to Dorchester already," Lesley said.

Meera shook her head, her breathing shallow. "I was just heading out when I got a call. From Traffic control in Dorchester."

"The van?"

Meera nodded.

"Tell me they've found it," Lesley said. "Tell me it hasn't moved since then. That someone's keeping an eye on it."

"It's in Bournemouth," Meera said. "Parked on the street."

"Number plates?"

"Still the same."

Lesley punched the air. "Day Watson, you are a stupid little bastard, and I love you for it." She composed herself. "Is it being watched?"

"Traffic control are observing it via CCTV. They'll alert me if it moves."

"That's not good enough."

Lesley looked around the room. Tina and Mike had left, heading for Dorchester: Fran's flat and the CSI lab. Stanley had gone too, presumably following up a lead on Vera Kelvin. There was just Dennis.

"Dennis," she said. "I know it's a while since you've had to do this, but I need you to keep an eye on a vehicle."

He stood up. "Watson's van. You've found it?"

"Traffic spotted it on CCTV," Meera said. She glanced down at her notebook. "Manor Road in Bournemouth."

Dennis flashed a look at Lesley. "That's near where you live."

"So? Get over there, Dennis. Talk to Traffic, make sure they tell you if it moves. If so, follow it."

"What if someone else accesses the vehicle? Not Watson?"

"That vehicle is the best lead on Watson we have. Even if someone else is driving it, they could lead us to him."

"Will Uniform be getting involved?"

Lesley jabbed her fingernails into her thigh. *Think.*

What if Watson was still with Collingwood?

"No," she said. "Just you. Keep me updated, will you? I want to know if Watson's still with Collingwood."

"No problem, boss." Dennis grabbed his tweed jacket.

CHAPTER FIFTY-FIVE

"IT'S NICE, JUST US," Mike said as he and Tina drove towards Dorchester on the Wareham Road.

Tina smiled, gazing out of the window as the fields whizzed past. It was a dull day and the traffic was lighter than it normally was at this time of year.

What did the grockles do when it rained around here? Some of the hardier ones went to the beach regardless, but the rest of them seemed to go into hiding. They couldn't all be in the pub.

"What d'you think Louis is doing right now?" Mike asked her.

Tina turned to her husband. "Playing with balloons still, I hope."

Mike chuckled. "He loves those bloody balloons."

"I think we might have to buy a bag of them."

Mike rolled his eyes. "I don't much relish blowing them up."

She gave him a playful thump. "Young fit bloke like you? Your lungs'll have no problem."

He pulled his arm away. "I haven't been to the gym since Louis was born."

"You've been busy. I haven't read a single book since I was seven months pregnant."

"D'you think we'll ever get our lives back?"

Tina felt a pang of panic run through her. "Do you regret having him?" *Do you regret marrying me?*

He turned to her, his face open. "Not for a second. He's the best thing that ever happened to me." He caught her look. "Apart from marrying you, that is." He turned back to look at the road. "It's just... it would be nice to be able to do normal stuff sometimes, you know? All we seem to do is work and baby stuff."

"Tell me about it."

"We should force ourselves to spend time together that isn't like this and isn't with him."

"When would we fit that kind of thing in, though?" Tina said.

Mike reached out and put a hand on her knee. "We should make time. Set a date night."

Tina rolled her eyes. "That's so corny."

"It isn't. It doesn't have to be every week. We get a babysitter, go out together, all talk of police work is banned."

"And talk of nappies."

"And sleep patterns."

"And poo habits."

Mike laughed. "Are we that boring?"

Tina joined in the laughter. "No! At least, I hope not. But who's going to babysit? My mum's miles away."

"My mum can."

"You're sure?" Mike's mum had never shown all that much interest in being a grandmother.

"I'm sure. As long as we make sure she's got plenty of snacks and a nice bottle of wine, she'll lap it up."

"Let's hope so."

They crossed the A35, the outskirts of Dorchester around them. "Where first?" Tina asked. "Fran's flat, or the lab?"

"*You* don't need to go to the lab."

"True. Can you drop me at the flat then? I'll look for anything that'll tell us more about Fran, and I'll check for signs of a struggle, too."

"I'll ask Gail if her team found anything there as well."

Tina considered. "You're right. Let's start at the lab, see what Gail has to tell us. Anything we need might already be in the evidence store."

"We still need to see her flat."

Tina nodded. "CSI are there already. But nothing beats being in the place where it happened."

"If it did happen there."

"True."

"Park here."

Mike nodded and parked the car. "Come on then. Lab first, then flat."

CHAPTER FIFTY-SIX

THE OFFICE WAS EMPTY.

Lesley sat down at Tina's desk, working through the case in her mind.

Dennis and Stanley were following up the strongest leads when it came to finding David Watson. The man was in Bournemouth, surely, and would be picked up soon. The question was whether he would have DI Collingwood with him.

And how Dennis would react, if he did.

Maybe she shouldn't have sent Dennis. Whoever arrested Watson would have to make a quick judgement on how to deal with Collingwood. The DI would no doubt claim that he was only with Watson in the interest of solving another case. Maybe a case against Rowan Angus, if the man was involved in Fran's death.

But Lesley was SIO on Fran's murder inquiry, not Collingwood. Carpenter had made that clear.

She didn't want to go running to Carpenter again. She could handle this without constant guidance from the top.

But this case, or rather these cases, were politically sensitive. They involved members of other units. And if she wasn't careful, her team might plunge in blindly, make an arrest, then find it impossible to make that arrest stick.

Lesley sighed, her elbows on the table and her chin resting on her hands.

She needed to know who'd killed Mackie, if her team was to remain safe.

She scrolled through her phone until she came to the message she needed. A phone number, sent to her with no context, by Sadie.

They both knew whose number it was.

Sadie, I hope you're not out there doing anything stupid.

Lesley dialled.

"William Phipps speaking."

He's answered. Which meant he didn't have her number stored in his phone.

"Detective Superintendent Phipps, my name is DCI Lesley Clarke. I'm sorry to bother you like this, but—"

"I've retired, DCI Clarke. I don't see how I can—"

"I gather you've been speaking to a journalist about the case you were heading up before you retired."

She didn't mention Mackie's name.

Silence.

"Detective Superintendent?"

"I've retired. Call me William."

"William." Lesley ran a hand through her hair. "I'm working on a case that involves the murder of a PSD officer who was involved in investigating police corruption surrounding the death of DCI Mackie."

"Fran Dugdale. Sorry business."

"Sir, did—"

"Not Sir, Lesley."

"William. Did you have contact with Fran, before she died?"

"Well, I would hardly have had any with her after she died, would I?"

"I'm sure you understand what I mean."

"I do, Lesley. And I have yet to see how it's relevant to your case. Am I a witness?"

Lesley leaned over her phone, lowering her voice. "I have reason to believe that Fran's death is related to a complaint she made. A complaint she may have spoken to you about."

"I don't know what you're talking about."

"What did Fran talk to you about?"

"Can you tell me exactly why you need to know this?"

"Sir... William. Fran was involved in an investigation into a member of my team. That officer was subsequently released without charge. I have evidence that Fran suspected another officer of being involved in the death of DCI Mackie, and that—"

"DCI Clarke, I'm not trying to derail your investigation into DC Dugdale's death. But you must understand that the kind of accusations you're throwing around here—"

"We also have DNA evidence suggesting Fran fought with another officer before her death."

"Another officer?"

"A DI Rowan Angus."

No response.

"William? Sir?"

"Bring me in under caution, if you need to speak to me."

"I'm sure that won't be—"

"Either that, or speak to your senior officer."

"Superintendent Carpenter. I've already—"

"Speak to him, Lesley. I can't tell you any more."

He hung up.

CHAPTER FIFTY-SEVEN

TYNEHAM VILLAGE WAS BECOMING like a second home to Meera.

The emergency vehicle access had been closed off and the gate locked, so she took the long way round, turning sharp right to take the narrow lane down into the village.

The village was empty. Or at least, it seemed that way. Her experience this morning had taught her not to assume there was no one here.

She parked her car by the telephone box and the row of houses at the entrance to the village, not bothering to drive all the way to the car park. A crow stood on top of the phone box, cawing at her.

"What have you seen?" she said, looking up at it as she passed the houses. "I wish I could stick a video camera on you."

If she'd known yesterday what she'd be coming across this morning, maybe she'd have left cameras here overnight, or asked Gail to.

She trudged past the ruined houses towards the old Rectory. The gate in front of it was still open, but the tarpaulin that had covered the building had been taken down. A sign warned that the building wasn't safe, but Meera would be careful.

She walked towards the building, scanning it as she went, careful to keep her footsteps light.

No sign of movement. No one in the trees. A lone palm tree rose in the woodland ahead of her: whoever had lived here before the place was abandoned had clearly had a taste for tropical plants.

She stepped through the door leading into the house and picked her way through the weeds to find the spot where Fran had been found. It was a patch of paving, probably someone's floor, decades ago. She could see traces of fingerprint dust and some paint from the CSIs' work.

She went on, stepping further into the house and out the other side, into the woods where she'd seen Collingwood.

Once she was through the house, she stopped.

Where had he been walking?

She looked back towards the wall she'd hidden behind while she'd been watching him, trying to reconstruct the angles.

She turned back. There was a clump of hedgerow just to her right.

She pulled on forensic gloves and approached it, preparing to pull the branches to one side. Hoping there would be something hidden there.

Nothing.

Meera forced herself to breathe.

Where are you, dammit?

She'd seen him digging here, or that's what it had looked like. She scanned the ground. It had been disturbed, but that could have happened anytime.

She turned, scanning the area. The woods were thick over here, and she knew he hadn't gone further into them. If he had, there would be signs of it: broken branches, trodden down grass.

She should have called Gail. They needed Forensics, to help analyse this scene.

She waded through more undergrowth, pulling aside bushes and grasses, searching.

Still nothing.

Meera looked up into the trees, her head full of frustration. She'd been trying so hard to make a good impression, to convince them to let her stay in the MCIT. But today she'd lost two key suspects and now the evidence she'd claimed to have seen was gone.

Collingwood had been here, openly. He'd spoken to the DCI and tried to inveigle his way into the case. And she'd seen him. Had he come down here deliberately, to cover his tracks and provide a legitimate explanation for his presence?

DI Angus, though. He hadn't been here. Not legitimately. And even if he had come as a visitor, he wouldn't have ventured into this building and this patch of woods.

And there was the object he'd handed to Watson. If Watson still had it, they might prove it had been here, in this spot.

It was a long shot. But first, they had to find the object.

CHAPTER FIFTY-EIGHT

"TWO FOR THE PRICE OF ONE," said Gail as Tina and Mike entered the lab. "Lucky me."

Tina gave her a smile. "The DCI has asked me to look into Fran's background."

"I thought you'd have already done that."

"Some new evidence has come to light."

Gail raised her eyebrows. "OK."

"And I need to know if you've found any more physical evidence, anything that might corroborate the DNA you found under her fingernails."

"Gav's at her flat now," Gail said. "He's taking samples."

"You think DI Angus might have been there?" Tina asked. Mike was standing next to her, looking around the lab.

"I don't think anything," Gail said. "Not my job. But I imagine you and Lesley will be wanting any physical evidence we can get before anybody interviews the man. You do know we found his DNA at other crime scenes, don't you?"

Tina nodded. Mike shook his head.

Gail sighed. "Of course, you were at home playing Daddy

Daycare during the Hamm case. Tina, can you fill him in while I check through the evidence store?"

Tina nodded and Gail walked away. Mike touched her arm.

"What's this about Angus and Hamm, then?"

Tina turned to him. "There were three crime scenes in that case. The lighthouse where we found Hamm's body."

"I knew that."

"Let me finish, will you?"

"Sorry." His gaze dropped to the floor, making Tina feel guilty. She was tired, and she'd caught herself snapping at him before.

"Then there was the huts," she continued. "And then Dawn Stephens's house."

"Dawn Stephens?"

"The third victim. She worked at the lighthouse, let them in so they could dump Hamm's body there. And Beef's DNA was at her house."

"Beef?" said Mike.

"It's his nickname, remember? Angus. Beef." Tina thought back. "The boss saw him at the scene after Dawn's death, so it was feasible it could have got there that way. And they'd been married. Long since divorced, though. But it was weird, the way he kept turning up at crime scenes like that. Ones his team wasn't involved with."

"Does the DCI think he was part of the conspiracy to break Hamm out of prison?"

"I don't know what the boss thinks. But it's odd that his DNA was under Fran's fingernails, too."

"More than odd."

Gail reappeared. "We've got the coat Fran was wearing

when she was found. No sign of any third-party DNA on it, from the tests we've run. No fibres either."

"None at all?" Tina asked.

Gail shook her head. "Some from another coat her mum's given us, it must have been hanging in a wardrobe next to the one she was wearing. Nothing else."

"If she was in a fight with her attacker, surely they'd have left evidence on her clothes," Mike said.

"You'd think that."

"Maybe it happened in her house," Tina suggested. "While she didn't have her coat on."

"But then how did her coat get on her before her body was dumped?" Mike asked.

Tina turned to him. "Good point." She looked at Gail. "What about her other clothes?"

"There's more cross-contamination of fibres from other garments we found in her wardrobe. No skin, no DNA though. Just what's under her fingernails."

"No blood from her attacker?" Tina asked.

"Sorry."

"What about anything that might have come from the vehicle she was transported in?"

"There's residue of metal on the back of her coat. That could have come from the floor of a vehicle."

"Not many vehicles have metal floors," Tina said.

"A van might," suggested Mike. He looked at Gail, who shrugged.

Tina frowned at him. "You're thinking about Day Watson's van."

He nodded. "We need to find it."

"We already know that." She looked at Gail. "Did you pick

up anything from her flat that might tell us more about her?
Mike, you went to her office, didn't you?"

"All I found was that notebook."

"OK. So... Gail?"

"There was nothing out of place, nothing disturbed. We
took some garments to check against. Just fibres from her other
clothes on them. But no, everything else is still there."

"We'll go there next," Tina said.

"What about the van?" asked Mike.

"We don't know for sure there was a van." Tina tried to
push the exasperation out of her voice. "And besides, the sarge
and Stanley are looking for that."

"Fair point."

Tina looked at him. "I'll call Gav, let him know to
expect us."

"I'll do that," said Gail. "Good luck. I hope you find something useful."

CHAPTER FIFTY-NINE

"Not again, Lesley."

"Sir. I'm sorry to bother you again." Lesley stepped into Carpenter's office just as he stood up from his desk.

He shook his head, rounding the desk to approach her. "Do you have any concrete evidence in the Dugdale case? Any forensics, witness statements?"

"Yes," she replied. "Both of those, as a matter of fact."

He was standing close to her, near the door. She glanced past him to the desk, and the sofa and easy chair beyond it. Normally he guided her there.

"Sir, is everything alright?"

He sighed. "Tell me about the forensics."

She nodded. "The CSIs have found a match for the skin found under Fran's fingernails."

His eyes widened. "There was a struggle?"

"It would seem that way."

"And the match is..."

She looked past him and into the corners of the room. She lowered her voice.

"A DI, Sir. From Blandford Forum CID."

Carpenter's face darkened. "You'll be after PSD's job next. I hope you haven't spoken to this officer, not after—"

"I'm being exceptionally careful, Sir. I know how important it is not to jeopardise the integrity of any arrest."

"Hmm. Well, that's something." He grabbed her arm.

Lesley looked down. His fingers were tight, gripping the fabric of her jacket. "Sir..."

"Sorry." He let go, moving towards her. He reached around her for the door handle. "We can talk another time."

"But I also need to speak to you about the witness statement."

Carpenter shook his head. "I'm about to go into a meeting." He moved closer again, forcing her to shift backwards.

What was going on?

"Sir, this case. It's—"

His eyes flashed. "Another time, Lesley. I really must be getting on."

She was in the corridor. Somehow he'd managed to move her out of his office.

The door closed, right in front of her. Lesley stared at it for a moment, half expecting it to reopen and a different version of the super to walk out.

What the hell was going on? And if Carpenter wasn't going to speak to her, who would?

CHAPTER SIXTY

DAVID WATSON's van was still in Manor Road, exactly where Traffic Control had said it would be.

Dennis let out a sigh of relief as he drove past the car, looking for a parking spot.

The boss lived around here somewhere, in a street behind this one. Her wife Elsa had owned the flat here when they'd met, and DCI Clarke had moved there from her cottage in Wareham before the wedding.

Dennis didn't understand that. When he and Pam had met, he'd been in digs in Weymouth – a studio flat, they'd call it now, but it was nowhere near that grand – and she'd been sharing a flat with a couple of girlfriends. They'd waited until they could save a deposit on their house before getting married, knowing it would be their home together.

That house had seen his son Jacob grow up, and would probably see the two of them leave this world. He wondered what Jacob would do with it after his parents were gone.

He spotted a space and pulled in, taking care to straighten his wheels and make sure he was the same distance from the cars in front and behind. He could see the van from here, its battered rear wheel arch unmissable.

He had a newspaper with him, the *Bournemouth Echo*, but he wasn't going to let himself get distracted by reading.

This was like old times. Dennis hadn't been required to observe a car, or sit outside the address of a witness, since at least 2008, when he'd become a sergeant.

He leaned back in his seat, adopted the most comfortable position he could without putting himself at risk of falling asleep, and settled in to watch.

CHAPTER SIXTY-ONE

STANLEY HAD mates across the county. Other coppers, in CID and Uniform. Officials in other public bodies: traffic wardens, social workers, teachers.

You never knew when someone you knew might spot something useful.

Most of his contacts were in his old patch in and around Poole, and Jheel Kaur was one of them.

Jheel worked for an estate agent in Bournemouth. Like Stanley, she had her own contacts and mates all over the place, and she talked to other estate agents in different firms and different towns.

If someone was moving house, chances were Jheel knew about it.

Stanley sat in his car outside the petrol station just before the level crossing in Wool, having nipped in to get himself a Snickers and a can of Coke. He was bloody starving. He listened as the on-hold music switched from Taylor Swift to Rick Astley.

He smiled. *Rick-rolled.* Was that even a thing anymore?

The phone clicked as Jheel picked up. "Stanley. I've got a viewing in five."

"Hey, Jheel. Good to speak to you too."

"You know what I mean."

"Yeah. Did you get any joy on that address for me?"

"You don't make things easy, do you?"

Stanley smiled and took a swig from his Coke.

"But," said Jheel, "you're talking to the best. So I got it for you. Wasn't easy, mind. People like Vera Kelvin don't find their next house on Rightmove."

"And?" Jheel had a viewing in four minutes now, Stanley knew she wouldn't want to mess around.

"She used a swanky agent in London, selling the Sandbanks pad and buying the new one."

"Tell me it's in the county."

"You're in luck. It's just outside Lulworth Cove."

Stanley smiled. "Jhee, you're a bloody star."

"I don't need you to tell me that. Here's the address." She gave him the house name and a postcode.

"Means nothing to me."

"You won't have visited the place. It's on a road that's only got two houses on it. Gorgeous property. I'd give my right arm to be the selling agent on a property like that."

"How much do you know about the security?"

A laugh. "Really, Stan? You're thinking of breaking in?"

"No."

"Well, place like that, it'll have everything. Alarms, cameras, the lot. Women like Vera Kelvin don't go in for anything less, do they?"

Vera Kelvin wasn't a name that was widely known amongst the public. She'd not been involved in organised crime since her husband had died. But Jheel wasn't any old member of the public.

"Anyway. Got to go."

"Thanks, Jheel. I apprecia—"

But the line was dead.

CHAPTER SIXTY-TWO

Fran Dugdale's flat was on the first floor of a small modern block on the northern side of Dorchester.

There was a CSI van parked on the road, and Tina could hear noises from inside the flat. She knocked on the door, already wearing her protective suit.

The door opened and the tallest man she'd ever worked alongside stood in front of her. He grinned at her, then at Mike, through the gap under his hood. "You two. Gail told me to expect you."

"Can we come in?" Tina asked.

"Course you can." He looked up and down their suits. "Be careful, though."

Tina glanced at Mike and rolled her eyes. He gave her a shrug in return.

She stepped inside, Mike behind her.

"Where do we start?" Mike muttered.

"Gav?" Tina said.

The CSI turned to her. "Yeah?"

"How long have you been here?"

"Just a couple of hours. I'm dusting for prints, using UV to check for blood that might have been cleaned up."

"And?"

"Nothing yet."

That wasn't a surprise. Fran's body hadn't had any blood on it.

But her attacker's might.

"Any specific spot where you think something might have happened?" she asked.

"That's the thing. There's nothing." Gav swept an arm to take in the flat's living room where they were standing.

"This is my job," Mike muttered. Tina shook her head: they were a team, weren't they?

Mike squeezed past to stand next to her. "You're saying there's no sign of a struggle."

Gav blinked at him. "Nothing, mate. The flat's tidy. Looks like it's been cleaned recently, which of course could be someone trying to clean up after themselves. But the substances I've found on the surface match the cleaning products under the fridge, and there's no one area where there's a particular concentration of them."

"Which there would be if someone was cleaning up after a fight," said Mike.

"Exactly. Nothing's been broken, no scuffs to the wallpaper... nothing."

"What about DNA?" Tina asked.

"Prints are easier to get," Gav told her. "So we'll be looking for any matches with what we've got."

"Have you taken a lot of prints?" Mike asked.

"Not loads. I can't tell you whose they are till tomorrow though, sorry. I'm only here now cos I had to start late today."

"OK." Tina surveyed the room. "Thanks. Is it OK if I go into her bedroom?"

"Sure. That's clean too. Bed made, surfaces tidy, all the clothes put away. Your victim was a clean freak."

Tina left the living room and found her way to Fran's bedroom. Sure enough, the bed was made and the duvet smoothed down. A single soft toy sat propped against the pillows. Tina felt a sudden pang of sadness.

A chest of drawers sat opposite the bed. She opened the drawers and sorted through their contents.

In the top drawer, knickers and socks, sorted by colour and folded neatly. In the second, t-shirts, also folded. In the bottom, sweaters and fleeces.

She opened a wardrobe to find jackets, blouses and trousers, all clean and on their own hangers. A row of shoes sat beneath them, perfectly aligned.

"Was Fran OCD?" Mike's voice came from right behind her, making her jump.

"Don't do that," Tina breathed. "First off, a person *isn't* OCD, they *have* OCD. And no, I don't think so. There was nothing about mental illness or compulsive behaviour in her file."

"This wardrobe, though..."

"Maybe she was just tidy." She thought of their own bedroom at home. "Maybe you could learn something from her."

He gave her arm a playful punch. "Oi. I'm perfectly tidy."

Tina opened her mouth to reply, but Gav was in the doorway.

"If you don't mind, guys. I need to head off now."

"Fine." Tina scanned the room. "Can I just have five minutes?"

"You can have as long as it takes for me to pack up my van." He disappeared.

"You take that bedside table," Tina told Mike, "I'll take this one."

"We're looking for a diary or something, right?"

"Anything that might tell us what Fran was doing in her own time. How she felt about her colleagues."

"And who she might have pissed off."

"That would be even better." Tina went through the contents of Tina's bedside table: medicines, a vibrator, tampons.

No diary.

"Your side?" she asked.

"Perfumes and stuff. Nothing helpful."

Tina straightened up. "There aren't any other rooms."

"We can try the kitchen."

She nodded. Mike was closest to the bedroom door: he hurried out, making for the tiny kitchen.

The two of them opened cupboards, poking around behind food packets, crockery and jars.

"This room's just the same," Mike said. "Nothing's out of date."

Gav was in the doorway. "Time to go," he said.

Tina nodded, but didn't stop her search. She turned to see a small dresser against a wall.

She opened a drawer. What looked like bills. All folded in two, the date they had been paid written on them in the same green ink.

Fran Dugdale, you were an organised woman.

She opened a second drawer. This one was less neat, with greetings cards, letters and postcards. She turned a postcard over and her breath caught in her throat.

"Mike."

Mike turned from the fridge, closing it behind him.

Gav was looking at his watch. "I'm meeting some mates at the pub. Can you—"

Tina held up a hand. "I've got something."

She held out the postcard for Mike to see. With her other hand, she grabbed one of the greetings cards: it was nonspecific, just a drawing of a couple dancing.

"The name," she breathed.

Mike nodded.

Both cards were addressed to Fran.

And both cards were signed by the same person.

All my love, Rowan.

CHAPTER SIXTY-THREE

LESLEY PARKED her car around the corner from the flat, cursing the summer traffic. Normally she could park right outside, but in July, things got trickier. A new restaurant had opened nearby, to complement the two pubs already there, and it increased the number of people wanting to park here in the evenings.

Still, she shouldn't be grumbling. She and Elsa had eaten at the new restaurant the previous week, and it was good. Maybe good enough for a six-month anniversary celebration, in September.

She shouldered her bag, pulled her jacket tighter against the sea breezes, and made for the flat. After a couple of minutes' walk, she spotted a distinctive white van with its rear wheel arch bashed in.

Lesley pulled back and crossed to the other side of the road. Dennis's car was there, the DS in the driver's seat. He was watching the van, his eyes narrowed, but hadn't spotted Lesley yet.

When she was right by the passenger window, she bent down and knocked on the glass.

Dennis jumped, placing his hand on his chest.

"Boss." His eyes were wide. He fumbled for the window controls, opening first the driver's window and then the passenger one. Lesley watched, smiling.

"You startled me," he said.

"Sorry, I didn't mean to. No sign of him?"

"No sign of anyone."

She glanced over at the van. There were no shapes inside, no sign of occupation. "Maybe he's left it overnight."

"Only one way to find out."

"Dennis, you're going to fall asleep if you stay here like this. And that's not going to help anyone. Call it in to Traffic, get them to watch it." She pointed out a CCTV camera on a lamppost. "We can come back in the morning."

He shook his head. "I thought you wanted to keep this within the team."

"Traffic have already been watching out for this vehicle."

"And what if Watson turns up and there's no one here to take him into custody?"

Lesley looked over at the van. "We'll be alerted if he arrives. We'll make sure they track the van's movements so we can pick him up wherever he goes."

"I'm sorry, boss. But I'm not satisfied with that." He yawned.

Lesley cursed him inwardly. "Very well. But you're tired, and you're not alert. You're no good to anyone here. Go home, and get Stanley to cover."

"I'm sure Stanley has—"

"Stanley is a young man whose body will cope better with

being cooped up in a car at this time of night. And his mind will be fresh. Call him."

Dennis gave her a long look. At last, he looked away.

"Very well," he said.

"Good." Lesley straightened up: her knees were complaining at the crouching she was doing. "I'll see you in the morning."

She started walking, glancing at the van on the opposite side of the road as she passed it. She hoped Dennis would do as he was told: call Stanley and let the younger man take over. For one thing, the sergeant wasn't getting any younger, and sitting in a car all night wouldn't be good for him. For another, if he fell asleep and missed the van driving off, they'd never catch up with Watson.

A few minutes later, she let herself into the flat. "Hey, sweetie!"

Nothing.

Frowning, Lesley walked through into the living room. Elsa was sat on the sofa, a man sitting in the armchair next to her.

"Sir?" said Lesley.

"He's been waiting," Elsa said. "He wanted to speak to you."

Lesley nodded at her wife. She looked back at her boss. Carpenter was standing up, brushing down his trousers.

"Lesley," he said.

"Sir. What brings you here?"

CHAPTER SIXTY-FOUR

DENNIS DIDN'T LIKE the boss telling him to stand down. It was late, yes, and he was tired, but he wasn't the kind of man who shirked his duty. He felt a personal compunction to wait until David Watson returned to his van.

The man had eluded them enough times already. Dennis wanted to ensure he didn't do it again.

But Pam would be waiting for him. And he had felt himself nodding off a few times in the last hour.

He sighed and picked up his phone to call Stanley.

"Sarge, I'm at Vera Kelvin's new house. Fancy red brick pile just outside Lulworth Cove. Even posher than the Sandbanks house, if that's possible."

Dennis smiled. He didn't care how Vera spent her dodgy money, or the money she'd inherited from her son and grandson no doubt.

"Is there any sign of movement? Anyone coming or going?" he asked.

"Not so far."

"In that case, I've got another job for you. The boss wants you to replace me here watching David Watson's van."

"You alright, Sarge?"

"I'm fine. A bit tired, but who wouldn't be after the day we've had?" Dennis didn't wait for an answer: Stanley was twenty-three and probably didn't know what tired meant. "Anyway, you get over here and then I can head home."

"No problem, boss. What about Vera?"

"Vera will still be there in the morning."

"Fair enough. I'll be with you in half an hour."

It was an hour's drive from Lulworth Cove to Bournemouth. "No you will not," Dennis said. "You'll be here in an hour. Don't go driving like a madman along those lanes." He knew what the roads around Lulworth were like: high hedges, sudden bends, few passing places.

"Right, Sarge. See you in a bit."

CHAPTER SIXTY-FIVE

SHARON HADN'T BEEN to the Overcliff pub before.

She leaned in behind Rick as they entered, nervous. She was only just eighteen and didn't have ID on her. She'd get thrown out, without a doubt. And she'd told Rick she was nineteen.

Rick had tight hold of her hand, oblivious to her unease. He pulled her towards the back of the pub and a group of lads sitting around a table covered in empty pint glasses.

"Alright, lads?" He pulled Sharon out from behind him, putting her where his mates could get a good look at her.

"This your girl?" asked a lad with a mohican at the front. He grinned at Sharon in a way that made her uneasy.

"She's a bit young," added a skinny guy at the back.

Rick laughed and turned to her. "Virginal."

Sharon felt her skin tense and her face turn as hot as the sun. Had he really said that? She'd only told him when they'd been kissing in one of the shelters on Boscombe Beach the other week.

She certainly didn't want all his friends knowing.

"Sharon, this is Sammy," Rick said. "That's Lyle. Over there's Harry, and this idiot here," he ruffled the mohican in front of him, "is Azo."

Azo?

"Hi," Sharon said.

"And he's..." Azo said. "What name are you using these days?"

"Don't be daft." Rick frowned. He turned to Sharon. "I used to be Richard. I switched to Rick, a few years back. Didn't want to sound like a dickhead."

Sharon smiled. Rick wasn't like this when it was just him and her. There was no bravado, no showing off. He was calm, when they were alone. Considerate. He held doors open for her and pushed stray hairs away from her face. It made the blood rush to her head.

"Sit down, Shazza," Lyle said.

"Sharon," she muttered.

Rich turned to his friend and gave him a slap on the side of the head. "Did you hear the lady? Her name's Sharon. Not Shazza, you wanker."

Lyle laughed, ducking away from the slap. It seemed that low-level violence and insults were the norm, between Rick and his mates.

Was this the real Rick? Or did he reserve his true self for her?

Stop worrying. He was just putting it on, trying to impress them. Rick was alright. He cared about her.

He turned to her, his eyes darkening. "You look hot tonight."

Sharon smiled, looking him up and down. He wore a white denim jacket over black jeans. "So do you."

He gave her a wink. "Let me get you a drink."

"A WKD."

He raised an eyebrow. "Magic word?"

"Please?" she giggled.

"You sit down with the gang and I'll be right back."

Sharon took the seat that Harry pushed out for her, already wishing she'd gone to the bar with her boyfriend instead.

Five minutes later, Rick was back. The lads had ignored her while he'd been gone, too busy talking about football. Sharon knew plenty about football, but she had no clue about the Bournemouth team. Were they even a real team?

"You OK?" Rick asked as he sat down, his voice soft.

She shrugged. "I thought it'd be you and me, tonight."

He leaned back, giving her a surprised look. "You not having a good time?"

Another shrug. "It's just not—"

He placed a kiss on her lips, then pulled back to the sound of his mates cheering him on. Not looking at them, he held up his middle finger.

"If you don't want company, we can head off." He looked into her eyes.

Sharon felt her chest flutter. "That sounds... better."

Rick stood up. He downed half of his pint and slammed the glass onto the table. He held out his hand and Sharon took it.

She smiled into his eyes. She'd been right. Rick wasn't like the other lads.

"Come on, gorgeous," he said. "Just you and me."

CHAPTER SIXTY-SIX

"I wasn't expecting to see you here, Sir." Lesley looked from Carpenter to her wife. "How long?" she mouthed at Elsa.

"I've only been here ten minutes," Carpenter said. "And if you're concerned that DS Frampton out there might have spotted me, he didn't. He was asleep when I passed his car."

Lesley scowled. It was one thing Dennis dozing off while watching for a suspect, another thing entirely if he got caught doing it by the super.

"I—" she began.

"It's fine, Lesley. DS Frampton's had a lot on his plate. And the van he's observing has shown no sign of anyone approaching it, anyway."

"You were watching it?"

"I've been keeping an eye on your case. I knew you were looking for it, and when I spotted it on the street outside your flat, naturally my interest was piqued."

"I'm sure it's just a coincidence, Sir."

"I'm sure it is." Carpenter glanced at Elsa. "Anyway, that's not what I came to speak with you about."

"No." Lesley caught Elsa's puzzled look. "Anything you need to say to me, my wife will keep confidential, Sir."

He smiled. "I'm sorry, but I know your wife's profession." He turned to Elsa. "And I'm sure you wouldn't want to find yourself on the wrong side of a conflict of interest."

Elsa gave him a nod. "I'll head out for a bit."

"It's getting dark," Lesley said.

"I'm a big girl, aren't I?" Elsa checked her watch. "I'll give you half an hour." She headed out of the room. Lesley heard the jangle of her keys being picked up from the hall table, followed by the slam of the front door.

She gestured towards the armchair Carpenter had been sitting in when she'd arrived. "Take a seat, Sir."

"Don't mind if I do."

Lesley perched at the nearest end of the sofa, waiting.

"You wanted to ask me about DI Robert Collingwood and any connection he might have to DCI Mackie," Carpenter said.

Lesley blinked. She hadn't been expecting him to get to the point so quickly.

"Well... yes."

Carpenter raised an eyebrow. "You're right that Fran Dugdale made a complaint about the man. But I believe you've seen all there is to see of that complaint. It's anodyne. Relates to the correct following of procedure rather than any accusation of him being involved in crime."

"My theory is that Fran made that complaint to give herself a legitimate reason to speak to officers outside PSD about Collingwood. Once she was face to face with someone like yourself, she would voice her real concerns."

"Did you speak to DC Dugdale about this supposed plan of hers?"

"Of course not." Lesley hadn't known the woman existed until she'd died. "But I did speak to her fiancé."

"Mr Gill."

How did he know so much about the case? "Yes."

"And what did he tell you?" Carpenter asked.

"He said that Fran believed her DI to be working with organised criminals, and that he'd been behind the death of DCI Mackie."

"That's quite an accusation."

"From your reaction in your office yesterday and earlier today, I don't believe it's an accusation that's new to you." Lesley spotted the shadow crossing Carpenter's face. "Sir."

He smiled. "I really don't—" He frowned. "Do you need to get that?"

Lesley's phone was vibrating, on the sofa next to her. Police HQ.

"It can wait a moment, Sir."

"It might be an emergency."

"I'm off duty."

"You're in the middle of a tricky murder investigation." He looked at her phone, which was still vibrating, in danger of sliding off the sofa. Lesley put a hand on it to still it.

She heard another phone ringing and looked down. Hers was still vibrating, on silent mode since she'd got home.

Carpenter was reaching inside his pocket. "That's me." He frowned at his phone. "Also HQ."

He looked at her. "Yours rang first."

Lesley picked up her phone. "DCI Clarke," she said, just as Carpenter took his own call.

"Ma'am." It was a voice she didn't recognise. "This is Command, sorry to bother you. But there's been another body found, not all that far from the crime scene you're investigating."

Lesley looked across at Carpenter. His eyes were as wide as her own.

"Where?" she asked.

"Durdle Door. The beach below the cliffs."

Lesley felt the breath catch in her throat. "Who?"

A pause.

"Who?" she repeated. "Male, female, young old, black, white?"

"Sorry, Ma'am. It's a bit of a shock, see. I used to work with him in Blandford Forum."

Lesley stood up. Carpenter had walked towards the windows and was muttering into his phone.

"Who is it?" she breathed.

"It's DI Angus," said the woman at the other end of the line. "DI Rowan Angus."

CHAPTER SIXTY-SEVEN

STANLEY HAD BEEN WATCHING the van for just ten minutes when he spotted the indicator lights flashing.

He sat up in his seat, scanning the street for someone holding out a remote key fob.

He spotted them, and held his breath.

Two people. A young man, and a woman... not much more than a girl. They were walking unsteadily, clutching at each other, laughing. They stopped a few feet away from the van and shared a kiss, then continued walking.

He dipped down in his seat, just high enough to see but low enough to hope they wouldn't see him. It didn't matter. The couple were too wrapped up in each other, oblivious to him.

The young man walked round to the passenger door of the van, the girl following him. He wore a white jacket and black jeans, and his hair had been slicked back.

He didn't look like he had last time Stanley had seen him, but it was him alright.

Day Watson.

The girl was short, maybe in her late teens. Maybe younger. She wore a short white skirt and a black blazer, and her hair was pulled back into a knot. She was totally focused on Day, looking into his eyes like her life depended on it.

Poor kid. She had no idea what Watson was really like. Or at least, Stanley hoped she didn't.

He watched as Watson opened the passenger door and ushered his companion in, making a show of being chivalrous. He kissed her hand as she climbed into the van, then closed the door after her.

Quickly, he hurried around the front of the van to the driver's door. He glanced up and down the street, but didn't appear to see Stanley.

The van's lights came on and the engine started. Stanley put his hand on his ignition key. He wouldn't start his own car just yet. He knew better than that.

He smiled to himself. *Day Watson, you little scumbag, I've got you.*

CHAPTER SIXTY-EIGHT

SHARON GRIPPED the door handle as Rick sped through the streets of Bournemouth, making for the seafront.

"Where are we going?" she asked.

"I've got a mate, in Wareham. He's got a flat, it's empty this week."

She bit her bottom lip. "A flat?"

He turned to look at her, smiling. "You said you wanted it to be just you and me." He gestured out of the windscreen. "We can't go down to the beach again, it's fuckin' freezing."

He was right. And she had told him she wanted to get away from his friends.

Besides, all they were doing was going to his mate's flat. It was up to her if that meant anything else was going to happen.

"OK," she said. "It's not far to Wareham. My mum used to have a house there."

The car jerked, Rick briefly losing his grip on the wheel. "Oh. Right."

"Yeah. She hated it, though. She – we all – live at her wife's flat in Bournemouth now. Well, I guess it's her flat too, now."

"A flat?" he asked, his voice pinched.

"Yeah. It's nice. Not far from where you picked me up."

"You'll have to show me sometime."

Sharon shrugged. She didn't imagine her mum reacting well to her bringing Rick home. She'd probably arrest him, soon as look at him.

She laughed at herself.

"What's funny?" Rick grabbed her hand.

Sharon let him squeeze it. "Just thinking about how you and my mum would get along."

He laughed.

"What?"

"Nothing. Let's just think about you and me, eh?" He lifted her hand and kissed the back of it. "You look so hot in that skirt."

Sharon felt herself blush. She looked out of the windscreen, focusing on the roads. She'd only had one drink, but it was going to her head. She wanted to know where Rick was taking her, to look after herself. If she needed to get home by herself later...

Or maybe in the morning...

She smiled to herself. She had a condom in her bag and was feeling confident.

She leaned back in the seat. "That WKD you got me, was it a new flavour?"

He glanced at her. "Yeah. You like it?"

She nodded. "Sour. Just a little bit. But I liked it." She wound down the window, glad of the cool air on her face. "This is awesome, don't you think? The sea air on a warm night?"

He opened his own window and waved his arm out of it.

The van slowed.

"What's up?" Sharon asked.

Rick was looking in the rear-view mirror. "Nothing."

Sharon turned to look behind them. "What?"

"Don't do that." His voice had hardened. "Hang on."

He hit the brake and turned into a side road, the motion sending her swaying across the van. Once in the side street, he braked again and turned into a car park.

Shit. There was no flat in Wareham.

"This is..."

Rick put a finger to his lips, closing his window. "Shh. Shut your window."

Sharon did as she was told. "What's up?" She could feel her skin turning cold.

She leaned forward to look around the car park. There were only four other cars, and no people.

But she was near the seafront. And she'd followed the signs and knew exactly where she was.

"Why have we stopped, Rick?"

"Hang on."

He got out of the van and walked to the back. She shifted to one side to watch him in the wing mirror.

What's he doing?

He opened the back doors, rummaged inside the rear compartment, and closed the doors. Walking more slowly this time, he returned to the front seat and handed her a screwed-up tissue.

She unravelled it to find a necklace inside. "For me?"

He grinned. "Like it?"

She turned it over in her hands. "It's lovely." It was gold, with a ruby at the centre." of the pendant.

"Put it on." He held out a bottle. "And drink this."

She raised her eyebrows as she did up the clasp of the necklace. A lock of hair was caught in it, making her flinch. Had this belonged to a previous girlfriend?

"Another one of your WKDs," he said. "We can share it."

She looked at him. The hair in the necklace clasp was tickling the skin on the back of her neck. "You're driving."

He raised both eyebrows. "True. All the more for you, then. Drink up."

He turned the key and started the car up. Sharon untwisted the lid of her bottle as he headed out of the alleyway and back onto the street, heading for Wareham again.

CHAPTER SIXTY-NINE

THERE WAS a faint spill of light over the hill to Lesley's left at Durdle Door. The sea in front of her glowed as it began to turn blue in the morning light.

Lesley stood at the edge of the beach, holding her arms around herself and shivering as she watched a small team of uniformed officers erect a tent. This was an exposed spot and a very public one, and they had to close it off to the public and protect any evidence as quickly as possible.

She'd arrived over an hour and a half earlier, just as the paramedics were leaving. It turned out Command had been wrong about the discovery of a body, but only in terms of timing. Rowan Angus hadn't been dead when he'd been discovered, just gravely injured. The paramedics hadn't wanted to move him because of suspected spinal injuries, and they'd worked on him right there on the beach while Lesley and Carpenter stood back, waiting, hoping.

It hadn't worked. Angus had been pronounced dead at three am. Dr Bamford had been called and would be with them eventually, but the paramedics were able to tell her the

DI had died as a result of acute spinal injuries following a fall from the cliffs behind her.

Despite having been here for almost two hours now, Lesley still hadn't had access to the body. Carpenter had stood beside her throughout, watching in silence. They had come in separate cars and there had been no discussion of DI Collingwood, DCI Mackie, or how DI Angus's injury and subsequent death might be related to it all.

She shivered again, and not just because of the cold. She hadn't been working in Dorset when Mackie had died, but tonight – dead police officer, early hours of the morning, fall from the cliffs – it all felt much too familiar. She had to ignore that, once the investigation was underway, and focus on the facts.

The officers erecting the tent were struggling. Angus's body had landed at the base of the cliffs, half on the sand, half on the rocks. Working around the side of him towards the cliffs was tricky.

She wondered if that tent would be strong enough for Gail's needs. Gail hadn't been roused yet; there was no point until they knew if there was an investigation to pursue, but it was looking more likely that she would be needed.

Finally, the tent was up. Lesley turned to Carpenter.

"Do we think it's linked?"

He glanced at her. He was wearing a thick Barbour jacket and hadn't shivered once since their arrival.

"I'm not sure *we* think anything at all."

"Let me reframe that. Do *you* think it's linked?"

"To...?"

"To Fran Dugdale's death." She hesitated. "To Tim Mackie's."

Carpenter shook his head. "Don't let the parallels suck you

in. We're at the other end of the county and almost three years on."

"But my team have found evidence that DI Angus was in a relationship with Fran Dugdale. His skin was under her fingernails. We can't deny a connect—"

Carpenter turned to her. "Follow the evidence, Lesley. You'll be SIO on this. If the two cases are connected, you'll need to prove why, in terms that make sense to a jury. If not, then it's simply a tragic coincidence."

"I'll need to get my team in."

"It's early. Don't two of them have a baby?"

"That doesn't affect their dedication."

"Glad to hear it. Yes, get your team in. Open an investigation. But if I were you, I'd get the CSIs down here first. The pathologist. Find out what you can from them before you decide on your plan of attack."

Carpenter put a hand on her shoulder. "Sorry to abandon you, but I need some sleep." He gave her shoulder a squeeze and turned towards the path up to the car park.

Lesley watched as he made slow progress up the path. If anyone had told her two years earlier, when she'd started in this job, that one day Anthony Carpenter would stand next to her as the sun broke above the sea and squeeze her shoulder like that, she'd have laughed.

She still didn't understand the man. But she was coming to believe, despite all her instincts, that she could trust him.

CHAPTER SEVENTY

LESLEY PUSHED OPEN the door to the flat to find Elsa standing in the hallway, staring at her face in the mirror. She flinched as she saw Lesley.

"Oh, love, you gave me a scare."

Lesley put her arms around her wife. "I'm sorry. You OK?"

"Just worried about you. It's been hours."

It was six am and Lesley was back at the flat for a change of clothes. Gail had arrived at the crime scene and Bamford was expected in a couple of hours.

"Sorry. A man died at Durdle Door last night. It was... well, you don't need to know the details."

Elsa gave Lesley a sympathetic smile. "Sorry."

Lesley shrugged. "Comes with the job. But..."

"But what?"

"He's police. Was. Potentially a suspect in my other investigation."

"The DC who was abandoned at Tyneham?"

"Yes." Lesley hugged Elsa tighter. "Sorry I didn't call. I should have told you where I was."

"That's OK. But I'm worried about Sharon."

Lesley pulled back. "Sharon? Why?"

Elsa's eyes roamed across Lesley's face. "She didn't come home last night."

Lesley felt bile rise in her throat. She glanced at the closed door to Sharon's bedroom. "You're sure? Sometimes she sneaks in, she—"

"I checked her room, just ten minutes ago."

Lesley strode past her wife and opened the door to her daughter's bedroom.

It was empty. The bed was neat and tidy, just as it had been when she'd smoothed it down the previous evening.

Sharon never left her bed like that.

Lesley went back into the hallway and grabbed her phone off the table. She jabbed at the screen, searching for messages.

Nothing.

She looked at Elsa, who had been following her movements.

"Have you heard from her?" Lesley asked.

Elsa shook her head. "I was going to call you at six. But you walked through the door at one minute to."

"It's not your fault. She's... I don't know what she's doing." Lesley gritted her teeth. "That girl is going to be in so much trouble."

"Don't be too hard on her."

Lesley felt panic grip her. "She knows the rules, Elsa. We're not strict. She's expected home by midnight, and if she's going to be late, she has to call." She felt her breathing grow shallow. "It's not difficult."

She picked up her phone and dialled Sharon's number. It rang out. She fired off messages: text, WhatsApp, Instagram.

She stared at the screen but there was no response, no dancing dots. No sign that any of her messages had been read.

"I don't bloody well have time for this," she said. "I'm in the middle of two murder investigations."

Elsa stroked her arm. "I'm sure she'll be home soon. She's just stayed out with friends."

"That boyfriend she's started up with. Has she told you anything about him?"

"No. Sorry. I didn't even know there was a boyfriend."

"She's been coming in late, getting upset over nothing. Hiding her phone when it pings. There's a boyfriend."

"Or a girlfriend," Elsa suggested.

Lesley looked at her. "I hope so."

"You'd prefer...?"

"Teenage girls get preyed on by young men. I don't like—"

Elsa held Lesley's face in her hands. "That's the copper talking, sweetie. Most teenage girls lead perfectly normal lives, without being the victims of crime. I'm sure Sharon's no different."

Lesley looked up at the clock: half past six. She needed to get to work. "I'll keep calling her," she said. "Tell me if she comes home?"

"Of course." Elsa leaned in and kissed Lesley's cheek. Lesley received the kiss passively, her mind elsewhere.

CHAPTER SEVENTY-ONE

DENNIS LOOKED up as he pulled into the car park, towards the windows to the DCI's office. Her car was here already, along with only six others. At seven thirty am, there wouldn't be many staff at HQ yet.

He couldn't see her through the wide windows, but that didn't mean she wasn't up there.

If she'd arrived early, did that indicate some kind of break-through in the case?

There was no sign of the other team members' cars. He'd come in early because he wanted to speak to the boss, alone. And it looked like he'd get the opportunity.

Ten minutes and a brief chat with Tony on the front desk later, he was in the team room. He could see the DCI in her office, speaking into her phone. She gave him a terse wave as he placed his jacket over the back of his chair.

Stanley had called him at half past eleven the night before. He'd been watching Watson, who'd arrived back at his car with a young woman. Stanley had followed them through Bournemouth, but Watson had turned without warning into a side street and Stanley had been forced to drive on so as not to give himself away. By the time he'd turned back to search for him, Watson was nowhere to be found.

Dennis knew he had to take responsibility. He'd been the one assigned to watch Watson initially, and he'd only been replaced because he'd been falling asleep at his post.

The boss would be livid. He needed to apologise, before Stanley got in.

He took off his glasses, wiped the lenses with the handkerchief he kept in his trouser pocket, and replaced them on his nose. He wrinkled his nose to shift them into the correct position.

He took a deep breath and walked to the boss's door.

She was placing her phone on the desk, looking away from him. She seemed agitated.

Dennis raised his hand to knock on the glass. She spotted the movement and looked up. She frowned then strode to the door and pulled it open.

"Dennis."

"I wanted to speak to you before the rest of the team arrive. We lost David Watson." He looked down. "I owe you a personal apology."

She stared at him. "David Watson?"

"We were watching the van, in Bournemouth, boss." He waited. She gave a sharp nod and he went on. "Stanley took over, and Watson came back and drove off, but he lost the man." He licked his lips. "He knew he was being followed, boss."

"Yes. David Watson." She seemed preoccupied.

What was going on?

She looked him up and down. "We need to talk, Dennis."

Dennis felt his throat constrict. Was he about to be reprimanded? It hadn't been him who'd personally lost David Watson – twice – but he was the one who'd been given responsibility for tracking the man down.

"What's... what's the problem, boss?"

"There's been another death." Her face was pale, her eyes wide. "Another police officer. Don't just stand there by the door, Dennis. Come into my office. We need to talk."

CHAPTER SEVENTY-TWO

SHARON'S LEG HURT.

She squeezed her eyes together, grimacing at the pain.

Her leg hurt, and her arms were cold.

She yawned, not wanting to open her eyes any further. She was too tired. But she and Rick had left the pub well before closing time, and then they'd...

She felt a jolt of uncertainty run through her.

They'd *what*?

They'd got in his car. There had been some weird stuff where he'd driven into a car park, then he'd given her the necklace and the bottle of WKD, and then they'd headed to his mate's flat.

His mate's flat. That must be where she was.

The bed was bloody hard. And the duvet was bloody flimsy.

And she couldn't remember the flat.

She felt for the duvet, pulling it up around her.

It wasn't a duvet. It was a blanket. A very scratchy blanket, that smelt musty.

Who has blankets?

Sharon turned over to face away from the window. The sun was streaming in, her closed eyelids red.

It was bright out. Someone needed to shut the curtains.

Slowly, she opened her eyes.

She jolted, closing them again.

No. What?

She put out a hand, feeling the bed around her.

It wasn't a bed. It was a platform, made of rough wood. She could feel cold air coming up through gaps in the wood.

And when she'd looked down...

No.

Don't be ridiculous.

She opened her eyes again, slowly this time, her grip firm on the edge of one of the slats of wood.

Hold on, Sharon. You aren't going to fall.

And besides, she was imagining things.

But she wasn't.

Below her, through the slats, was green.

Grass?

Whatever it was, it was a long way down.

She was on a raised platform of some kind, lying under a blanket.

Where the hell...?

She rolled over onto her back, her arms out to the sides to keep her steady. She needed to find out how big this platform was. Whether she was at risk of rolling off.

She took a few deep breaths.

You're imagining things. It's just a bed.

But she wasn't imagining the sky above her head. The sun shone down, filtering through trees to her left.

She tensed. She'd heard something.

"Rick?" she croaked. "Rick?"

She turned onto her other side. Maybe he was with her, right next to her.

She concentrated. She couldn't remember anything after the van. They'd driven inland, following the signs for Wareham. She remembered going past the harbour at Upton, the darkness out to their left.

But she didn't remember taking the turn at Lychett Minster. And she didn't remember driving through the woods, towards Wareham, where Rick had said his mate's flat was.

What had happened? And where was Rick?

Lying on her right side, she scanned the area in front of her. She was on some kind of climbing frame, in a wood.

It was higher than any climbing frame she'd seen before.

There was another platform, past her feet. She pushed herself up, craning her neck to see.

There was someone on that platform.

Sharon felt her panic subside.

"Hello?" she called.

The person had their back to her, hunched over, sitting on the platform. They were wearing... it was unclear... was that an orange fleece?

She rubbed her eyes and sat up, feeling a rush of vertigo.

"Hello? Where am I?"

The person on the other platform turned to look at her.

Sharon felt her stomach lurch.

That was no person.

CHAPTER SEVENTY-THREE

MEERA SAT at the kitchen table, watching over Suzi.

"Eat your porridge," she told her daughter, for the fiftieth time.

She yawned and checked her watch. Twenty to eight. She needed to get into work.

Jill pushed open the door and gave her a smile.

"You look smart."

Jill looked down at her pale grey suit and black shirt. "I've got that interview, remember? The cold case team."

Meera's hand went up to her face. "Oh, I'm sorry."

Jill bent down to kiss her cheek. "It's OK. You're busy."

"It's not OK."

Suzi dumped a spoonful of porridge on the table. Jill looked at it, then at her suit, then at Meera. Meera shrugged and scooped it up with her hand, back into Suzi's bowl.

The things you do when you have kids.

"I was going to get you a card," she said.

"And you didn't." There was an edge to Jill's voice. Meera

knew she'd been neglecting their relationship lately. Too focused on work, and on their daughter.

She stood up, her hand lying softly on Suzi's head. "I'll buy you flowers."

Jill's eyes flashed. "Only if I get it."

"Regardless of whether you get it. You deserve something nice." She looked Jill up and down. "If you were wearing something brighter, I'd get flowers to match."

Jill frowned. "You know I feel more professional in grey."

"So you should. And it suits your blonde hair. But not as much as your blue suit."

Jill wrinkled her nose. "That's too bright." She picked up Suzi's spoon and held it out to the girl. Suzi opened her mouth and accepted the spoonful of porridge.

"I thought we'd agreed not to spoon feed her anymore," Meera said. "She's too old."

Jill looked up at the clock behind Meera. "She needs to be in nursery in fifteen minutes."

Still.

Jill looked down at her outfit, smoothing down her skirt. She was preoccupied, expecting Meera to take care of everything else.

Was this how it would be, if Jill got that job? She was the more senior of the two of them, bringing in the most money.

But they'd agreed they'd share all this.

Meera opened her mouth to speak. She wanted to tell Jill about her day yesterday, to talk about how useless she was feeling. Jill had been up late preparing for her interview, reading up on Dorset history. In recent days she'd been regaling Meera with tales of the diesel train that ran along Weymouth Harbour, and how they'd sometimes had to push cars out of the way so it could pass.

Jill's phone beeped.

Meera closed her mouth.

Jill looked at her. "Sorry, hun. Can this wait?"

"Course."

Jill rummaged in her bag and grabbed her phone. It was a message.

She turned to Meera. "Do you know about this?"

"About what?" She stared at Jill, her mind racing. Had they found David Watson? Had they arrested someone in the Fran Dugdale case? Even if Meera hadn't been involved in whatever success they'd had, she'd be relieved.

Jill thrust the phone into her hand. "Rowan Angus. The CID DI who worked with your sergeant back in the day."

Meera frowned. How did Jill know that?

She took the phone. "What about him?"

"He's dead. Found on the beach at Durdle Door." Jill looked at Suzi. Her face fell. "I guess I'm dropping her at nursery, aren't I?"

CHAPTER SEVENTY-FOUR

"THERE ARE some things I need to tell you, Dennis." Lesley gestured to the chairs in front of her desk. "Why don't you sit down?"

She walked around the desk to sit in her own chair, then thought better of it and joined him in the second of the two chairs opposite it. Dennis was licking his lips and rubbing his palms on his trousers, looking worried.

She gave him a smile. "This is nothing for you to worry about." She glanced past him, into the team room. No one in yet. She'd call them all in as soon as this was done, tell them about Angus.

"It doesn't look that way." Dennis's face had paled.

Lesley leaned forward. "You wanted to apologise. I know it's a setback that we've lost Watson again, but to be frank, I think it's the least of our worries right now." She surveyed him, watching the blood slowly return to his face. "In fact, I'm going to have to take you off the hunt for him. We need all the people we can get."

He rubbed his forehead. "Why?"

"There's been another death. Late last night, at Durdle Door."

The colour left his face again.

"DI Rowan Angus," she said. "He was in a relationship with Fran Dugdale, we'd be—"

"Rowan?" He stared at her.

Lesley nodded. "I'm sorry. You knew him."

"I worked with him." Dennis's breaths were faint. "He's a good man."

Lesley raised an eyebrow. "Really?"

"He was an excellent detective, and someone who held the team together."

"And as you know, he'd been married to a suspect in the Hamm murder."

Dennis's shoulders dipped. "I'm aware, boss."

She carried on, ignoring him. "Dawn Stephens. She died. I bumped into him at her house. We... we suspected him of being involved in her death, Dennis. And Trevor Hamm's."

Denis shook his head, very slowly. "I know, boss. And his presence at all the crime scenes. But Rowan Angus was a good officer. The last man I'd expect to be corrupt." He shrank back. "How did he die?"

Lesley swallowed. Dennis hadn't reacted well to DCI Mackie's death at the cliffs near Swanage. Another similar death might tip him back into panic attacks and depression.

"I'm sorry about this, Dennis."

"He went off the cliffs," Dennis said, his voice terse.

"He did. He was found by a member of the public at the base of the cliffs." She could feel her own heart rate increasing. "The paramedics tried to save him, but it was no good."

"How...?"

"I have no idea, Dennis. Not yet. But Gail's team are

already at his home, making sure we have access to any evidence."

"His home?"

"If he left a note..."

Dennis eyed her. "Rowan would never have committed suicide."

Just like Tim Mackie would never have committed suicide, she thought. But for months, that was what everyone had thought he'd done.

"Like I say," she said, "we'll need more resource. I'm offering you the choice. You can join the investigation into Fran Dugdale's murder, or you can take a role in this new case."

"I'd like to be involved in investigating Rowan's death, if that's all the same with you."

"Certainly. I'm glad you feel that way."

She eyed him. Could she trust him with her suspicions?

She owed it to him.

"I've got something else I wanted to talk to you about."

"David Watson," he said. "I've already got an alert out for the van. We'll find him."

"Was he alone?"

"Stanley saw him with a woman, going back to the van."

"Anyone Stanley recognised?"

"No. Sorry, boss."

"Watson's probably got himself false plates by now."

"We will find him, boss."

Dennis had been saying that to her for days.

"That's *not* the other thing I wanted to talk to you about."

"Oh." Dennis leaned back, his nostrils flaring.

"I... I have some suspicions. About Fran Dugdale's death, and how it might be related to another case."

"The Angus case."

"That, yes. But another one. From three years ago."

Dennis's jaw clenched. "DCI Mackie."

Lesley leaned forward. She wanted to put a hand on his. He pulled his hands back, clenching them together in his lap. "What are your suspicions, boss?" He glanced out to the team room, still empty.

"I'm working on a hypothesis that Fran knew something about the people behind Mackie's death. That she was killed because she was about to reveal what she knew."

A frown. "Which was?"

"Fran worked for DI Collingwood." Lesley watched Dennis for a reaction. "She believed that he was behind Mackie's death. That Mackie was investigating links between Collingwood and organised crime, and that Collingwood arranged for Mackie to be... to be taken out of the picture."

"That's quite a hypothesis."

"Dennis, I know you were talking to Mackie in the days before he died. Did he say anything to you about an investigation?"

"He'd retired, boss."

"I know that. But you've already told me he was giving you advice on cases. It doesn't sound like his retirement was all that... thorough."

Denis shook his head. "That was just a burglary in Swanage. Nothing to do with organised crime."

"Was there anything he was working on before his retirement? Anything he might have continued investigating, without telling anyone?"

"There was... No."

"What, Dennis?"

Dennis looked into her eyes. Was that fear she could see?

"What is it, Dennis?"

"We've already put this incident to bed."

"What incident? Is this about your arrest?"

"No, boss. It's about... It's about Johnny."

Lesley leaned back, surprised. DC Johnny Chiles had been a member of the MCIT when she'd started here. A few months later, he'd been moved to the Met when she'd discovered he'd been coerced into providing information to Arthur Kelvin, who was blackmailing him over his drug addict brother.

"Johnny?" she said.

"Mackie knew there was a CID officer providing information to Kelvin. He'd planted incorrect information, to see if Kelvin's gang followed up on it." He readjusted his glasses. "Sometimes they did, sometimes they didn't." He looked at her. "None of it made sense."

"Dennis, why didn't you tell me about this before?"

"Because you aren't involved in the investigation into DCI Mackie's death."

Lesley wanted to laugh. "Dennis, no one's involved in that investigation anymore. Phipps was taken off it."

A shrug. Dennis was being far calmer than she'd expected.

"So the work Mackie was doing didn't lead to Johnny after all?" she asked.

"It didn't."

"In which case, who?"

"He didn't share that with me."

No, because his suspect was a senior officer to you. Not to mention a decidedly dangerous one.

"Were DI Collingwood and DI Angus acquainted?" she said.

"They attended training college together, a year before me. Rumour had it they fell out over a woman."

"Dawn Stephens?"

"I don't think so."

Lesley licked her lips. She had Collingwood and Angus and their historic rivalry, the fact that Mackie suspected an unnamed CID officer... and Carpenter behaving oddly. She had Fran's suspicions, too, but that would never be more than hearsay now.

It wasn't enough.

She sighed. "OK, Dennis. The rest of the team will be in shortly. We need to update them on the Angus death. But what we've discussed about Mackie stays between us, OK?"

"Of course."

CHAPTER SEVENTY-FIVE

LESLEY WAS in the team room, about to pick up her phone, when Meera walked in, her footsteps brisk.

"I heard," the DC said. "Are you alright, sarge?"

Lesley looked from her to Dennis.

"I'm alright, thanks Meera," he said. "Eager to get on with this case." He looked at Lesley. "Get me doing something."

"I've already attended the crime scene," she said, "and the CSIs are at Angus's house. The best thing we can do is wait for the rest of the team to come in so we can set a plan of action."

"Really?"

"Really. Dennis, you call Tina, Mike and Stanley. Get them in asap. I need to see Carpenter."

Five minutes later, she was knocking on the super's door. She'd already checked the car park from her office window and seen his car out there. His PA Carla wasn't in yet, which meant there was no one to stop her going straight to his office.

"Come in."

Lesley slid inside and closed the door behind her. Carpenter was alone.

Good.

"I feel like you and I are in serious danger of spending far too much time together," he said.

"We didn't conclude our conversation." Lesley stood with her back to the door, her hands clasped behind her back.

The super gave a half-smile. "You're nothing if not tenacious."

"I believe that's why you hired me, Sir."

"Fair point. Very well. Sit down."

Lesley walked to the easy chairs, not waiting to be told to sit opposite his desk.

"What progress have you made on the investigation?" he asked as he sat down.

"The CSIs are at the scene and at Rowan Angus's house. The pathologist will be arriving in half an hour or so. I've informed two of my team and asked DS Frampton to call the other three in."

"They're already working on the Dugdale case."

"DS Frampton and DC Brown are working on the Hamm case still. Tracing David Watson."

"I thought you had a fix on him outside your flat."

"We lost him."

Carpenter coughed. "Again?"

"He evaded us, Sir. He knew he was being followed."

A sigh. "He'll be out of the county already."

"DC Brown has a lead, we're hoping that brings fruit."

"Good. Well, don't wait for him to come in to chat about the Angus case. Get him out there, chasing Watson down."

"With respect, Sir, I need more resource."

He eyed her. "And you'll have it. But first I need to ask you something."

"Sir." Lesley leaned back, hesitant.

He cocked his head, his voice lowering. "What the hell do you believe gave you the right to make contact with a retired Chief Superintendent from another force?"

Phipps.

"I didn't make contact with him, Sir. It was—"

"The journalist, Sadie Dawes. I know. Her manager called me this morning."

Lesley frowned. "Has there been a development?"

"No, DCI Clarke. Just a BBC manager wanting to corroborate a source." He narrowed his eyes. "You do know that Dawes can't report anything pertaining to an ongoing investigation, don't you?"

"I think she's saving it all up. Gunning for a Pulitzer Prize."

"She'll struggle with that, given she isn't American."

"I'm not sure what the British equivalent is."

"Nor me." Carpenter shook his head. "If you need to speak to someone like Phipps again, you come to me first. And you'd better have a bloody good reason before you even ask. In the meantime, I suggest you focus on the Angus investigation."

Lesley wanted to scream. *So why did you come to my flat last night? Why did you talk to me about Mackie's death?*

"Sir, I know this is extremely sensitive. But I believe that I myself and, more importantly, my team, are potentially in danger from whoever killed DCI Mack—"

He held up a hand, his eyes wide in alarm. "Enough. Focus on your case."

Carpenter stood up and approached her. He bent down briefly, his mouth close to Lesley's ear.

"Leave it, Lesley," he whispered. "Leave it with me."

CHAPTER SEVENTY-SIX

SHARON STARED at the creature on the other platform, barely able to believe her eyes.

This was no flat in Wareham. It wasn't even the garden of a flat, or of a house for that matter.

Not unless Rick's mate in Wareham kept orangutans in his back garden.

Where the hell was she? And how had she got from Rick's van, to here?

The orangutan sat with its back to her, scratching its head and armpits. Its movements might have been endearingly human, had she not been shut in here with it.

Were orangutans dangerous?

Sharon had never seen one in the flesh before, so she had no idea.

She'd seen them on wildlife documentaries, David Attenborough giving a lecture about how they were endangered, but she'd never been this close to one.

At least it hadn't seen her.

She heard a noise from off to her left. There was a building below her, some kind of house for the creatures. An arm, if you could call it that, was emerging from it.

Another one?

How many of these things were there?

She turned around to scan the area. She was at the top of a huge wooden structure, a kind of play frame for apes. The structure sat in the middle of an enclosure that was surrounded by a wire fence and, at the top of that, a circular construction that seemed designed to prevent the orangutans climbing up and over it. It was smooth, and jutted out from the top of the fence.

If the orangutans couldn't get over that thing, there was no way she could.

Should she call for help?

No. That would just attract the creatures.

Sharon turned back towards the first orangutan, focusing on her breathing. She couldn't afford to pass out, or to lose focus.

The creature still had its back to her, but instead of scratching itself, it was staring towards the brick building.

Sharon followed its gaze.

Another orangutan was emerging through a plastic curtain that covered a doorway in the brickwork.

She felt bile rush into her throat.

The orangutan below her, the one that was coming out of the building, was much bigger than the first one. It was huge, with a massive head and vast, hair-covered body.

She looked back at the first creature. It had swung itself down to the next level of the climbing frame, its eyes still on its companion.

Was it scared? Or was that its mother?

Sharon didn't know much about wildlife, but she did know

that some creatures could get violent when they thought their young were threatened.

She looked back at the fence, and the barrier at the top.

She had only one chance.

To get down from here, over to the fence, and then attract someone's attention.

But there was no one around.

What time was it?

Fuck. She hadn't worn a watch: she'd put on a thin gold bracelet instead. She'd thought about how well it coordinated with the necklace he'd given her.

She'd never be that vain again.

If she waited till someone appeared, would she have time to get down to the fence before the orangutans reached her?

She had no idea how fast they were.

The larger creature, the one in the doorway, began to move. It ambled across the grass and swung itself up to the climbing frame.

Sharon squeezed her eyes shut, then opened them again. *Don't come up this way. Don't see me.*

They hadn't noticed her yet.

She had to keep it that way.

She had a plan. She'd wait till a keeper appeared, maybe with the creatures' breakfast, and then she'd make a run for it. She had no recent experience of climbing frames, but she was relatively fit, or at least, she had been last time she'd forced herself to do any exercise.

She'd just have to hope she still was.

CHAPTER SEVENTY-SEVEN

ON HER WAY back to her office, Lesley pulled out her phone to call Elsa.

"Any news?" she panted into it, all but running.

"Sorry, sweetie. I've called all her friends, anyone I could think of."

"She doesn't have many." *And how did you get the numbers?*

But Elsa was a lawyer. She was resourceful.

"I need to report her missing," she said.

"Lesley, it's not even nine o'clock. She stayed out for a night, with her mates. And she's only just eighteen."

"She's the daughter of a police officer. It puts her at risk."

"You're doing it again."

Lesley was at the door to the team room. Everyone was inside.

That's something, at least.

"I've got to go," she said. "If she's not home by ten, I'm reporting it. And can you call the college?"

"I tried, they're not picking up yet. Don't worry, love. I'm on it."

"Thanks."

Lesley hung up, pulled her shoulders back and entered the team room. As one, the team turned to look at her. She was glad she'd taken a moment to compose herself.

"Right, folks," she said. "In my office."

They still didn't have a board, which meant there was nothing visual she could direct their attention to. She missed it.

Surely things were desperate enough now?

No. Collingwood couldn't be trusted not to swing by.

"Right," she said. "You all know about DI Angus's death."

Solemn nods.

"We went to Fran's house last night," said Mike.

Lesley frowned. "Let's just focus on—"

"It's relevant," said Tina.

Mike nodded. "He sent cards to her. Angus did. They were an item."

"She was engaged," Lesley said.

Tina shrugged. "She had two blokes on the go."

Stanley whistled. Lesley gave him a warning look.

"OK." She considered. Did that mean Satvinder Gill might be a suspect, after all? Was this a double murder committed out of nothing but jealousy?

"Someone needs to pay a visit to her fiancé, in that case," she said. "Tina, you've met him before."

"No problem, boss." Tina made a note in her pad.

"It also means Angus had a reason to be with Fran before she died," said Mike.

"And for his DNA to be on her body," added Tina.

"So maybe Rowan isn't a suspect in Fran's death," Mike concluded.

Lesley smiled. "Have you two been talking about this at home?"

The couple exchanged glances. "Louis had a quiet night," said Tina.

Lesley nodded. "I can't get past the fact that we keep finding Rowan Angus's DNA at crime scenes, but then he's always got a reason to be there."

"Like I said, boss—" began Dennis.

"I know. He was a fine, upstanding officer." She caught Dennis's expression. "Sorry, Dennis. If anyone's a reliable character witness, it's you. So if Angus didn't kill Fran, who did?"

"It has to be Satvinder," Tina said. "Jealous rage."

"She was dumped at Tyneham Village," Lesley pointed out. "That took planning. And there was no blood on her. But yes, we can't rule it out." She looked at Mike. "Are we any closer to having a cause of death?"

"I'll call the pathology lab as soon as we're done here."

"You do that."

"What's Angus's cause of death?" asked Stanley. Dennis let out a grunt.

"Much more straightforward," said Lesley. "Spinal damage from the fall. But Pathology will still be examining him for substances."

"Someone might have drugged him then pushed him in the direction of the cliff," said Meera.

Another grunt from Dennis.

"Everyone," Lesley said. "If you don't know it already, you should be aware that the sarge here worked with DI Angus. He tells me that he was a good man, a good copper. And I think we should work on that basis." She looked around the DCs. "We should also show a bit of respect."

"Right, boss," said Meera. "Sorry, Sarge."

"Nothing to apologise for," muttered Dennis.

"Right," said Lesley. "Meera, I want you with me at the crime scene. We need to catch up with the CSIs and look for any vantage points over those cliffs. Might anyone have seen something suspicious, or could it have been caught on CCTV?"

"No problem, boss," said Meera.

"Stanley, I'm going to spare you for the Watson search just for a couple more hours. Go back to Vera Kelvin's house, just in case he or anyone else we're interested in turns up."

She hadn't forgotten that she'd seen Collingwood meeting Aurelia Cross, when they'd been investigating Hamm's murder. And Aurelia Cross was the Kelvins' lawyer. There could be a connection there.

Tina raised a hand.

"It's not school, DC Abbott," Dennis said.

"Sorry. I've just had a text. DI Angus's car was missing, the CSIs have found it between his house and Durdle Door."

"Where did he live?" asked Dennis.

Tina looked down at her phone. "Sorry, Sarge. I'll find out."

He grunted.

Lesley nodded. "Tina, you're already talking to Satvinder. Mike, you get over there. Find out who broke into the car. See if there's any CCTV from when it was taken."

Mike nodded. Lesley thought of her conversation with Elsa, her own missing person.

Sharon, where the hell are you?

She wiped her forehead: it was damp.

"Boss, are you alright?" Dennis asked.

She frowned at him. "I'm fine. Just got a lot to think about. Everyone get to it. Report back here in two hours, either in person or by phone. Sooner, if you find anything important."

The team walked to their desks, muttering between themselves and picking up jackets and notepads.

"Get a move on!" Lesley shouted. Tina looked back at her, perplexed. Lesley blew out a quick breath. *Get out, everyone. Leave me alone.*

When the DCs had left, Dennis walked over to her. "You don't seem yourself."

"It's…"

"What is it? Is it about Mackie?" He glanced at the door.

"It's Sharon. She didn't come home last night. She's got a new boyfriend and I'm worried she…" Lesley grabbed a chair for support.

Dennis pulled it out. "Sit down. I'll get you a glass of water."

He walked away from the chair just as the team room door burst open: Stanley.

"Watson's van's been spotted, Sarge." The DC's face was alight with excitement.

"Where?" Dennis asked.

"Monkey World."

"That's only a couple of miles away," Lesley said. She looked at Stanley. "You're sure?"

"Positive, boss."

"OK. Dennis, you get over there. And for God's sake, don't let him get away again."

CHAPTER SEVENTY-EIGHT

ELSA HUNG up the phone for the third time. She'd been trying to get through to Sharon's college since it had opened at nine am, but all she'd managed to reach so far was the answerphone.

She didn't need to leave a message, or at least, not another after the one she'd left at one minute past nine. What she needed was to speak to a human being who could tell her if Sharon had showed up for college today.

She was about to head into the kitchen to make a coffee – anything to calm her jangling nerves – when the doorbell buzzed.

Elsa looked down at herself. She was still in her dressing gown.

Whoever it was would have to take her as they found her.

She answered the door to find a tall grey-haired woman in a pink suit standing in front of her.

"I'm sorry," she said. "We don't buy from door-to-door—"

The woman held up an ID card. "I'm not a salesperson," she said. "My name is Doris Ullerson. I'm the attendance officer at Bournemouth College." She looked past Elsa into the flat. "Can I come in?"

"Sharon's not here."

Ms Ullerson's eyebrows flicked up. "Why am I not surprised? Do you know where she is?"

"I've been trying to find that out from your college for the last half hour."

A frown. "I'm sorry?"

"Sharon didn't come home last night. We're worried about her."

"Are you Mrs Clarke?"

"I'm Ms Short. Her stepmum."

"Is her mother at home?"

Elsa resisted the urge to snap at the woman. "She's at work. Do you know where Sharon is?"

"I was hoping to get that information from you."

Elsa wanted to shake the woman. "I'm sorry," she said. "I have no idea why you're here, if you can't tell me where Sharon is."

Ms Ullerson gave her a piercing look. "I'm here to tell you your daughter – stepdaughter – hasn't attended college for two weeks. If she doesn't give us a good reason why and start attending very soon, then I'm afraid she'll lose her place."

CHAPTER SEVENTY-NINE

DENNIS PULLED up in the Monkey World car park. The site
wouldn't be open to the public until 11 am, and the car park
was quiet, just a few staff vehicles and four branded vans.

Past all the other vehicles, set a fair way apart from them,
was a different van.

A very familiar van.

He approached it and walked around it, checking the
bashed-in rear wheel arch and the numberplate that hadn't
been changed.

There was no one inside.

He looked up and scanned the area. No sign of Watson.

Surely he wasn't inside the attraction.

Dennis made a call to Control and requested a unit to
impound the vehicle and examine it for evidence. Evidence of
what, he wasn't sure. But he wanted to be sure David Watson
wouldn't have access to that van again.

He'd wait here, and watch. Watson would come back to his
vehicle eventually, and Dennis would arrest him.

He went back to his car and moved it so he had a better

view of the van, but wherever he parked, the van was shielded from his view by one or other of the staff vehicles. He opened the driver's window for some air and turned on the radio. There was no chance he'd be dozing off again.

After a few minutes, he caught movement in his rear-view mirror. He shifted in his seat so he could see without being seen.

It wasn't Watson. Instead, two uniformed Monkey World staff were running out of the main entrance.

What was going on?

Puzzled, Dennis got out of his car. He held up his ID and approached them.

"Is everything alright?" he asked. "Can I help?"

One of the two people stared back at him. A woman, young, not more than twenty. "There's a girl," she said.

"A girl?"

She nodded. Her face was red and her forehead damp.

"What kind of girl?" Dennis asked.

Stanley had said that Watson had a girl with him when he'd returned to the van. Could this be her?

"She's in the orangutan enclosure," the young woman said. "I've called the fire brigade."

"The fire brigade? Why?"

The man with her, also in a Monkey World uniform, stared at Dennis. "Someone has to get her down, of course. She's right at the top, and the orangutans are circling her."

Dennis looked towards the main entrance. He looked at Watson's van. Then he looked at the entrance again, and the open gate.

He ran for it, hoping he wouldn't be too late.

CHAPTER EIGHTY

SATVINDER WAS behind the counter in Wheelers again. Tina had phoned ahead and was surprised to find that he wasn't at home, dealing with his grief.

Was that suspicious? Or was it just a young man trying to distract himself?

The queue was shorter today, and Tina waited for a pair of middle-aged men in lycra to order their flat whites before speaking to Satvinder.

"Hello again." His voice was flat, but he didn't seem wary or scared.

"Hi, Satvinder. I'm sorry to bother you. D'you mind if we have a chat?"

He looked across the café. The only occupied table was the one with the two lycra-clad men.

He opened the door to the stockroom. "Jaz, I need to take a break. You keep an eye on the till for me?"

"No problem," came the reply.

Satvinder removed his apron and walked out from the

counter, his movements slow but fluid. He gave Tina a sad smile. "Let's go outside."

There was a row of picnic bench-style tables outside the café, with a small jar of flowers on each. Satvinder led Tina to the one furthest from the door. They were shaded by a wall beside them, but otherwise the harbourside was bathed in sunlight.

"Sorry to take you away from your work."

He shrugged. "It's OK. Have you got any news about who killed Fran?"

"It's not that, sorry."

"Oh. You've got more questions."

"Something like that."

"I spoke to her dad last night, he said he was expecting a call from you, have you got his number?"

"We have. It's not that."

"Oh." Satvinder slumped, looking down at his hands on the table. The nails were bitten.

Tina leaned forwards. "We've discovered something about Fran that you might not have known."

He looked up. "Is this about DI Angus?"

Tina felt her stomach dip. How was Satvinder so calm? "Yes."

"Yeah. I found out about that on Friday. She left one of his cards lying about in her flat. We... we had a row." He sniffed and brought his hands up to his face. "That was the last time we spoke."

"You knew she was having a relationship with DI Angus?"

Satvinder lowered his hands. His eyes were wet. "Not before Friday, no."

"How did that make you feel?"

He stared at her. "You... you think I killed her, don't you? You think I killed her out of, what, jealousy?" He sniffed, then wiped his nose with his sleeve. "I loved Fran. Still do. She told me that her thing with... with him... was over. We talked... we talked till two in the morning. Then I left the flat. But it was OK. We were going to work through it."

Tina tried to imagine how she'd feel if she discovered Mike was having an affair with a colleague. She wasn't sure 'working through it' would be her first instinct.

"DI Angus has also died," she said. "Last night."

Satvinder's hands dropped to the table. His mouth opened.

Tina waited.

"He's dead?" he whispered.

"I wanted you to know."

He stared at her. "You wanted me to know because you think I killed them both." He turned away. "Oh, fucking hell."

"Did you ever meet DI Angus?"

"No. And I never wanted to." He turned back to her, his muscles tense. "When did he die?"

"Last night. In the early hours of the morning."

"Well, I've got an alibi."

"You have?"

He nodded, his movements firm. "Tony, that's Fran's dad. He's staying at my house. Her mum wouldn't let him back at theirs."

Tina wasn't surprised by that. "Were the two of you both awake?"

"Yes. We stayed up late, drinking whisky and listening to sad music. He was telling me how shit he felt about taking up with that... I can't remember her name."

"Ruth."

"Ruth. I didn't tell him about Angus. I don't want their memory of Fran..." His voice broke in a sob, and then he looked into Tina's eyes. "Tony Dugdale and I were up drinking all night at my house in Bridport. He can vouch for me."

CHAPTER EIGHTY-ONE

CHAPTER EIGHTY-ONE

MIKE HIT hands-free as he drove towards East Lulworth,
where Rowan Angus's car had been found.

"Mike, you're on the ball today," Dr Bamford said.

Mike wondered whether he should take that as suggesting
he wasn't on the ball on other days. "I was wondering if
you've got any further with the cause of death in the Dugdale
case."

"I'm at the Rowan Angus crime scene right now, a bit
busy."

"Of course. Sorry."

"It's fine. As a matter of fact, some results came through
overnight."

"Oh?"

"Fran died of nonylphenol poisoning."

"What's nonylphenol?"

"It's a non-ionic surfactant."

"A what?"

"It cleans things. Nasty stuff, though, it's restricted these
days. Mildly toxic in the body in small doses, it can cause prob-

lems with the reproductive system. But in large doses, it's a poison."

"So we'd know who's using it?"

"Not necessarily, but we'd know who's supplying it. It's been phased out in recent years."

"So that's definitely what killed her?"

"Yeah. Pretty high concentrations, too."

"OK." Mike tapped his fingers on the steering wheel. They'd have to find out who stocked this stuff and how easy it was to get hold of. "Is it common?" he asked. "Am I going to find out half the businesses in Dorset have a bottle or two of it on the shelf?"

"It's restricted, so no."

"Restricted, but not banned."

"Sorry. That's better, though. If it was banned, there'd be no record of supply at all, as it would be illegal."

Mike punched the wheel. "Good."

Bamford laughed. "I thought you might say that. Good luck finding someone who still has it. It's probably lurking in a few storage rooms around the county, but you won't find much of it."

"Thanks."

"Do you want to know how we're getting on with Rowan Angus?"

"The boss is there, isn't she? And Meera?"

"Your DCI called me to let me know she's on her way. But meanwhile your forensics people have discovered scuff marks at the top of the cliff. And footprints. Two sets."

"That's not pathology."

Another laugh. "I listen in, Mike. Sometimes the forensics help to make sense of the pathology. Thought you might want to know."

"Yeah. Thanks." Mike hung up, putting his foot down. He wanted to learn what he could about Angus's car, then head back to the office where he could find out some more about this cleaning stuff.

CHAPTER EIGHTY-TWO

"You AGAIN," Gav said. "Not got your fella in tow this time?"

Tina had left Satvinder's café and headed to Rowan's house, which was just five miles away on the north side of Weymouth.

"Just me, I'm afraid." She gave the CSI a smile. "How are you getting on?"

"The place is a tip. Your Angus bloke was a slob."

Stepping inside, Tina found herself faced with piles of takeaway cartons and magazines on the floor, and clothes slung over the back of chairs. The ground floor of the terraced house consisted of one room containing a sofa, armchair and kitchen, and there was barely room to walk through it.

"I'm being methodical," Gav said. "Starting in the front corner furthest from the door and working my way in. I'm not tidying up, though. Just going through stuff looking for anything that might help."

"Signs of a struggle?"

He shook his head. "There's been no struggle in here. The

mess is too uniform. If someone had a fight in the middle of this, you'd see piles swept to the side, stuff pushed over. Clothes on the floor." He straightened up, his hands in the small of his back. His hair brushed the low ceiling. "This might look like a mess, but it's actually quite an ordered mess. Angus knew where everything was, I'd bet."

Tina nodded, finding it difficult to believe that. There were times when she thought Mike was messy, but now she'd never accuse him of that again. At least you could see their carpet.

"I'm going to take a look upstairs," she said. "That OK?"

"Be my guest. But tread carefully."

Tina retreated from the living space into the tiny hall and up the stairs, taking care not to touch anything even though she was wearing a full forensic suit. At the top were three doors: bedrooms to the front and rear, and a bathroom in the middle.

The bathroom was clean but messy, with bottles strewn on counters and no fewer than six toothbrushes in a mug. Five of them were old, the bristles splayed out.

Rowan Angus, were you a hoarder?

She entered the front bedroom, which was empty. Not just empty of belongings: empty of furniture. The room was entirely bare other than a thin set of curtains at the front window.

So why hadn't he stored some of his junk up here?

She tried the back bedroom. The bed was unmade and clothes were piled up at its foot. Shoes filled the space under the window.

One door of the wardrobe was hanging off its hinges.

A struggle?

Tina went out into the hallway and called down the stairs. "Gav? Have you looked up here?"

"Just briefly. You're wondering about the wardrobe."

"Yeah."

"So am I. Don't touch anything."

"Hello?" A man was standing in the open front doorway, peering inside. Tina hurried down the stairs and pulled down the hood of her suit.

"Hello," she breathed. "Please don't come in."

"Is everything alright?" The man was in his sixties, wearing a fleece and a pair of torn jeans. "I saw your van here and I wondered... Is Rowan OK?"

"Are you a neighbour?" Tina asked.

The man glanced over his shoulder. "I live over the road. Is Rowan OK? Who are you?"

Tina gave him a smile. "DC Tina Abbott, Dorset police."

"I thought you might be police. Has something happened here? Has there been a break-in?"

Not again. How many people had Tina had to inform of a death in the last week?

"I'm sorry, Mr...?"

"Dobson. Sid Dobson."

"Mr Dobson. I'm really sorry to have to tell you this, but Rowan is dead."

A gasp. Sid put his hand out to the doorframe.

"Please don't touch anything," Tina said. "Sorry."

He frowned. "OK. Someone... did someone kill him?"

"We don't know yet. But we're examining his house, to help us find out."

"Right. Only..." He glanced past Tina, towards the living room. "Rowan was a hoarder. It'll take you a while." He smiled.

"Were you friends?"

"We were. But that's not why I'm here."

"No?"

"No." He looked back at Tina. "My doorbell. It's got a camera. It picked something up, last night. Something I imagine you'll want to look at."

CHAPTER EIGHTY-THREE

STANLEY WAS STARTING to get used to sitting in his car, watching stuff.

It made him feel like a cop out of one of those American TV dramas from the eighties. The only thing missing was a bag of doughnuts.

Stanley would kill for a doughnut right now. He wondered if that cafe he'd gone past on the way through Lulworth sold them, or anything like them.

Irrelevant. He needed to stay here, watch the house.

Vera's new home, unlike the harbourfront place her son Arthur had lived in in Sandbanks, didn't have a gate separating it from the road. Which meant Stanley had to be extra careful not to be seen. He'd parked towards Lulworth, beyond a bend in the road and under a tree. The road was a dead end, so anyone coming or going would have to pass him.

He picked up his phone to call the sarge. Voicemail. "I'm here, Sarge. Just up the road from Vera Kelvin's house. There's no gate, but it's a dead end. I'll tell you if anything happens."

Stanley felt bad about losing Watson last night. There was no way he'd let the man go again.

He had some Red Bull in the back seat. He grabbed a can and swigged it, settling in for the wait.

CHAPTER EIGHTY-FOUR

DENNIS RAN through the open gates of Monkey World, then skidded to a halt.

He turned to see the young woman from the car park running after him. The man was still out there, standing by the entrance and waiting for a fire engine.

"Orangutan enclosure," he said to her. "Where is it?"

"It's that way." She pointed to her right. "But I don't think—"

"I'm a police officer," he told her. "This girl, is she in danger?"

"She's pretty high up. If she tries to jump down—"

"But the animals? Will they hurt her?"

The woman grimaced. "Orangutans are gentle. They find people fascinating, they'll probably approach her. But if they get too close, while she's on that platform..."

He nodded. "Which way?"

"Follow me." She started running. They ran into a grassy clearing with picnic tables and a playground, then took a sharp left along a path surrounded by bushes. He could hear monkeys calling, their shrieks echoing through the woods, just about audible over his own heartbeat.

"How far?" Dennis breathed, trying to keep up with the young woman.

She looked back, not breaking stride. "Not far. The orangutans are just past the shop."

Dennis focused on his breathing. He was fifty-nine years old, not built for this kind of thing. He should have called Uniform.

But then, this girl in the enclosure. She needed urgent help. She couldn't afford to wait.

He grabbed his phone and dialled Control.

"There's a girl trapped in one of the enclosures at Monkey World. Staff have called for fire service but I'll need Uniform backup."

"They're already on their way."

Dennis shoved his phone back in his pocket, realising he was lagging behind. He turned a bend to find a group of staff gathered in front of an enclosure. Two of them were at the open door to a low building beside it, and the others were huddled against the fence, watching.

"Police! Let me through." Dennis pushed his way through the crowd, ignoring the fact that his legs felt like jelly.

He looked up, through the fence. Three orangutans were on the ground ahead of him, gathered around a pole that formed part of the support system for a vast climbing frame. They were all looking up at something.

Dennis followed their gaze, and felt his heart leap into his mouth.

There was a girl up there. Long blonde hair, wearing black. She had her back to him.

Should he call out? Would that panic the creatures?

He turned to a man standing next to him. "How do we get her out of there?"

"The best thing is to get the animals out. We can corral them in the indoor enclosure, then bring her down when it's safe."

The girl stood up. Dennis put a hand to his face, staring up at her. She shuffled to the edge of the platform she was on and peered down.

He felt his chest jolt.

Oh my word.

He knew her.

The girl. He knew her.

And he had to get her down.

CHAPTER EIGHTY-FIVE

THE ATTENDANCE WOMAN HAD LEFT, finally convinced that Elsa wasn't an irresponsible stepmother and that either she or Lesley would have stern words with Sharon about college attendance when she finally turned up.

Elsa had no idea that Sharon had been skipping college. She'd been going out in the mornings, taking her rucksack with her, then returning home at what felt like a reasonable hour. Elsa knew that sixth form colleges didn't expect students to be on site all day the way schools did, so she hadn't thought about the specific times Sharon had come home. And she'd been out a lot herself, scouting for business premises, meeting new clients.

She and Lesley hadn't known. They hadn't known about the college non-attendance, and they hadn't known about the boyfriend.

The boyfriend.

He had to be behind this. Sharon was skiving off college so she could spend time with him.

Elsa pushed open Sharon's door. Lesley liked to respect the

girl's privacy, and didn't go through her things. Elsa usually followed Lesley's lead.

But this was different.

She pulled open the drawers of Sharon's bedside table. Underwear, jewellery, tampons. Nothing about a boyfriend. No diary, no letters.

Sharon would have her phone with her. But there was a tablet...

Where did she keep it? And would it have her messages on it?

Elsa spun round to survey the room. She flung open the door to Sharon's wardrobe. The girl was surprisingly neat. Clothes had been hung properly, folded and put on shelves. Elsa hadn't done that when she was a teenager.

She rummaged through the piled-up clothes, then amongst the shoes in the bottom of the wardrobe. When Sharon returned home she would see what Elsa had done, but that didn't matter.

There was nothing there.

She turned back to the bed, then dropped to the floor. When she'd been a teenager, she'd hidden makeup and contraband cigarettes under her bed.

She reached in and felt around. Her hand landed on something.

A book.

It had to be a diary.

Elsa pulled it out.

"Sorry, Sharon," she said as she opened the cover, "but this is for your own good."

She flicked through the pages. She was looking for a name, an address.

Something fell out. She bent to pick it up: an envelope.

A letter, from the boyfriend?

Elsa pulled out the contents of the envelope.

It wasn't a letter.

It was better than that. It was a photo.

And Elsa recognised the man in it.

CHAPTER EIGHTY-SIX

STANLEY SAT up in his seat as a car drove past, slowing to pass him in the narrow lane.

He bent over, facing away from the car, not wanting the driver to see his face.

After a moment, the car continued. Stanley turned back towards it.

Bugger.

The problem with turning away so he couldn't be seen was that he hadn't been able to see them either.

He had to know who it was, before they went inside the house.

He darted out of the car and ran up the street. There were trees and bushes lining the road so it wasn't hard to find a hiding spot where he could see right up Vera Kelvin's drive.

Thank God Lulworth had less security than Sandbanks.

The car had parked at a haphazard angle in the centre of the drive, and a man was getting out. He wore a beaten-up leather jacket and a pair of jeans, along with sunglasses.

He took his sunglasses off and whistled as he peered up at the house. Briefly, he turned round.

Stanley punched his thigh.

Day Watson. It's bloody Day Watson.

He swallowed down his excitement, anxious not to make a sound, and dipped down further below a hedge. There was a house behind him, and he hoped its occupiers hadn't noticed the man crouching outside.

He waited, peering through the leaves at Watson as he strode towards the red brick house. The front door opened and an elderly woman wearing a bright pink trouser suit walked out.

Vera Kelvin.

In Sandbanks, Arthur Kelvin had employed a housekeeper who would always answer the door. Apparently, his mother had to do it herself here.

Stanley pushed forward into the hedge, trying to hear their conversation. The day was still and sunny and fortunately the sea, not far beyond the house, wasn't loud.

"You took your time." Vera's voice carried. She was the kind of woman who was used to being heard.

"I had business to attend to."

"You didn't do it."

"I did. She's currently in the orangutan enclosure, probably wondering if she's going to get eaten."

A laugh. "Orangutans don't eat people."

"She won't know that. And besides, I put her right at the top."

"How the bloody hell did you do that?"

"There's climbing gear, kept in the offices there. It's not hard."

"Well, I just hope you weren't picked up by CCTV. Bloody idiot. Police are all over you."

"I know. I've already lost them twice this week."

"Only thanks to Collingwood and his quick thinking."

Watson grunted.

"Anyway," Vera said, "I don't want you here. You'll draw attention to the place. Bugger off."

"I haven't got anywhere else to go. My flat, they'll be—"

"I don't care about your fucking flat. Just get out of my hair. If I need to speak to you again, I'll contact you. Don't come here again."

She looked past him into the street, then turned her back and closed the front door. Her gaze didn't snag on Stanley, and he allowed himself to breathe again as Watson walked back to his car. His gait was less cocksure now.

Who are you talking about? What's all this about orangutans?

Stanley needed to speak to the sarge.

He waited for Watson to get back into his car, then for him to drive away.

Watson didn't.

The car, a battered red Astra with 2013 plates, sat in the driveway, the engine off.

Was he ever going to move?

Stanley couldn't shift from his spot until that car drove away. As soon as he got out from behind the hedge, he'd be seen.

Damn.

But he needed to tell someone about Watson and Vera's conversation.

He picked up his phone and dialled the sarge.

Voicemail again.

If the sarge hadn't turned his phone on since Stanley's last call, then he wasn't about to do so anytime soon.

He didn't want to call the DCI, not yet. She'd been in a funny mood when he'd left the office.

He dialled Mike.

CHAPTER EIGHTY-SEVEN

LESLEY STOOD ON THE BEACH, watching as Dr Bamford examined Rowan Angus. She'd arrived with Meera and sent the DC to the car park at the top of the hill, in search of witnesses or CCTV. Two uniformed officers were helping her.

The beach was quiet, its only inhabitants the pathologist and his assistant, Gail and two of her crew, and Lesley. Three uniformed constables walked its perimeter, searching. Above them, a squad car was parked across the entrance to the car park and PC McGuigan was turning people away.

The pathologist looked up. "It's definitely his injuries that killed him."

"Are there any other marks on his body?" she asked.

"None that I can find without stripping off his clothing." He stood up. "We'll get him to Dorchester, do a proper PM." He nodded at Lesley. "I'm sure it'll be fast-tracked."

Two police officers dead within a week. She bloody hoped it would be fast-tracked.

"I need to know if he jumped off those cliffs, or if someone pushed him," she said.

"The ten-million-dollar question," he replied. "Don't worry. We've got a physical cause of death, but the coroner will need to pronounce on the legalities. I'll give him a through once-over back at the morgue, and if there's evidence of him being pushed around or forced to walk, I should find it."

"Check for drugs, too. Start with the cleaning product you found in Fran's system."

"That'll be my first request on the toxicology form."

Lesley looked at him. "You can't do it yourself?"

"We can screen for certain substances, but not all of them. The lab's in Exeter."

"Your old stamping ground."

"Indeed." He licked his lips. "Look, if you really think the nonylphenol's an issue, I can get one of my team to drive a sample over there for you, get it—"

"It's OK. Knowing what was in Angus's system won't help us find out who killed him."

"It might help to—"

"We're already looking into it, thanks to Fran," she told him. "Don't worry."

Bamford nodded and packed his equipment into his bag. He stood up. "Right, I'll get the transfer organised and then we'll schedule in the PM for this afternoon. It's not going to be easy getting him up this path, but we've done worse."

Lesley nodded. She knew he had.

Her phone rang as the doctor was walking away: Elsa.

"Hey, love. Any news on Sharon?"

"She's not home yet, sorry."

Lesley felt her stomach hollow out. "Where is she, Els?"

"I know where she isn't, and that's at college. I had a visit from an attendance officer."

"You had what?"

"She hasn't been to her classes for two weeks."

'What? I'll bloody kill her."

"Lesley..."

"Of course I won't. But she can't just skive off. It's that boyfriend, isn't it?" Lesley pulled at her hair. "She's with him. Who the hell is he, Els?"

"That's why I called."

"You've spoken to him."

"I haven't spoken to him. But I do know who he is."

"Tell me." Lesley gripped her phone tighter. Behind her, a crew of pathology assistants and uniformed officers were getting into place, preparing to move Rowan's body. She stepped back.

"Who, Elsa?" she said.

"You're not going to like it."

"Just tell me."

"I found a photo of him in her room, and I recognised it from the photos of one of your suspects in the newspaper."

Lesley took a step back, her balance unsteady. "Suspects?"

"I think his name is David Watson, Lesley. Do you know him?"

CHAPTER EIGHTY-EIGHT

MEERA WAS at the top of the steps up from the beach at Durdle Door, talking to the man in the kiosk.

"So you don't have CCTV here," she said.

"Sorry, mate." His accent was Australian. "But," he said, pointing, "the holiday park up there, I think they do."

She looked past him at the rows of caravans at the top of the hill. They'd have sweeping views over the sea, but they didn't make the view look very pretty themselves.

"Can I get in from here?" she asked him.

"Yeah. There's a path over there, see. And if you can't find anyone, their number's on the sign by the campervan pitches."

"Cheers." She pocketed her notebook and headed towards the path.

"Meera!"

Meera looked round to see the DCI approaching, her breathing heavy and her gait uneven.

"Boss, are you OK?"

"I've got to go."

"Err... OK."

"Are you making progress on witnesses?"

"The two constables are knocking on doors up at the caravan park. It's busy, so we're hopeful. And the guy in the kiosk over there has just told me where I can find CCTV."

"Brilliant. You carry on with that."

"Of course." Meera could see that the boss's face was red. "Are you OK, boss?"

The DCI gave her a vague smile. "I'll be fine, Meera. It's just... it's Day Watson. We have another lead on him."

"Good. About the other day, I'm sorry I—"

The boss put a hand on her arm. "Don't worry. These lanes are a bugger to follow people on. It's not your fault."

"Thanks. I still feel bad, though."

"Don't. Look, I've got to go."

"Of course. What's the lead?"

The boss looked at her for a long moment. "It's my daughter."

Meera frowned. "Your daughter?"

"She's been missing, overnight. And I think she's been seeing Day Watson."

"She's been watching him too?"

The DCI shook her head. The redness had gone from her face. "No, DC Vedra. She's been dating him. And I think he might be behind her disappearance."

CHAPTER EIGHTY-NINE

MIKE WAS at Rowan Angus's car, which had been parked on the road down to Lulworth Cove from West Lulworth.

The car was in good condition, the remote key fob sitting in the storage well between the front seats. It didn't look like it had been broken into.

So how had it got here?

He looked up as a car pulled up behind his: the DCI.

"Boss," he said. "I wasn't expecting you."

"I just left Durdle Door." She looked at Angus's car. "What's the story with this?"

"No sign of forced entry. No damage. Keys still inside. It doesn't look like it was broken into."

"So how did it get here?"

He shrugged. "Can I help with anything else, boss?"

She shook her head. "Have you heard from Dennis?"

"Not from the sarge, boss. But I did get a call from Stanley."

"He's watching Vera."

Mike nodded. "Day Watson turned up at her house."

Her eyes widened. "Why the hell didn't he call it in?"

"He tried the sarge, but got no answer. Then he called me."

"And were you going to let me know?"

Mike bit his lower lip. "With respect, boss. This is the sarge and Stan's case."

"The cases are linked. That's looking pretty obvious now."

Mike nodded. He wasn't about to go correcting the DCI, not with the mood she was in.

"Hang on," the boss said. "Stanley says Watson was at Vera's." She looked behind her. "That's back near Durdle Door."

"But his van's at Monkey World," Mike said. "The sarge is there."

The DCI gave him a look. "Did Stanley say Watson had anyone with him?" She coughed. "A girl?"

"He was alone." He thought of something. "I heard something, on the radio, about Monkey World. An emergency call, something about a girl."

"What?"

He shrugged. 'Sorry, boss. I don't know any more."

"Damn." The DCI looked away, to the side. Was there red, around her eyes?

"Is there anything I can help with?" he asked.

"Meera's at Durdle Door, finding witnesses, looking for CCTV cameras. You can help her."

"No problem, boss." He turned towards his car.

"Mike."

He turned back. The DCI looked perplexed. He'd never seen her like this.

"Yes, boss?"

"Watson's van was at Monkey World. That's where Dennis went."

Mike shrugged. "That's good."

"Maybe she's.... Oh, shit." She slapped her forehead.

"Boss?"

"You go to Durdle Door. Oh, *shit*. I'm going to Monkey World."

CHAPTER NINETY

Tᴉɴᴀ sᴛᴏᴏᴅ in the hallway of Rowan Angus's neighbour's house. This place was quite a contrast to the house she'd just been inside. Instead of piles of junk and a general sense of chaos, this house was like a pin.

Nothing was out of place.

Sid looked around, following her gaze. "I know what you're thinking."

She nodded.

"I only set foot inside Rowan's house once," he told her. "I... I found it difficult, being in there."

"I bet you did."

His gaze lowered. "We shouldn't speak ill of the dead."

"No. Anyway, what was it you wanted to show me?"

"It's my doorbell. It's got a camera on it. It pinged me this morning, which is why I came over to Rowan's to see if he was alright."

Tina felt her heart rate pick up. "It pinged you?"

A nod. "Come in. It's on my phone. I'll show you."

Tina followed the man through to the kitchen section of

the living space. There was a small square table with four chairs, a phone lying on its surface. He sat down and she joined him.

Sid fiddled with his phone for a moment, muttering under his breath.

"Can I...?" Tina asked.

He handed it to her. "I was hoping you'd ask. I hate the thing. My daughter makes me have it. But the doorbell app is good for security."

Tina nodded. She brought up the app and its timeline, then scrolled through to the time when the app would have pinged Sid.

2:18 am.

She looked up: "Did this alert you in the middle of last night?"

"I keep the phone down here, when I'm not using it. I don't like the idea of radio waves near my head when I'm in bed at night. Rowan laughs at me about it." Sid picked at the skin on the back of his hand. "Laughed. God, I'm going to have to get used to that. What am I going to do on Saturday nights, now?"

Tina looked up from the phone. "Saturday nights?"

"Rowan and I play poker. It's my one vice. We play here, of course. Is it relevant?"

"Did you play last Saturday?"

Sid smiled, his eyes sad. "We did. If I'd known..." He wiped away a tear.

"What times was Rowan here between?"

"Ummm..." Sid tapped his front teeth with a fingernail. "He came at six pm, he always does. He had a run. I wanted to get my winnings back, so it was a late night." He looked up. "One am."

Tina glanced at him. So DI Angus had an alibi for Fran's murder.

She picked up Sid's phone and brought up the footage from last night. A man, standing at Rowan's door. He had his face away from the camera and wore a suit.

A suit, at two am?

Tina watched as Rowan answered the door. She zoomed in. They spoke for a moment, then Rowan locked his door and walked to his car.

The man in the suit walked to another car, parked on the street.

After a few moments, both cars moved off. The visitor's went first, followed by Rowan's.

As the man had got into his car, he had turned to look up and down the street. Checking for witnesses. Not realising he'd been caught on camera.

Tina had got a look at his face.

And she knew who he was.

CHAPTER NINETY-ONE

LESLEY SLAMMED her car door and ran towards the gates to Monkey World. A young man had been turning visitors away at the main car park entrance and she'd had to show him her ID. Dennis's car was parked near a small group of vehicles by the gates, and a fire engine had pulled up right by the turnstiles.

At the very end of the row, away from Dennis's car, was David Watson's van. Lesley ran to it, her stomach lurching. It was empty, the doors locked.

She ran to the gates, which were barred by a metal barrier.

"What the...!" Lesley slammed against the barrier and gripped it with her hands. "Let me in! My daughter's in there!"

Nothing.

"Shit."

She pulled on the barriers again. No one came.

She ran to the fire engine and a set of turnstiles beyond it. This was the exit, but maybe...

The turnstiles were impassable, only turning the wrong way, but Lesley could see people on the other side.

She waved her ID.

"Police! You need to let me in."

A man in a Monkey World t-shirt hurried to the turnstile, unlocked a barrier at the bottom and turned it the wrong way, letting Lesley through.

"Where is she?" Lesley asked.

"Who are you?"

"DCI Clarke. That's my daughter in there."

The man's face paled. "Oh. Your colleague's already arrived."

"DS Frampton. I know."

"Come with me."

Lesley ran behind the man, past a set of toilets, into a building housing a gift shop and out the other side. At last they emerged into a clearing filled with people: fire fighters and Monkey World staff.

No sign of Sharon. Or of Dennis.

One of the firefighters turned to her. "You're police?"

"I am." She wasn't about to tell another person her daughter was in there; she knew the drill was to keep parents away from scenes like these.

He pointed towards the fence all the people were staring at. "Your colleague's in there."

"Dennis?" Lesley shoved through the crowd to the fence. Sure enough, Dennis was climbing a huge wooden frame at the centre of a grassed enclosure.

She looked up to see Sharon above him, standing on a wooden platform.

Lesley shoved her fist into her mouth.

Two firefighters emerged from a low door in the building to the left of the enclosure. They carried harnesses and ropes.

"What are you doing?" she called.

The firefighter who'd spoken to her was standing behind her now. "They're getting your colleague out. And the girl."

"What's my sergeant doing in there?"

"He slipped in when Todd opened the doors to get the orangutans inside," said a young woman with red hair.

"Orangutans? They're still in there?"

"They're not dangerous," the woman replied. "They're gentle. They're more at risk from those two." She jerked her head upwards.

"One of those two is my daughter."

"Oh." The woman's face reddened. "Sorry."

Sorry, indeed.

Lesley looked back up. The two firefighters were inside the enclosure now, approaching Sharon.

Bring her down, Lesley thought. *Bring her down safely.*

CHAPTER NINETY-TWO

Meera stood in the reception hut of the caravan park, tapping her foot on the floor. The elderly woman behind the counter stared into a computer screen, her tongue between her lips.

"I'm sure it's on here somewhere," she said in a Brummie accent.

"It would be easier if you let me."

The woman gave Meera a disapproving glance. "The boss doesn't let us allow other people onto the system."

"I'm police."

Another glance. "You're other people. I'm not losing my job." She smiled. "Here it is."

"Can I look, at least?"

"No need to be sarcastic."

Meera bit back a retort.

"Yes," the woman said at last. "Shuffle round here, it'll be fine."

Meera squeezed round the back of the desk. The hut was

cramped and there wasn't much space for her and the woman, let alone the stands full of holiday paraphernalia and postcards.

Meera bent to peer into the screen. The computer must have been at least ten years old and the picture was grainy. But the woman had told her that the security system was new. So once they got these pictures onto a decent screen, they'd be clear.

She just hoped they would be clear enough for now.

"When d'you want from?" the woman asked.

"Last night. Two thirty am." Tina had called her with news of the CCTV from Angus's house. She was hoping that around fifteen minutes later, which was how long it took to drive here, both Collingwood and Angus would arrive.

Bingo.

At exactly 2:32 am, according to the time stamp onscreen, two cars drove into the car park.

"Where is the camera located?" Meera asked the woman.

The woman looked out of the windows towards the beach. "On the side of the toilets. It's supposed to prevent people using them camper van spots without paying. More trouble than they're worth, those bloody pitches."

Meera tried to remember the layout of the buildings around the car park. There'd been two shacks uphill, presumably selling food when the area wasn't closed to tourists, the toilet block near the caravan park, and another cabin where they were selling pitches on the park. She couldn't remember any campervan pitches.

It didn't matter. The important thing was getting the two cars on screen.

She watched as the cars pulled up right next to each other, despite the car park being deserted. The door of one, an Audi, opened, and a man got out.

Collingwood.

He walked around the other car and opened the driver's door. A man got out, his movements unsteady. Collingwood reached down to help him stand.

Angus.

And he didn't look in a good way.

"Who are they?" the woman asked, then her face fell. "Oh. I'm not sure I..."

She stood and walked out of the hut, lighting up a cigarette to smoke outside.

Good. Meera worked better when she wasn't being watched over by members of the public.

She pushed out a shaky breath, aware of what she might be about to witness.

DI Rowan Angus, someone she'd worked with for a year in Bournemouth CID.

Being pushed to his death.

But she didn't know that yet.

Onscreen, the two men walked across the car park together, Collingwood propping up Angus. They approached the path down to the beach.

Were they about to walk down there together? Had Angus not died from a fall at all, but from something else? An attack on the beach? A blow to the spine?

That made no sense. She'd seen the angle his body had fallen at.

They stopped at the point where the path dipped down towards the beach. She'd done this walk with Jill plenty of times, bringing Suzi down to the beach. On a sunny day it would be thronged with families enjoying the sunshine and the unique view of Durdle Door from the beach. Some hardy souls even swam under the archway.

The two men stood at the top of the path, huddled together. It was difficult to make out what was going on, but their faces seemed to be towards each other.

Talking?

Then they moved.

She watched them walk along the top of the cliff, away from the path. Towards the spot where Angus would have had to go off, for him to land where he was found.

Meera felt her chest go weak.

The men stopped. Right at the correct spot.

Meera rubbed her cheek.

If they'd acted quicker, if they'd found Fran's murderer... but was this connected?

"Sorry, Sir," she muttered, putting her fingertips to her lips.

The men swayed, then Angus ducked. Collingwood punched downwards, his arm hitting the other man. Then Angus was gone.

The woman rushed back into the shop. "You OK, love?"

Meera looked up at her. She shook her head.

"Did you hear yourself? You screamed."

Meera could barely breathe. "I'm sorry."

"It's OK. Did you...?" The woman looked at the screen.

Meera nodded.

Tears came to the woman's eyes. "You poor girl. Wait a minute, I'll get you a strong cup of tea."

Meera looked back at the screen. She hadn't seen the moment when Angus had gone off the cliff. Couldn't tell if he'd jumped or been pushed. But one moment, he'd been standing there, and the next... not.

Onscreen, Collingwood gazed out to sea for a moment, not looking down, then walked to his car. He started it up and drove away, as if nothing unusual had happened.

CHAPTER NINETY-THREE

STANLEY WAS STILL WATCHING David Watson's car. Still sitting in the damned hedge.

If he stayed here any longer, he'd be scratched to shreds. And he was in danger of needing the toilet.

He shifted his weight a little, careful to stay hidden. Watson sat inside the car, not turning on the engine.

Stanley frowned. What was he waiting for? Vera had clearly told him to bugger off. He had nothing to gain by hanging around.

He heard engine noise from off to his left. A car was approaching.

Oh, fuck.

He lay down on the grass, hardly breathing, hoping whoever was driving wouldn't think to look this way. He waited for the car to pass.

He heard it drive past him, then it slowed, and then there was the sound of tyres on gravel.

Vera Kelvin's house had a gravel driveway.

So the car was going in there. Not driving on for the next house along the road.

Was that what Watson had been waiting for?

He heard a door slam.

Sit up. You've got to see.

Slowly, he rose from his spot lying on the grass. He needed to sneeze.

Don't.

The door of the new car was opening. It was an Audi.

The urge to sneeze vanished.

Stanley watched, open-mouthed, as a tall man in a suit got out of the Audi. Watson emerged from his car and walked around it to join him.

They spoke, their voices low. Stanley couldn't hear what they were saying.

He watched the man in the suit, his mind racing.

It was always possible he was here on legitimate business.

He might be investigating a case.

Vera Kelvin might be a witness.

If Vera Kelvin's volunteered to be a witness, I'm a monkey's uncle.

The man in the suit – DI Collingwood – walked to the front door, which opened before he had a chance to ring the bell.

Vera Kelvin looked past Collingwood at Watson, a scowl on her face. Then she looked at Collingwood.

Her expression shifted into a smile.

She stepped out of the house and gave the man a hug.

Stanley resisted a yelp.

Since when did PSD officers hug witnesses?

CHAPTER NINETY-FOUR

LESLEY'S PHONE RANG. She grabbed it, her eyes on her daughter. The firefighters were at the base of the climbing frame now, calling up to her.

Dennis was off to one side, on another platform, watching them.

She held her phone to her ear, not bothering to check who it was. "Make it quick."

"Boss, it's Stanley."

"I'm at an emergency. This had better be urgent."

"Err..."

"Stanley! Just tell me what it is. Now."

A couple of the Monkey World staff standing closest to her shrank back.

Good. Now I can see better.

"Er, yes. Sorry, boss. I'm at Vera Kelvin's. I've been trying to get hold of the sarge. He's not picking up."

"That's cos he's— never mind. What's happened?"

"Collingwood's here. And Watson."

"DI Collingwood?"

"He turned up a few minutes ago in his Audi."

"Can you see him right now?"

"Yes."

"Good. Take photos, if you can. Stay hidden. Call Command, get a response unit out there on the hurry-up. You need to catch the three of them together."

"Will do boss. And...?"

"I don't have time for anything that isn't an emergency, Stanley."

"I was just going to say I hope your daughter's OK. I heard she's gone missing."

"She's right here in front of me, Stanley. She's going to be fine."

Lesley ended the call and shoved her phone into her pocket. She hoped she was right about Sharon.

And as for Collingwood... she didn't have the time to process that now.

She took a step towards the enclosure and leaned on the wire mesh. Sharon was making her way down, attached to a harness one of the firefighters had slipped onto her. She was halfway down, taking it slowly.

Good girl. You can do this.

Should she call out, encourage her daughter? Or would the sudden noise distract her?

Leave her with the firefighters. They know what they're doing.

She scanned the frame for Dennis.

Dennis, you bloody fool. Why did you go up there after her?

But although she wanted to slap him for being such an idiot, she was touched. And grateful. He'd risked his own life to save her daughter.

Where was he?

She scanned the frame.

Ah.

He was climbing up a ladder, making his way towards another platform. From there, he could use a rope and a pole to get down. If he wasn't Dennis Frampton, fifty-nine years old and not known for his agility, she'd be relieved.

Stay where you are, you fool. Wait for the firefighters.

One of them had moved away from Sharon and was heading for Dennis.

"Sir!" he called out.

Dennis turned, letting go of the rope he was hanging onto.

He swayed.

Lesley felt a gasp leave her mouth. She raised a hand to the wire fence.

"Dennis!" she called, not thinking.

He turned in the direction of her shout. He hadn't seen her, didn't know she was here.

His body was tilted to one side. Lesley could see him trying to shift his weight the other way.

His eyes widened, and he swayed again.

"Sir!" the firefighter called. "Stay where you are."

Dennis looked round, but it was no good. The swaying, the sudden movement one way and another, had caught his balance.

Almost in slow motion, Lesley watched as one of his feet left the platform, and then the other. He threw out an arm to catch himself, but it caught on the rope and then slid out.

"No!" she cried.

Dennis stumbled, his weight tipping over the edge of the platform. His mouth opened and his arms flailed out.

"Sir!" the firefighter called, running towards him.

Dennis's head jerked to one side, trying to spot the fire-fighter. But it was too late.

Lesley let out a scream as her friend fell from the platform, and landed, unseen, in the grass with a sickening crunch.

CHAPTER NINETY-FIVE

"EVERYONE, IN MY OFFICE." Lesley walked through the team room, ignoring the stab of eyes on her back.

They were all there: Tina, Mike, Stanley, Meera.

All except Dennis.

In her office, she sat at her desk, unable to meet their gazes. She waited until Stanley had closed the door.

None of them sat. Meera looked at the chair in front of Lesley, which Dennis normally used.

Lesley felt a lump rise in her throat.

"Do you all know?" she said.

"I got a call from the fire brigade," said Tina. "I told the others."

Lesley nodded, forcing herself to look at her team. "It was my fault."

Stanley frowned. "It wasn't, boss. You couldn't help that he went up there after your daught—"

"I called out to him. Like a bloody idiot. I distracted him. And then..." She looked down. "And then he fell."

"Day Watson took your daughter there, boss, is that right?" Tina's eyes were red-rimmed.

Lesley nodded.

"He can't have wanted to hurt her, then," said Stanley. "Orangutans are gentle."

"Shush," hissed Tina.

Lesley looked at him. "Orangutans may be gentle. But falls from platforms four metres above the ground are not."

Meera let out a sob.

"He wanted Sharon to die?" Tina muttered.

Lesley sighed. "I've no idea, DC Abbott."

"How is she?" Mike asked.

"She's fine. Shaken up. Badly. And she'll need some psychiatric help, no doubt. But the firefighters got her down in one piece."

"Unlike the sarge," muttered Stanley.

"Stop it," hissed Meera.

"He's under arrest," said Stanley. "Watson. And we've got Vera Kelvin too."

Lesley's head snapped up. "You have? On what charge?"

"Watson on false imprisonment."

"What about Vera?"

"They found drugs in her cellar. Possession with intent to supply."

"Not Collingwood?"

"He'd left by the time Uniform got there. I wasn't about to arrest him on my own."

"Good call." Lesley gave Stanley a smile. "You got photos?"

"Plenty. Video, too."

Lesley blew out a breath. "Bloody hell." She glanced at the empty chair. "Sorry."

"He'll be alright, won't he?" said Mike. "I heard he was in Dorset County Hospital."

Lesley looked up at him, her vision clouded. She needed to call Elsa. To tell her Sharon was OK. She needed to go to the hospital in Dorchester to see her daughter.

And she needed to visit Dennis, at the same hospital.

"I really don't know, Mike. He was unconscious when they took him away in the ambulance. They think there was damage to his spine. I'm waiting to hear from the doctors. And his wife."

As one, the team looked down at the floor.

Lesley stood up. "I need to go over there. I want you all to carry on working, if you can. We've got two prisoners to process, and each of them is going to be a challenge. I want the I's dotted and the T's crossed.

There was muttering.

"Unless," she continued, "you need time to yourselves. Anyone who needs it can take time off if they need it, as of this moment. I don't want to keep you here if it's too much for you."

"We'd rather keep working," said Tina. She looked at Mike, who nodded.

"Yeah," said Stanley. "Pin down the bastards who did this to the sarge."

Meera sniffed.

"Meera?" Lesley was aware that Meera knew DI Angus. "Are you sure you'll be alright here?"

"I won't be alright, boss. But I'd rather stay here. I'd rather make a contribution."

"Very well." Lesley made for the door. "If any of you finds it too much, just go home, no questions asked. You don't need to wait for my say-so."

"Thanks, boss," said Tina.

"I'll let you know as soon as he wakes up." Lesley reached out a hand to squeeze Tina's. "He's going to wake up, I promise."

CHAPTER NINETY-SIX

"Darling!" Lesley hurried to her daughter's bed and wrapped Sharon in a hug. Elsa was already there, sitting in an armchair.

"I'm sorry, Mum." Sharon winced and pushed her mum away.

"Does it hurt?" Lesley asked, looking her daughter up and down. She had bandages on her arms and her face was bruised.

"I'll be fine. I got scrapes, from the wooden platform. They're worried about infection. No one's been close enough to those orangutans for long enough to get diseases from them."

Lesley looked at her. "That sounds... worrying."

Sharon shook her head. "The animals get regular checkups. They're healthy. I'll be fine."

"So why the bandages?"

"They put lotion on the scrapes, it's a bit yucky. And gave me some steroids. They make me feel great."

"Good." Lesley took her daughter's hand and held it softly. "I'm so glad you're OK. And I'm sorry I didn't get there sooner."

"Dennis did, didn't he? And they spotted me when they came with the morning feed, called the fire brigade." Sharon's face fell. "Is Dennis going to be alright?"

Lesley had come straight to Sharon, and hadn't had a chance to find out about Dennis yet. "He's going to be fine," she said. "Don't worry."

"Good. I like Dennis."

Lesley wasn't sure how many times Sharon had even met Dennis.

She looked at Elsa. "Thanks for coming."

A shrug. "I couldn't not."

"Still..." Lesley looked back at Sharon. "No more animal sanctuaries for you, my girl."

"And no more dodgy boyfriends," said Sharon. "Elsa told me all about Rick – David. I'm sorry, Mum. I was an idiot."

"You weren't an idiot. He was clever and manipulative. That's what men like him do. I'm just glad you're alright."

"I'm not in trouble then? Elsa said you were going to kill me cos I didn't go to class."

Lesley gave her daughter a smile. "We'll talk about that." She gave her another hug, more gently this time. "But I'm not cross with you. I'm just glad you're safe. Now, if you don't mind, I need to go and see Dennis. He's three wards along."

Sharon's face brightened. "Thank him for me. I know he didn't get me down, but what he did was very brave."

Lesley felt a lump rise in her throat. "I will, love. I will."

She stood up and felt Elsa's hand brush against hers. She turned to look at her wife.

"Good luck," Elsa whispered.

"Mum?"

Lesley looked round to see Sharon reaching out for something on her bedside table.

"Yes, love?"

"You might need this. He gave it to me."

Sharon held something out. It was a necklace. Gold, with – was that a ruby?

Lesley looked at her. "Where did you get this?"

CHAPTER NINETY-SEVEN

"I'm sorry, love. Close family only."

Lesley peered past the nurse into the intensive care ward. She'd placed the necklace in an evidence bag and it was in her pocket.

"I'm his boss," she said. "DCI Clarke."

The nurse smiled. "We rarely have police in here, patients aren't in any fit state. And Dennis hasn't woken up yet."

"Can I at least look at him?"

"Sorry. His wife's with him at the moment, but we don't want anyone else in there. The place is calm, and we like to keep it that way."

Lesley bit down her frustration. She was tempted to lie to the woman, to say she needed to speak to Dennis's wife about the case. But that wouldn't be fair on Pam.

"Can I leave a note for him?"

"He won't be able to read it."

"His wife will."

The nurse shrugged. "Fair enough."

Lesley grabbed a pad out of her bag and scribbled a note. She scrunched it up into a ball then started again.

After three attempts, she had a pocket full of paper and no note.

"It's not easy," the nurse said. "I need to go in, though."

"Just – get this to him. Please."

Lesley scrawled: *Call me when you're awake.* She thrust the note into the woman's hand.

It wasn't the world's greatest get well soon note. But it conveyed her hope and belief that Dennis would pull through.

"I'll give it to his wife." The nurse retreated through the glass doors.

Lesley stood for a moment, staring at the doors. She couldn't get in there even if she tried; the nurse had used a pass.

She turned and walked back to the hospital entrance. She needed to update the team. Then she'd be back for Sharon.

As she approached to her car, she noticed a man standing next to it: Carpenter.

"Sir? Are you here to see Dennis?"

"They won't let anyone in. I phoned. But they did tell me there was a blonde woman trying to get past the system." He smiled. "I thought that sounded like someone I know."

She shrugged. "They wouldn't let me in."

"He'll be alright, Lesley. He's made of tough stuff."

But Dennis wasn't, not really. He'd struggled through, these last two and a half years: Mackie's death, his arrest, his mental health problems. She'd kept most of it from the super.

"I need you to do something for me," he said, "before you go back to your team."

"Sir?"

"Follow me."

He turned away and got into his car, parked three along from hers. He pulled out of the space and opened his window.

"You won't regret it, Lesley. Follow me."

CHAPTER NINETY-EIGHT

"I can't focus," Tina said, staring into her computer screen.

"Me neither," said Mike. He stood up from his chair and stretched out his arms.

"D'you think we can call the hospital?" Meera asked.

Tina looked at her. "The boss will let us know as soon as there's news."

Meera nodded. "I'm working through these CCTV files and my eyes keep glazing over."

"D'you want some help?" asked Stanley.

She turned to him. "OK. But it feels like we can't make any progress until we know how everything else is going to pan out."

"We've got a suspect," Tina said. "The CCTV from Angus's house and from Durdle Door show him taking the victim to the cliffs at the right time."

Mike had rounded the desks and was standing next to her, his hand over hers on the arm of the chair. The warmth was comforting. "Yeah, but he's PSD."

"None of us can arrest PSD," said Stanley.

Tina shook her head. "We can't yet. But there'll come a point when the boss is satisfied we've got enough to make an arrest, and she'll go to the super. Then we'll get his authority." She grinned. "I'd be happy to go and arrest him."

"Me too," muttered Mike.

"After what happened to the sarge..." Stanley said.

"Exactly," Tina said. "If Collingwood hadn't been working with Vera Kelvin and Day Watson, then Sharon would be fine."

"How so?" asked Mike.

She looked up at him, pulling her hand away. "Vera clearly wanted to scare the boss off. She was worried, because we were close to uncovering Collingwood's involvement. And Collingwood was worried enough to kill Angus himself." She looked around the team. "With the old DCI, I don't reckon he did that."

"You don't think he killed DCI Mackie?" Meera asked.

"It's similar. I don't..." She sighed.

"Which leaves us nowhere," Stanley said.

"I don't know," said Tina. "I'm sure the sarge knows things about it all that he hasn't told us, though."

The team went quiet. After a moment, Mike said, "He and the DCI were close."

Tina swallowed, then wiped a tear from her cheek. "Mackie was his mentor. I wasn't in the team at the time, but even I could tell how much he missed him, after he went off the cliffs at Ballard Down."

"Yeah," muttered Mike.

Tina's phone rang. She fumbled for it, almost letting it fall off her desk.

"It's the DCI," she hissed. Everyone fell silent, watching her.

"Boss," she said. "How is he?"

"I haven't been allowed to see him, I'm afraid. He's stable, but that's all I know yet. I'll keep you updated, but I just need to follow up a lead first."

"How's Sharon?"

"She's fine, thanks, Tina. She'll be home in a couple of hours. And she gave me a necklace, one that Watson gave to her. It's got hair in it, that isn't hers. And soil on the back. Ask Meera to check those photos she took, of Collingwood handing something to Watson."

"Er... yes, boss." Tina punched a fist in the air, then caught herself. "It's horrible, what he did to her."

"It is. But David Watson is going to go to prison for a long time. And he won't be the only one."

"Is the necklace enough, boss? Can we arrest Collingwood?"

"Not yet, Tina. But I'm hoping that might change very soon."

CHAPTER NINETY-NINE

CARPENTER DROVE to the Ship Inn, not much more than a mile from the office. Lesley had been there before, with members of the team. Back when the rest of them would go out drinking without her and she wasn't sure she'd ever fit in.

She parked in the car park and walked inside. The pub was busy and it took her a moment to spot him.

Carpenter was sitting at a round table away from the door and the bar, as secluded a spot as he could find.

He wasn't alone.

She approached the table. "Sir." She turned to the second man. "Sir."

"We've been through this, Lesley. It's not 'Sir' anymore. I've retired. Call me William."

Lesley said nothing, but sat down. Both men had drinks in front of them: Carpenter's a Coke, Phipps a half pint of bitter.

"Can I get you a drink, Lesley?" Phipps asked.

She shook her head. "I'd rather just get straight to it."

He raised an eyebrow. "You've been trying to talk to me, I know. You're not the only one." He glanced at Carpenter.

Carpenter leaned in, lowering his voice. Lesley pulled her chair closer to the table.

"I didn't want to speak to you in the office, Lesley, and I certainly didn't want to bring William in there. I believe someone is listening to me."

"I suspected that, Sir."

"You knew?"

"I saw the way you were behaving in your office. I noted that you came to my home or spoke to me in the car park when you wanted to be more frank with me."

He smiled. "We can see why you're a DCI."

If all it took to make DCI was to notice someone acting like they were scared, the force would be full of them. "I assume this isn't a social chat, Sir," Lesley said.

"No." Carpenter looked at Phipps. "Tell her."

Phipps licked his lips and shifted in his chair. "You know I retired abruptly, DCI Clarke. And that the investigation into DCI Mackie's murder was dropped immediately after."

"I do."

"And you probably wondered why that was. Why they didn't just hand the case over to someone else."

"I did."

"Of course. That's why you called me." He glanced around the pub. "I'm afraid they got to me."

"Got to you, Sir?"

He raised an eyebrow.

"William, then."

He nodded. Waited.

"The Kelvins," she said.

"And..." he replied.

Lesley hesitated.

"You can say it, Lesley," Carpenter told her.

She looked at Phipps. "Collingwood?"

"I had evidence linking DI Collingwood to Arthur Kelvin, via Aurelia Cross. I had DCI Mackie's notes that he kept at home. I believe you saw some of those."

"Pam let me have them."

"Well, you don't have all of them. I confiscated a few." He glanced at the super. "I've given them to Superintendent Carpenter here."

"I've only had them for a few weeks," Carpenter said. "Since William approached me."

"I had to know who to trust, you see," Phipps said. "It wasn't easy."

"You knew that Collingwood and Angus weren't to be trusted."

Phipps looked puzzled. "No. Why would you think that?"

Lesley shrank back. "But..."

"Collingwood, yes. He's as bent as a boomerang. But Angus, no. Angus was an upstanding detective, who just happened to find himself in the wrong place at the wrong time."

"That's quite a coincidence," Lesley said. It hadn't just been the wrong place at the wrong time, not when it came to the Hamm case. It had been a lot of wrong places at a lot of wrong times.

"Not coincidence. He'd worked for Collingwood in the past, looked up to the man. Collingwood gave him his orders."

"But Collingwood was PSD. Angus was CID."

"It doesn't always work like that, does it, Lesley?" said Carpenter. "I mean, look at you and your DI up in Birmingham. Zoe Finch."

Lesley felt heat rise to her cheeks. She was loyal to her team. Her Dorset team.

She had a sudden flashback to Dennis falling from the orangutan platform.

"Lesley? Are you alright? You trembled." Carpenter was peering at her, concerned.

"It's been a hard day, Sir. You know about DS Frampton."

"Ah. Yes." Carpenter looked at Phipps. "Severe injuries sustained in the line of duty. Tragic."

"He's not dead yet," Lesley snapped.

"No. Which is good."

Phipps was looking at his watch. "I shouldn't stay any longer." He looked at Lesley. "Anthony has told me about the CCTV footage you have. Relating to Rowan Angus's death. A team from outside Dorset will be brought in, given that the prime suspect is a Dorset officer. A Devon officer whom you know, I believe."

"DI Patterson," said Carpenter.

"DS Patterson." Lesley had worked with Hannah on a Lyme Regis case. Or rather, she had sparred with the woman.

"She was promoted," the super said. "She'll bring him in."

"Surely a more senior officer—"

"... will attract his attention," said Phipps. "I was too big a target, Lesley. You couldn't miss me. Hannah Patterson will be able to finish your work without drawing undue attention to herself."

"You'll be interested to know," Carpenter added, his voice low, "that a wrench with Rowan Angus's skin on it has been found in DI Collingwood's car boot."

"But there's no warrant." Lesley looked between the two men. "If this case isn't pursued properly—"

Phipps shook his head. "It's police property, Lesley. Don't worry."

"He set Angus up?"

"That's what I believe. We can't prove it yet."

She swallowed. *Don't let them mess this up.*

The wrench. The necklace. The van.

She looked down at her lap, thinking of Dennis. After a few moments she looked up.

"And what about DCI Mackie's death?"

Carpenter's expression turned grave. "William has evidence linking Collingwood to it. Based on what we've seen with regard to DI Angus's death, we believe Collingwood pushed DCI Mackie off the cliff at Ballard Down, or at least coerced him into throwing himself off."

Lesley frowned. "How?"

"There's CCTV, Lesley. Fibres on the clothes Mackie was wearing that night."

"They were missing."

He shook his head. "They were moved to another evidence store."

"Why?"

"Too close. They're no longer in the county."

She licked her lips. "Mackie wrote a suicide note. Petra said it was coerced."

"Petra?" Phipps looked puzzled.

"Dr McBride. A forensic psychologist. You don't need to... she said it smelled off, to her."

"That sounds like Petra," Carpenter said. "Hannah Patterson will be able to follow that up." He chuckled then looked at Lesley, his face grave again. "Go back to your team. Wait to hear from me. That's all I can tell you to do, right now."

Lesley nodded. "And Vera Kelvin?"

"Oh, we've got her for drug supply," Carpenter said. "The Organised Crime team will be speaking to her too."

"Not DI Gough."

Carpenter frowned at her. "Not Jim?"

"No. He's... I'm not sure, but I think there's a chance he's in cahoots with Collingwood."

"In cahoots," Phipps said. "There's a phrase I haven't heard for a while." He looked at the super. "Anthony?"

"Another officer will make the arrests," Carpenter said. "You've proved yourself, since you came here, and I'm going to trust you on this."

"Thank you." Lesley stood up. Her head was spinning and she needed to be alone.

"You won't get the credit for any of this, Lesley," Carpenter said. "But we will know. Without you, we'd never have brought Collingwood in."

CHAPTER ONE HUNDRED

PAM CAME to the door wearing a black blouse and grey skirt. When she saw Lesley, the worry on her face brightened a little.

"DCI Clarke," she said. "Come in."

"It's Lesley. You know that. How are you?"

Pam shrugged. "Come on through." She sniffed and took a tissue from her sleeve. She wiped her nose with it then shoved it back up her sleeve.

Lesley followed Pam into the house. She'd been here before, chasing Dennis because he wasn't at work in the midst of his mental health problems.

The dining room was no longer a dining room. Instead, it had been turned into something that looked more like a hospital ward. A vast bed sat at the centre of it, surrounded by equipment and boxes of drugs.

In the bed was Dennis. His eyes were half-closed and he lay on one side, snoring lightly.

Pam went to the side of the bed. She pressed a button and Dennis shifted position, sitting up a little.

"Dennis," she murmured in his ear. "You've got a visitor."

Dennis blinked a few times, then frowned. "I'm in no state."

"It's DCI... Lesley." Pam smiled back at Lesley.

"And I've got the rest of the team outside on the street," Lesley said. "They all wanted to see you, but only if you're up to it."

Dennis turned over to face her. "Pam." He batted at his wife's arm. "Get the DCI a cup of tea. Let the others in." He smiled, but it wasn't much more than a flicker.

"How are you?" Lesley asked as Pam left the room, whispering "coffee" to her.

He groaned. "I've been better."

"What you did. Climbing up after Sharon like that." Lesley wiped away a tear. "I'll always be grateful."

He shook his head, then winced. "How d'you get this thing more upright?"

Lesley approached the bed and looked at the buttons on its side. She pressed the button that looked most like it would help him sit up further. It worked.

Dennis looked into her eyes. "I'm a copper, boss. I was only doing my job."

"You did more than your job."

"How is your daughter?"

"Sharon's fine. She's moved to another college, one that suits her better, and she's got a new boyfriend."

"That's risky."

"She introduced him to me on the first date. I think he was a bit freaked out by it."

"Did you run him through the system?"

She lowered her voice, shaking her head. "He's clean."

A smile. "Good."

Lesley cocked her head, watching Dennis's face. Smiling

was clearly an effort for him, and his legs hadn't moved under the covers since she'd arrived.

"What do the doctors say?" she asked.

He closed his eyes. "They're unsure. There's a seventy-five per cent chance I'll have the use of my legs again. But I'll have to do a lot of physio."

Lesley felt her heart well up. "Thank you, Dennis. I'm so sorry this—"

He waved a hand. "Shush. I did what I'd do for anyone."

She swallowed. "I think it was my fault."

He frowned. "Of course it wasn't. You weren't even there."

Lesley paused. Had he not seen her? Or heard her?

"I was," she said. "I spoke to Mike and put two and two together. I called out to you. You turned, and then you slipped."

"Nonsense. I slipped because I was trying to see the firefighter." He shifted his weight, looking at her. "It isn't your fault."

Lesley said nothing. She and Dennis had disagreed on plenty in the past, and it looked like that wasn't going to change.

"So I'm retiring early," he said. "I get an extra ten months and an extra three thousand a year on my pension. Which is a bonus."

"Not much of one."

He reached for her hand. "I'm going to walk again, boss. I get to spend time with my wonderful wife, and your daughter is safe. She's got so much life ahead of her. That's what matters."

Lesley blinked back tears. The door behind her opened and she wiped her face on her sleeve.

Mike came in, followed by Tina. Lesley turned to look at them.

"Be gentle," she said. "The sarge is—"

"Not the sarge anymore," said Dennis. "I'm retiring."

"Good for you, Sarge," said Mike.

The door opened again, and a tall man with blond hair walked in. Tina gasped and threw herself at him, clinging on for a hug. "Johnny!"

"Watch out," DC Johnny Chiles said, giving Mike a wink. "I've heard you're DC Legg's missus now."

"I am!" she cried. "But it's so good to see you."

There were two more behind him: Meera and Stanley.

"Move out of the way, Mike," Tina said. "We can go in the living room so everyone gets a go."

"It's OK," Lesley told her. "I'll get out of the way." She looked back at Dennis and mouthed a *thank you* to him.

As she left the room, she heard an explosion of laughter inside. She smiled; hopefully they would visit Dennis frequently. It would certainly help his recovery.

Pam was coming out of the living room. "Everything alright in there?"

"It's fine. I've given them some space."

"He loves those young people. Doesn't show it very well, but they're what he lives for." Her face darkened. "Far more than our son."

"How is your son?"

"Oh, you don't want to talk about him." Pam looked up at Lesley. "Anyway. I came out to bring you in to hear the radio news." She jerked her head sideways. "In the front room."

Lesley followed Dennis's wife. An armchair sat in the window, next to a low table with a radio, a cup of tea and a plate of biscuits. The radio was on. The two of them stood and listened.

"In local news, a Dorset police officer has been arrested on suspicion of murder and conspiracy to murder. The arrest relates to the recent death of DI Rowan Angus and the death three years ago of DCI Tim Mackie. We're unable to name the officer arrested for legal reasons, but he is believed to be a member of the Professional Standards Unit."

Lesley looked at Pam, feeling her jaw drop.

"You got him," Pam said.

Lesley blinked at her. "Not me."

Pam smiled at her. "It was you alright. I always knew my Dennis was innocent. You got him off, and you got the man who killed poor Tim." She gripped Lesley's hand. "Thank you."

CHAPTER ONE HUNDRED ONE

"I ORDERED A KNIFE AND FORK MEAL," Elsa said as she sat down at the table in the tearoom in Corfe Castle. "Sharon tells me that means I can have a pint."

Lesley laughed. "You remembered that?"

Sharon shrugged. "It was my first day in Dorset. And your first day solving murders down here."

Lesley leaned back in her chair, eyeing Elsa. "I heard a scream. We both did. Turned out it was a young woman called Layla Ford, who'd just found her boyfriend dead."

"And then Layla ended up dead, too," added Sharon.

"Don't sound so excited about it," Lesley told her.

Sharon grimaced. "Sorry. It's just, you seem to attract murder."

Lesley shook her head, just as a waitress placed a plate of scones, jam and cream in front of Sharon. "Not anymore. It's been four months now without a single murder."

"You're clearly losing your touch," Elsa said.

A scream rang out over the tea shop. Lesley pushed back her chair and stood up, her senses alert.

Sharon laughed. "Sit down, Mum. It's just that little girl. Someone probably gave her scones with currants in, or something."

Lesley turned to see a woman comforting a crying toddler. She blushed.

"Sorry," she said, lowering herself into her chair. People were turning and giving her odd looks.

"You need a change of scene," Elsa said.

"You know I can't. Not until the court case is finished."

"Fish and chips?" The waitress was back, holding out a plate.

"That's me," said Elsa. "And I ordered a pint of Rogue."

The waitress wrinkled her nose and surveyed the table. All Lesley had was a coffee.

"I'll go and get it," she said.

"You did that just to wind her up," Lesley said.

Elsa's eyes widened. "I wanted a beer. It's just the thing for a cosy evening in a Dorset tea shop."

"It's only half past four," Sharon said. "I've got a date with Walt in two hours."

"We need to get you home, then," said Lesley. "Elsa, eat up."

Elsa saluted. "Aye aye, cap'n." She winked at Sharon, who giggled.

Elsa tucked into her fish and chips. Lesley reached out to steal a chip from time to time, but focused mainly on drinking her coffee. She enjoyed watching Elsa: her wife was still as beautiful as she had been the day Lesley had first seen her in the Duke of Wellington pub. And now she was a successful lawyer with her own firm and a growing roster of clients.

"Right," said Elsa between mouthfuls. "Once this court

case is over and bloody Robert Collingwood is in prison, we need a holiday. Where are we going to go?"

"I can't take time off," said Lesley. "They're recruiting Dennis's replacement. I can't poss—"

"You keep grumbling that they're not involving you." Elsa swallowed a mouthful. "So where are we going?"

"I can't come," said Sharon. "Too busy at college."

"Fair enough." Elsa held out her fork, a chip on its end. "Lesley? Where d'you fancy?"

Lesley wrinkled her nose, considering. They'd been to Scotland, on their honeymoon. Going abroad was too much... too much effort. And besides, this was what she liked. Rolling hills. Cosy tea rooms. Pubs that served beer without making you eat a 'knife and fork meal'.

"Can't we stay right here?" she said.

Elsa put the chip in her mouth then gave Lesley a slap on the thigh under the table. "No."

"OK." Lesley ran through destinations in her head. "I know. A friend of mine has just moved to a part of the country I think we might enjoy."

"A friend?" Sharon asked. Elsa looked sceptical.

"Well. A former colleague."

Elsa cocked her head, smiling. "That could work."

"I'm glad you think so," said Lesley. "We'll take a trip to Cumbria. And we can take the opportunity to spend a bit of time with Zoe and Carl."

READ A FREE PREQUEL NOVELLA, THE BALLARD DOWN MURDER

How did DCI Mackie die?

DS Dennis Frampton is getting used to life without his old boss DCI Mackie, and managing to hide how much he hates being in charge of Dorset's Major Crimes Investigation Team. Above all, he must ensure no one knows he's still seeking Mackie's advice on cases.

But then Mackie doesn't show up to a meeting, and a body is found below the cliffs a few miles away.

When Dennis discovers the body is his old friend and mentor, his world is thrown upside down. Did Mackie kill himself, or was he pushed? Is Dennis's new boss trying to hush things up? And can Dennis and the CSIs trust the evidence?

Find out by reading *The Ballard Down Murder* for FREE at rachelmclean.com/ballard.

READ THE DORSET CRIME SERIES

Buy now in ebook, paperback or audiobook

ALSO BY RACHEL MCLEAN

The DI Zoe Finch Series - Buy in ebook, paperback and audiobook

Deadly Wishes, DI Zoe Finch Book 1

Deadly Choices, DI Zoe Finch Book 2

Deadly Desires, DI Zoe Finch Book 3

Deadly Terror, DI Zoe Finch Book 4

Deadly Reprisal, DI Zoe Finch Book 5

Deadly Fallout, DI Zoe Finch Book 6

Deadly Christmas, DI Zoe Finch Book 7

Deadly Origins, the FREE Zoe Finch prequel

The McBride & Tanner Series

Blood and Money, McBride & Tanner Book 1

Death and Poetry, McBride & Tanner Book 2

Milton Keynes UK
Ingram Content Group UK Ltd.
UKHW041938070923
428085UK00005B/40